Anthony Price was born in Hertfordshire in 1928, was educated at King's School, Canterbury, and studied history at Merton College, Oxford. Apart from some temporary peace-time soldiering he has been a journalist all his life, beginning as a reviewer on the *Oxford Mail*, then Deputy Editor and finally Editor of the *Oxford Times*.

He won the Crime Writers' Association's Silver Dagger for his first novel *The Labyrinth Makers* and later their Gold Dagger for *Other Paths to Glory*. All his novels reflect his intense interest in history and archaeology, and in particular in military history.

By the same author

ANTHONY PRICE

Gunner Kelly

PANTHER
Granada Publishing

Panther Books
Granada Publishing Ltd
8 Grafton Street, London W1X 3LA

Published by Panther Books 1985

First published in Great Britain by
Victor Gollancz Ltd 1983

ISBN 0-586-06175-4

Printed and bound in Great Britain by
Collins, Glasgow

Set in Times

For Simon Price

PART ONE

How Colonel Butler's breakfast was spoilt

Colonel Butler loved all his three girls equally, but (as he was accustomed to tell himself when they presented their problems to him) differently. Because, notwithstanding the identical red of their hair, they were entirely different people.

And that was why Jane had his attention now across the breakfast table, absolutely but unequally with the disquiet which he might have diverted from his *Times* to Sally or Diana.

'I said, Father,' she repeated, '*I think I have done something rather silly.*'

'Yes.' Butler nodded gravely, just as he would have done for Sally or Diana, but without the pretence which paternal gravity would have required for them. 'I heard you the first time, Jane.'

He stopped there, and the difference widened with his silence and hers. With Sally and Diana he would have added some soothing verbal placebo. But then, with Sally it would have been merely something to do with horses, and with Diana merely something to do with men; but it was *the* horse that Sally loved, not (in spite of temporary infatuations) any particular horse; and Diana, whose physical resemblance to her late mother went disturbingly more than skin deep, seemed to feel much the same way about men; and in both cases Colonel Butler and his money had together proved more than a match for any emergency in the past.

But Jane was different.

'Tell me – ' Butler overcame his Anglo-Saxon reticence with a conscious effort ' – darling.'

With Jane it was different: with Jane, from the moment

7

when she had ceased to be a thing and had become a person, life had been reason and calculation, not emotion. With Jane, Butler had never been sure whether she was the least loving or the most loving of his children – whether, because she felt most deeply, she had armoured herself most carefully against feeling, or whether, because she felt nothing, she was impervious to life's shot and shell. And so, because he loved her *equally*, he had found himself worrying about her more, because she brought him fewer problems, and those almost purely academic, balancing one relative benefit coldly against another: *Mathematics* or *English* (she excelled at both)? *Oxbridge* or *Bristol* (mathematician or barrister, and no serious question about entry, but a faint sympathy in Butler himself for other mathematicians or prisoners at the bar eventually . . . just as his ultimate sympathy in her sisters' cases was not truly with them, but with the horses and men they chose to ride into the ground, which were the animals with which – with whom – he himself could identify, having been similarly ridden in his time)?

But she was still his daughter – his flesh and his red hair and his responsibility and his equal love; and now – his instinct and experience both told – *she was in deep trouble at last, who had never been in such trouble before*.

The realization of that, cold as the shrill, distant sound of Chinese bugles blowing the charge against the last handful of his company in Korea, stripped all Butler's worries away from him momentarily (the true leak at Cheltenham, which was not the one the Russians had so carefully let them have . . . Mitchell and Andrew could only handle that at a pinch; but the problem with the Americans could only be dealt with by David Audley, whose own private links with the CIA would have to be cashed in when he got back from leave . . . So he would have to give St John Latimer *carte blanche* at Cheltenham – the more he disliked Latimer, who hated Audley, the more he inconveniently needed both of them to do what had to be done – even though Audley coveted that job . . .).

But for the moment it was Jane who mattered –

'Tell me, darling.' This time he managed something close to encouragement, if not sympathy.

'Yes . . .' Some other process of reasoning, very different in content, but equal in duration and sufficient to nerve her to answer him, animated Jane '. . . Father, you remember when I took the little car last week . . . ?'

As though summoned by the memory, Sally breezed out of the kitchen into the breakfast-room, carrying her enormous horsewoman's breakfast.

'I remember. It was last Saturday, to be exact,' Sally agreed. 'Because I had to get a lift to the gymkhana the other side of Winchester that day – '

'Go and eat in the kitchen, Sal.' Jane looked at her sister uncompromisingly. 'I've got business to transact with Father.'

Sally gave her younger sibling one quick, sharp glance, and then picked up the plate again and was gone before Butler could say a word. And that, if anything had been required to consolidate Butler's disquiet, confirmed it beyond question: however much they might be at odds on day-to-day matters, they never failed to decode each other's Most Urgent signals in an emergency.

Silly was what worried him now. Because, where Sally and Diana were given to hyperbole, Jane's weakness was understatement, so that she would not admit to being unwell until she was too ill to walk.

Suddenly, he found himself simultaneously suppressing reasons for panic while discounting them: *she was only nineteen years old, but hard-headed and sensible with it . . . but she was still only nineteen years old –*

The Mini was still in pristine condition – he had washed it himself on Sunday, and it bore no marks of any chance encounters – and Jane wasn't the hit-and-run type –

Or . . . *No –*

No. Butler had staked his life on several occasions when the odds were better not computed, but he was quite happy to stake it again this morning across the breakfast-table that his youngest daughter wasn't pregnant. All the known facts of circumstance and character were against it, apart from the cheerfulness of her greeting only a few minutes before –

Only a few minutes before? Butler's eyes dropped to the table, to beside her plate on it: one letter, but hand-written, not official – just a few lines on a single sheet of paper, without even an address so far as he could see at the distance and upside-down – hardly more than a brief scrawl, but signed with a flourish –

He raised his eyes to meet hers, with his imagination up against a blank wall of incomprehension.

'I went to see David, Father.'

'David?' Jane had no boyfriend named *David*. In fact, Jane had no boy-friend, full-stop.

'Uncle David, Father.'

Butler was there as she spoke. *David* was David *Audley* – and, somewhat to his surprise, that in itself was reassuring: no matter how eccentric, even maverick, Audley might be in professional matters, when it came to Jane he had no doubt that the man would behave responsibly. Even . . . with the untimely death of Jane's godfather, Audley rather quaintly regarded himself as an unofficial substitute for that rôle, for which only one other parent had regarded him suitable, to his chagrin.

So, for once at least, and in this instance in particular, Audley could be trusted, surely –

Surely? He looked at Jane. 'You went to see David Audley?'

'About Becky, Father – Becky Smith.' Jane nodded.

'Becky Smith?' Butler repeated the name blankly, aware that he might have registered any young man's name for future reference, but that no female from school or university would have fixed herself in his mind unless

10

he could add a face to a name. And there was no file in his memory on any *Becky Smith*.

'Rebecca Maxwell-Smith – you don't know her, Father, but I've mentioned her. She's reading Law with me – we live in the same hall of residence . . . I had dinner with her grandfather once – you remember, I *told* you, Father.'

Something faintly registered now, but only faintly.

'So?' He was ashamed to admit the faint registration.

'So she had this hare-brained idea – more than hare-brained, bloody *mad* . . . But she was hell-bent on it, and there wasn't anything I could do to stop her – absolutely bloody *mad* . . . But I thought I had to stop her *somehow* . . .' She tailed off, and the very imprecision of her account of what Rebecca Maxwell-Smith was hell-bent on re-animated Butler's concern, for all that it was safely one step away from her now; because if there was one thing that Jane Butler was – apart from being nineteen and hard-headed and sensible – it was to the point. And at the moment she was circling the point like a mongoose round a snake.

Even Butler himself was infected by her caution. 'Why didn't you come to me?' She would come to the vital answer in her own good time, with no need for the question.

'You didn't come home on Friday.' She excused herself by accusing him. 'Becky phoned – I was going to ask you, but you weren't there . . . And you always said, if there was a problem Nannie Hooker couldn't solve, and you weren't here, we could phone Uncle David.'

True, thought Butler. But that was for *you* – and *your* problems. And the odds on this one are that you probably wouldn't have asked me anyway . . . Yet, at the same time, it was the old fatal error he had made, of giving a precise command imprecisely, so that she had been able to obey him in circumstances he had not envisaged, disobediently.

'So what did he say?' This time, as he phrased the

11

indirect question with false sincerity, leaving Rebecca Maxwell-Smith's as-yet-unrevealed madness even further behind, he felt that little frisson of excitement he always did where David Audley was involved: no one could ever be quite sure what Audley would do in any situation, including Audley himself.

'He said he'd help – of course.' Jane's expression indicated that she had only just discovered what her father and others had learnt by experience. 'But now I've received this from Becky – !'

She pushed the letter across the table towards Butler.

There were only a dozen or so words on it, with no sender's address, as he had already noted, and no date either.

Jay – Thanks a million for sending us your David.
Now we really have a chance of pulling it off –
Love, Becky.

Butler looked at his daughter interrogatively.

'He wasn't meant to *help* them,' said Jane. 'He wasn't meant to help them pull it off – he was meant to *put* them off.'

She was coming to it now, at last, thought Butler. But, whatever 'it' was, at least she wasn't directly involved in it.

He concealed his overwhelming relief behind a frown.

Jane frowned back at him. 'They're planning to murder someone, Father,' she said.

Colonel Butler closed the door of his library behind him, shutting out the sound of the girls' argument over which of them was going to drive the Mini, and went over to the huge mock-Tudor window.

One of Sally's horses was cropping the grass right up against the white fence on the other side of the forecourt. As he stared at it, the animal seemed to sense his presence and looked up towards the house incuriously for a moment. Then it lowered its head again and the grass-tearing sound re-started. On the far side of the paddock, the other two horses were similarly engaged in their endless breakfast-lunch-tea-dinner, and beyond them, the field by the road was dotted with cows which at this distance reminded him of Brittain's farm toys with which the girls had played when they were little and untroublesome.

Butler turned his back on the scene. It had served its purpose, because now he no longer wished to commit a murder of his own, both to pre-empt that which was allegedly in train and to punish the would-be murderers for the ruination of the quiet weekend with his girls, to which he had been looking forward.

Now commonsense and reason, disciplined by duty, had reasserted themselves. There were even books there on the shelves to remind him – *there*, high up on the left – that the rebellious American colonies had been supposedly lost because of the devotion of King George III's ministers to carefree weekends . . . and *there*, two shelves down and to the right, that 'lose not an hour' had been Horatio Nelson's watchword.

His eye travelled along the shelves, down to the other end of the long room: and *there*, also, was the gazetteer in which he could pinpoint the village of Duntisbury Royal, to direct him in turn to the right inch-to-the-mile Ordnance Survey map from the shelf below, on which he could pin the gazetteer's point exactly, if necessary.

The Mini's engine roared outside. (Whichever of them was at the wheel, she would take the drive too fast, and the corner at the entrance too dangerously, with all the reckless immortality of youth, untainted by experience and protected only by youth's split-second reflexes.)

(David Audley had the experience, and to spare, and a rare quality of intuition. But he also had his blind spots, and he no longer had the reflexes for field-work, unescorted.)

He listened to the engine-note, gauging the car's exact position until it finally snarled away in the distance, on the main road, holding his breath until then. (There was nothing he could do about the girls; they were their own women now, for better or for worse, and he could only come to them when they called him. But there was a great deal he could do – and *must* do – about David Audley.)

If necessary.

No certainty animated him yet, as he moved round the big desk, and sat down behind it, and reached decisively for the red telephone, with its array of buttons. Others, more gifted with that wild Fifth Sense than he, might be able to move from the known via the unknowable to the most likely. But he could only advance by experience and the map references of information received.

He lifted the red phone and pressed two of the buttons simultaneously. Two red eyes lit up, one steady, one blinking insistently. He watched them until they both turned green.

'Duty officer? I wish to speak with Chief Inspector Andrew. When you get him, patch him through to me on this line, please.' He drummed his fingers on the desk. 'Thank you.'

He replaced the receiver, so that one of the green eyes went out while the other turned red again, holding the scrambled line. Then he reached out, almost reluctantly, for the other phone – the ordinary humdrum Telecom instrument, beloved of Diana, Sally and Jane to his great quarterly cost, and dialled his required number, for all to hear who wanted to hear.

'The Old House.'

The childish treble rendered his next question super-fluous. 'Cathy – are either of your parents home?' It pained Colonel Butler's super-ego that he was glad his little god-daughter had been closest to the phone.

'Uncle Jack! Yes – Mummy is.' The breathlessness of

her evident pleasure turned the pain into a wound. 'Are you coming to my birthday party next Saturday?'

'Your birthday party?' Butler feigned surprise. 'Have you got *another* birthday? How many birthdays a year do you have? Are you like the Queen? Is this your *official* birthday – or your *real* birthday? You can't expect me to keep track of all your different birthdays – I'm much too busy for that, young lady!'

'But I haven't – ' The child caught herself a second too late, birthday-excitement betraying intelligence ' – if you're too *busy* . . . then that's *your* hard luck – *you* don't get any of the cake – *and* you don't come to the *dinner* afterwards, with Paul and Elizabeth, and pineapple Malakoff and Muscat de Beaumes de Venise in the funny bottle – *okay*?' Cathy added her special birthday pudding and its attendant wine to her other favourite grown-ups like a visiting Russian nobleman and his exquisite French mistress, joining in the game. 'But Daddy's not here, anyway – he's in Dorset, digging up Romans and looking at tanks . . . but Mummy's here, if you want her – '

Conflicting emotions warred in Butler's breast: his much-loved and super-intelligent god-daughter had given him what he wanted – Audley was in Dorset, *digging up Romans and looking at tanks*, whatever that meant, if it was true – even though he hadn't asked for that information, and though he had intended to play foully to get it, hoping it would come from her mother without his asking for it –

'Here's Mummy, anyway – ' The rest was lost in the surrender of the receiver, from daughter to mother.

'Jack?' Faith Audley was matter-of-fact, as always. 'If you want David, he's not here.' Then the ever-defensive and slightly-disapproving wife asserted herself. 'But he's on leave, as you well know.'

'In Dorset, digging up Romans and tanks?' Butler chuckled deceitfully at her.

'Yes.' The matter-of-fact disapproval crystallized itself.

'You can get him at Duntisbury Royal 326 – but only if you have to, Jack.'

Duntisbury Royal 326

'I haven't the slightest interest in Duntisbury whatever – and even less in Romans and tanks, Faith dear – ' *What had Romans and tanks got to do with Duntisbury Royal and General Maxwell, lately deceased*? ' – and least of all with your husband . . . I am at home, attempting to enjoy my weekend, if you can believe that . . . I was merely calling about next weekend, as a matter of fact. Your daughter's birthday, remember?'

There was a pause. Butler's eye ranged over his desk, and as it did so one of the blank red eyes on the console of the red telephone started to blink at him redly, off and on, on and off, to inform him that the duty officer was back on that line, holding Chief Inspector Andrew for him, from another ruined weekend somewhere.

'I'm sorry, Jack. Of course! But . . .' It started as an apology, then the voice became edged with doubt '. . . he is on leave, isn't he?'

There it was, thought Butler with bleak sympathy: the bomber pilot's wife's question, redolent with uncertainty about the actual whereabouts of her husband, who could be drinking in the Mess with his crew this morning, but then *Flying Tonight*: that, even after a dozen years' safe landings, and in spite of his age and seniority, was the nightmare with which Faith Audley lived, on her pillow in the dark, in her washing-up bowl in the light, and everywhere she went in-between when he was out of her sight, and nothing would change that.

'If he isn't, it's news to me.' That at least was true! 'I was just calling to confirm next weekend – ' he lowered his voice conspiratorially, covering the untruth of a phone-call he would not have needed to make if Jane had not spoken to him with the truth of what he had already done in honour of his god-daughter's birthday ' – I've got her a first edition of Kipling's collected poems, and a signed

16

copy of *Little Wars*, plus something for her bottom-drawer, which she can put into her savings account.'

'Jack – ' Her voice trailed off, and he heard her despatch Cathy out of ear-shot ' – Jack, that's much too generous – '

'Nonsense. She's my god-child. Just don't tell David that I've called – ' Butler's eye strayed from the winking red light on the red phone to the gazetteer, wedged blue-black in its shelf: *Duntisbury Royal* – Faith and Jane both agreed on that, and Cathy had added *Dorset* – and *Romans,* and *tanks* –

What the hell was David Audley up to, adding *General Maxwell* to all that – ?

And *murder* – ?

Faith was mouthing good-mannered platitudes at him and he had to get rid of her gently and circumspectly: Diana was well, and enjoying her job . . . and Sally's horses were well, and appeared to be enjoying what Sally made them do . . . and Jane was enjoying Law at Bristol University, together with all the other things that Law students did –

In the end he managed to extricate himself from her convincingly, if without the luxury of honour, and returned to the red phone.

'Hullo, sir,' said Andrew cheerfully. 'Trouble?'

'Wait.' There was a red eye still, next to the green one. 'Thank you, Duty Officer – that will be all.'

The red eye closed abruptly.

'Andrew.' Weekend or not, Andrew had been accessible. And – what was better than availability – Andrew could be trusted. 'Maxwell. Major-General Maxwell – in the newspapers recently . . . and there was a routine circular on him.'

'Yes, sir.'

'What do you know about him?'

There was only a fractional pause. 'Not a lot, sir. You want the Anti-Terrorist Squad for him.'

17

'If I wanted them I'd be talking to them.'

Another pause: as a detective-inspector, Andrew had been one of the brightest sparks in the Special Branch, but it still sometimes took a moment for him to adjust to the eccentric politics of Colonel Butler's service. 'Right, sir.'

'Very well. It was a car bomb in Bournemouth, about a fortnight ago, as I recall. We accused the IRA Provos or the INLA, with the odds on the INLA. They both denied responsibility. Go on from there.'

'Yes, sir.' Only the very slightest South London whine betrayed Andrew's Rotherhithe origins: for some people he turned it on full, complete with the rhyming slang, as a tactical device, but with Colonel Butler he never tried it on, it was the Honours graduate in Law who spoke. 'It was an Irish bomb, undoubtedly, Inertia-type – pop the parcel under the seat, and just withdraw the pin . . . Good for soft, unsuspecting targets: off they go, and the first time they slow down *up* they go . . . It's one they've used before – not too difficult to put together when you know how, but not crude.'

'Professional?'

'Professional – yes . . . to the extent that there are three known training schools in the Soviet bloc which include it in their syllabuses – schools which handle foreign trainees . . . one in East Germany, one in Czechoslovakia . . . and the KGB one, naturally.'

'So it doesn't have to be Irish?'

'It doesn't have to be – no. Except that they're the only ones who've used similar devices, so far . . .'

'Yes?' Was that uncertainty in the man's voice?

'Yes . . . well, there is an element of doubt on this one, it's true. In fact . . . doubt is about all there is, apparently.'

'Doubt?'

'About it being Irish, sir.'

Butler's heart sank. David Audley was not an Irish specialist, and notoriously avoided any involvement with the Irish problems which came their way even peripherally. He had pinned most of his hopes on that, he realized now.

'Why?' And *why*, come to that, was Andrew so well-informed about the case, in spite of that "not a lot" disclaimer?

'No motive, sir.'

'Since when did the INLA need a motive?'

'No connection, then. General Maxwell never served in Ulster – he wasn't remotely Irish . . . and he was ten years into his retirement – more than ten years . . . before this lot of Irish "troubles", anyway. The nearest thing he had to an Irish connection was his servant, Kelly, and he hardly qualifies as Irish within the meaning of the word, any more than Maxwell himself does – did.'

'Kelly?' Butler could recall no mention of any Kelly, either in the newspapers or in the intelligence circular. But as a name Kelly was Irish of the Irish.

'*Gunner* Kelly.' Andrew emphasized the rank. 'Irish for the first seventeen years of his life, until he joined up at Larkhill in 1938, like his father before him – father went through the '14–'18 – DCM at Loos, bar at Ypres . . . son went through the '39–'45 – Dunkirk, Tunisia, Italy – Maxwell's regiment . . . Peace-time soldiering afterwards, then drove a taxi up north somewhere . . . Came back to the General about four years ago – totally devoted to him . . . What they say is, if he'd known the General's name was on a bomb, he'd have scratched it out and put his own in its place, most likely.'

Butler thought for a moment. 'Could he have been the target, then – a lackey of the bloody British?'

'A 60-year-old lackey?' Andrew echoed the idea scornfully.

'Since when has the INLA been choosy?' It was too feeble though – even for the INLA. Much too thin.

'If they're going to start blowing up all the Kellys, then they'll need a nuclear bomb, not a pound of jelly under the seat . . . sir.' Andrew paused. 'But they did check him out. Because it's true he could have gone up with the General – in fact, if the General hadn't sent him off on some errand, he *would* have gone up . . . He was going to drive, but the old boy wanted a parcel of books collected – all above board and kosher, in front of witnesses . . . But that isn't the point, you see.'

'So what is the point?' For Kelly to be a non-starter there had to be a point, of course: that was implicit in Del Andrew's scorn.

'They weren't expecting this bomb, sir – neither the Provos nor the INLA – that's the fact of it, the word is . . . It caught them both with their trousers down – right down by their ankles.'

'How so?' 'Not a lot' was indeed turning out to be quite a lot. So now he also needed to know why Andrew had done so much more than read the circular on General Maxwell's assassination.

'Well, sir . . . after the Hyde Park bombing there was a lot of recrimination – killing Brits was one thing, but killing horses was another – that was bad medicine on the other side of the Atlantic . . . like, in the cowboy films you can have the Indians bite the dust, and the cowboys, and the horse-soldiers . . . but you can't have the *horses* with their guts blown out, or trying to stand up on three legs – that's the unacceptable face of terrorism . . . And if there's one thing the Irish themselves are soft on, it's horses – they can put their shirt on them, and lose it, but they can't blow six-inch nails into them and then stroll away whistling about Donegal and Connemara, like nothing has happened . . . So we got more mileage out of those pictures of dead horses, and Sefton in his stable, than we did from Airey Neave and Earl Mountbatten being killed, you see.'

'Yes.' That was another plus for Chief Inspector Andrew: he saw life as it was, not as it ought to be, with a hot heart but a cool head.

'Yes. So they weren't planning anything for the rest of this summer. And after the heat had gone off, when things had settled down a bit, they started to reorganize quietly – both the Provos and the INLA . . . But then, out of the blue, General Maxwell's bomb goes up in the middle of Bournemouth, and all hell breaks loose again when they weren't battened down – as they would have been if they'd planned it, sir.'

Butler waited, although he already knew what the point was now, from the recent circulars which had passed across his desk as a matter of routine.

'So as a result the squad picked up three of them who were out in the open – the Provo bagman who was delivering funds in London, and the girl who was setting up that new safe house . . . and the INLA hit-man – a real bad bastard we've been after for a long time, that the West Germans wanted too.' Andrew paused. 'Which our contacts in Dublin and Belfast both confirm – that the boyos there would like to get their hands on whoever did for the General quite as much as we would, and probably even more.'

That made sense . . . even if the sense it made was the mad and bad illogical sense of terrorism the world over, thought Butler bleakly. But now was the moment for a straight question.

'So how did you come into this, Andrew?'

This time it was a longer pause. 'Ah . . . I heard a whisper, sir – that it maybe wasn't an Irish job at all . . . But the bomb was a pro job, like I said.' Pause. 'And there was that paper of Wing-Commander Roskill's on bombs, not long ago . . . So I thought this one might end up on our plate – on *your* plate, sir . . .' Modesty disarmed Chief Inspector Andrew '. . . and I dropped in on the squad anyway, to talk about old times . . . just in case.'

Intelligent anticipation: another plus for the man. 'Could you go down there again?'

Pause.

'No, sir. If I go down there again . . . they're much too fly for that: they'll know it won't be just curiosity this time – especially as they're looking for someone to take it off their hands. They've already tried to unload it on the Dorset locals.'

'With what result?' If Audley hadn't been involved, Butler might have smiled: the experience was not unknown to him of having intractable problems left at his official door like unwanted babies, lusty and demanding.

'The Chief down there – the Chief Constable – he wouldn't have it. And quite right, too!' Andrew grunted sympathetically. 'He said there was no one on his patch who could set a bomb like that – and if there had been they'd never have set it under the old General. He was the last person anyone would want to blow up. So it had to be political.'

'And you go along with that, do you?'

'I don't go along with *anything* . . . sir,' replied Andrew cautiously. 'I don't know enough about it – this was just what I picked up over a few beers. But they certainly didn't have any local prospects down there with any sort of motive, never mind the know-how, apparently.'

'You mean he had no known enemies down there?'

'That's right. In fact . . . no known enemies *anywhere*, would be more accurate. He was a decent old stick – "much-loved local figure", as they say . . . only this time that was the exact truth: they couldn't find anyone who didn't have a good word for him. What the local vicar said, was that he disproved the parable about the rich man having difficulty getting into heaven: he'd get through the eye of the needle with plenty of room on both sides.'

'He was rich?'

'Rolling in it. Landed money, too – the sort that's gone through the roof the last few years.'

'Next-of-kin?' He knew part of the answer to that already. But there might be more.

'Just one grand-daughter – who adored him. And most

of his wealth was already in trust for her anyway, apart from that. Nobody stands to gain from his death, if that's what you're after. Most people think they *lost* by it.' Andrew sniffed at him down the line. 'Too good to be true, eh?'

'I said no such thing!' snapped Butler. One thing the years had convinced him of was the existence of pure evil. Fortunately, whatever the hell-fire preachers thought, it was very rare; but its corollary was the existence of pure good, though unfortunately that was even more rare.

'Well, that's what some of my old mates down the nick thought, having had some disillusioning experiences in that direction.' Andrew chuckled. 'This turned out to be equally disillusioning in its way – for them, actually.'

'How so?' Butler frowned.

'He wasn't as good as he seemed, was General Maxwell – "Squire" Maxwell – Major-General Herbert George Maxwell, CBE, DSO, MC . . . and Grade VII on the piano, and heaven only knows what else . . . and clever with it, sir.'

Andrew was clever too, Butler noted. But maybe he needed slapping down. 'Don't waste my time, Chief Inspector. Get to the point.'

'Yes, sir. He wasn't as good as he seemed – if anything he was better.'

'Better?'

'Yes, sir. No secret mistresses. No strange perversions. All they dug up was a lot of good he was doing by stealth – and a lot of good he'd done in the past, that no one had known about.' Andrew allowed an edge of incredulity into his voice. 'You know, there was even a letter – there were *two* letters – from his official enemies . . . They intercepted all the letters to his grand-daughter – '

'His enemies?'

'His *official* ones. One was from some branch of the Hunt Saboteurs – in his younger days he was a great one for fox-hunting . . . there's a Duntisbury Chase Hunt –

saying how courteous he'd always been to them, even while he was out-smarting them . . . and how he'd always listened to them, and stopped the locals beating them up, and so on – that was one of the letters.'

Good Gracious! thought Butler.

'And the other was from Germany, with money for a wreath – from some German Old Comrades' associations, from the war . . . They'd read about his death in the papers, and they remembered how well he'd behaved – how he'd looked after their wounded somewhere, and cheered them up by congratulating them on making a great fight of it, and fighting cleanly, and all that – which they'd never forgotten.'

Colonel Butler stared at his bookshelves, and remembered his own war, and the waste and the pity of it. And he could remember a German too, as they had remembered an Englishman –

'Sir?'

Colonel Butler blinked at his shelves, snapping free from the memories which for a moment – or for more than a moment – had taken him outside time, into a past which had had no future.

'Yes.' Only the present mattered now. 'Right!' And the first question to be resolved concerned Chief Inspector Andrew himself. 'Now . . . you tell me *exactly* why you became so interested in General Maxwell, Chief Inspector. Right?'

'Yes, sir.' Andrew was satisfactorily ready for the question. 'Well . . . I heard this whisper – like I told you – that it wasn't an Irish job . . . what I heard was that they didn't know what the hell it was, to be *exact*, sir.' The returned emphasis came back to Butler smugly, like a cool return to a hard service. 'So I had this feeling that we might get it, you know.'

That was a good and complete answer, even though it ignored the importance of their current preoccupation with the Cheltenham centre.

Or did it? The possibility that someone else might know about David Audley, never mind Jane Butler, chilled Butler.

'Just that? Nothing more?'

'No, sir. Nothing more.' The reply was stoutly delivered, with a very slight colouring of outrage at the suggestion that its honesty had been considered questionable.

'Right.' Butler refused to let himself be embarrassed. Loyalty in exchange for trust, trust in return for loyalty, was what he gave and expected to receive in his appointments, but in this wicked world nothing was certain. Yet in this officer's case the risk was worth taking. 'You're busy setting up the Cheltenham operation at this moment. I want you to drop that for twenty-four hours.'

'Yes, sir.' The faint red of outrage changed to the amber of expectation.

'I want you to get back in there somehow and pick up everything you can steal on General Maxwell, Chief Inspector.' Butler studied his books, looking for something which might inspire him, and felt belittled by them: there were so many clever men in those volumes, much more clever than he was, but many of them had come unstuck in spite of that. 'And I mean *steal* and I don't want anyone to know that you've done it. Is that understood?'

'Yes, sir.' It was understood – but could it be done? Butler waited while the Chief Inspector reconsidered the chances of doing successfully what he had already said he couldn't do. 'There is a way that I can maybe do that – indirectly.'

'All right.' Butler didn't want to know about the nuts and bolts of the deception. But it was time now to give the carrot of trust to make the whip-lash of loyalty more bearable. And he had already burnt his boats, in any case! 'You know where David Audley is at this moment?'

That stopped the Chief Inspector in his tracks, by God! 'He's on leave, sir. Writing another book. Do you want him?'

'No!' Butler recognized his mistake in that instant: it was no good blaming Jane – it was no good blaming Audley, even – no good telling himself that Audley ought to have behaved differently; that he ought to have behaved better, with his age, and his seniority, and experience, and intelligence – ought to have behaved *best*, not merely *better*.

David Audley had been born into the wrong age – that was what the man himself thought, and had never pretended otherwise: he always saw himself as a prince-bishop from his beloved Middle Ages, mediating between God and man, and meddling happily in the affairs of both to their discomfort.

Bletchley Park in the war would have suited Audley best – better than the Middle Ages, even – when he would have been safely bowed down not only by the responsibility and the importance and the challenge of the work, but also by the sheer volume of it, so that he wouldn't have had either the time or the energy to get up to mischief.

That had been his mistake: he had let Audley free-wheel for too long, while Cheltenham matured – the cleverest man he knew, whom he (of all people) should know was also most capable of behaving irresponsibly when he was bored with lack of responsibility. Jane had only lit that fuse – and perhaps he was lucky that Jane (of all people) had lit it!

Chief Inspector Andrew hadn't said a word this time. He had waited patiently for the next bomb-shell, with his head down.

'Audley's in Duntisbury Royal at the moment. I don't want him disturbed until I know what's happening down there.'

More silence from the other end of the line. It would be fascinating to know what Andrew thought of Audley: whether he knew enough yet to be as certain as Butler himself was that it could not be murder that Audley was contemplating. It would be something very different.

It would be the easiest thing in the world to find out: all he had to do was to recall the man and ask him what the hell he was up to – the easiest thing, and all the easier because it was in his own nature to do exactly that, to secure good order and discipline through common sense . . . just as it was in Audley's maverick nature to pursue his own insatiable curiosity in his own way, regardless of good order and discipline and common sense.

Colonel Butler looked down at his desk, at the note-pad near his left hand, and drew a deep breath. During his military career he had lived very happily by the book, being led and leading others, both of which conditions were as natural to him as breathing. But now the book was gathering dust . . . and Audley was a man who could be neither led nor driven, but whose unique value to Queen and Country lay in that restless free-ranging intuition. So it was his own plain duty to ensure that Audley functioned to maximum efficiency, however eccentrically, even if it meant temporarily ignoring the easiest thing in the world.

So that was it: he had to leave Audley alone, but not leave him alone; to show confidence in him while lacking confidence; to trust him while not trusting him; to do nothing while doing quite a lot; above all, to let him know none of that . . . somehow . . .

As the silence on the other end of the line lengthened, Colonel Butler moved the note-pad to his right, transferred the phone to his left hand, picked up a pencil, and started to write down names, and then to cross them out one after another, as the alternative to the easiest thing in the world became harder and harder.

PART TWO
Foxes in the Chase

1

Beside the ford there was a crude plank footbridge with a single guard-rail, and on the rail was perched a little blonde child in a very grubby pinafore dress.

Benedikt stopped the car at the water's edge and leaned out of the window in order to address her.

'Please . . .' He let the foreignness thicken his voice. 'Please, is this the way to . . . to Duntisbury Royal?'

The child stared at him for a moment, and then slid forwards and downwards until her toes touched a plank, without letting go of the rail.

Benedikt smiled at her. 'Please – ' he began again. But before he could repeat the question she ducked and twisted, and scuttled away like a little wild creature into a shadowy gap between the bushes on the other side of the water and an antique-looking telephone box.

Well, it was the way to Duntisbury Royal – it had to be, Benedikt reassured himself. *'Up the road about three miles'*, the man at the petrol station had said, and the map said so too. *'There's a turning on your left by a dead tree. Down the hill – and stay in low gear, because it's steep – and over the water-splash in the trees there, at the bottom, and it's a long mile from there, what there is of it. You can't miss it.'*

That was what they always said, *You can't miss it,* to reassure you at least for a time, until you had missed it.

'There are road-signs, yes?' He could read a map and find his way as well as any man, and better than most. But he had bitter experience of the irrationality of English directions and was suspicious of the man's confidence.

'No. Leastways . . . there were . . . but there aren't at the moment. But you turn by a dead tree, and just follow the

31

road. There ain't nowhere else to go once you're on it, see?'
The man had begun to regard him curiously then.

'Thank you. And there is an hotel there?' Curiosity, in
Benedikt's experience, was the father of information.

*'There ain't a hotel, no. There's a pub – they might have
a room, I dunno.'* The curiosity increased. *'They're a
queer lot there.'* The man spoke of the inhabitants of
Duntisbury Royal, who lived no more than five miles from
his petrol pumps, as though they were an alien race
hidden behind barbed wire and mine-fields.

'Queer?' All the same, Benedikt rejoiced in what he
guessed was the old correct meaning of the word, the use
of which he had been cautioned against in modern polite
speech: it was good to know that here, deep in the Wessex
countryside, the natives still guarded the language of his
mother, Shakespeare's tongue.

'Ah . . .' The garage man's face closed up suddenly, as
though he had decided on second thoughts that the
queerness of his neighbours was no foreigner's business.
*'That's £16.22, sir – sixteen-pounds-and-twenty-two-
pence.'* He adjusted the speed of his diction to that which
the English reserved for the presentation of bills to
foreigners, so that there could be no possible misunder-
standing, let alone argument.

'Ach – so!' Benedikt played back to him deliberately.
This might be the only garage for miles around, and if this
man was both a gossip and the local supplier to Duntisbury Royal, then so much the better. *'I may pay by credit
card, yes? Or cash?'*

The man looked doubtfully at the card, and then at
Benedikt, but then finally at the gleaming Mercedes and
its *CD* passport. *'Either of 'em will do, sir.'* He bustled to
find the correct form, and then squinted again at the card.
'"Weez-hoffer",' he murmured unnecessarily to himself,
as though to indicate to Benedikt that he would have
preferred cash from a foreigner and was noting the name
just in case.

'Wiesehöfer,' said Benedikt. 'Thomas Wiesehöfer.'

The man filled in the card number painfully. But his curiosity rekindled as he did so. 'On holiday then?'

'On holiday.' Benedikt nodded at the garage man and pretended to search for the right words and not find any. 'On holiday . . . ach so!' It galled him when he prided himself on being able to pass almost for English . . . or British, as Mother always insisted, who had been half-Scottish herself.

He studied the water-splash out of the driver's window, just a metre beyond his front wheels. The stream rippled across the tarmac in a patch of sunlight where the road crossed it, but it didn't look very deep. All the country hereabouts was open and empty, and he had dropped down from the high ridge in the low gear which the garage man had advised; but now he was on the miniature flood-plain of a little valley, and at this point, where the road crossed the stream, trees and bushes grew luxuriantly, making a secret place of it.

He looked up from the sun-dappled water, and caught a glimpse of the little girl watching him from her hiding place between the telephone box and the summer tangle of leaves. Of course, she would have been told not to speak to strange men in cars, so he couldn't rationally fault her behaviour. But he liked children, and was used to them, and prided himself on being good with them and was accustomed to their trust, so that – however irrationally – he recoiled from the rôle of strange-man-in-a-car and was disturbed by her fear.

Yet there was more to it than that, his momentary irrationality told him: the very young *were* innocent, and gullible and inexperienced with it, but they sometimes knew more than the very wise, picking up vibrations of danger with senses which atrophied as their experience of life increased; and now *he* was about to enter her secret little English valley –

33

But that was absurd fantasy! He broke contact with her and shifted the gear-lever into drive. It wasn't her valley, and it was only secret for the lack of a proper signpost – the busy main road almost within earshot, and it was only the foreignness of this small-scale countryside which he was foolishly letting himself be upset by, as he might be upset by some unpalatable local dish or custom to which he was unused, but which was unpalatable only because it was different from what he was accustomed to.

He felt the solid force of the water resist the forward thrust of the wheels, and then the Mercedes pulled free of the stream and surged ahead effortlessly into the dark tunnel formed by the overhanging trees. Then the road curved, to follow the line of the valley, and he could see open country ahead again, with one last glimpse of the child in his rear-view mirror as she broke cover to watch him go, and then took refuge inside the telephone box.

Beyond the ford the road meandered along the slope of the ridge, undulating with its gentle curves. Large single trees, which looked as though they had been planted for effect, rather than groves and plantations, obscured his view of the wider landscape. He became aware that he was in a different sort of countryside before he understood why it was different. Then he saw that there were no hedges, only a low iron railing on each side of the narrow road: it was as though he was passing through a private parkland –

Chase – of course, that was what all this land was: Duntisbury *Chase* – which he had looked up in Mother's massive double-volumed *Shorter Oxford English Dictionary*, ever to be relied on, and not least to be trusted as a sure reminder of their first and best owner, who had passed them on to him so long ago.

Chase –

3. *A tract of unenclosed land reserved for breeding and hunting wild animals ME . . .*

'ME' meaning 'Middle English', of the medieval variety, when, presumably, those Germanic tribes who had spoken 'Old English' – 'OE' – had settled their conquests well enough to start breeding and hunting for enjoyment –

4. That which is hunted ME . . .

And 5. Those who hunt (1811) . . .

That certainly covered everything he needed now (the *Shorter* could always be relied on): here he was, Benedikt Schneider, *alias* Thomas Wiesehöfer, in the chase, after the chase, and one of the chase, 3., 4., and 5., with all options catered for between the iron railings this fine English summer's midday –

But . . . no further along the chase at the moment, for the road was blocked ahead, with a tractor trying to manoeuvre a trailer loaded with hay bales almost broadside across it.

As Benedikt halted the car a heavily-built farm labourer appeared from behind the trailer, eyed the gap between the side of the vehicle and the gatepost critically, and shook his head in despair.

The tractor juddered forward slowly.

'Whoa!' roared the labourer to the youth at the wheel of the tractor. 'You'll 'ave the bloody post an' all! You just back up an' straighten 'er now, an' come out proper, like I told you.'

The youth looked from side to side uneasily – as well he might, thought Benedikt sympathetically, for both the road and the entrance to the field were narrow.

'Just take 'er easy now – like I told you,' shouted the labourer. Then he seemed to see Benedikt for the first time. 'Right 'and *down* – that's it!' He climbed the iron fence clumsily and came towards the car. 'Sorry, mister. Won't be long, though.'

'Please – it is no matter.' Benedikt peered at him, conscious again of his thick spectacles, and smiled as he adjusted his voice to the noise of the tractor's engine. 'I am in no hurry.'

'Ah . . .' The labourer nodded, studying the trailer's

painful progress. 'Get on with it then, Bobby! We ain't got all day.'

Benedikt wasn't so sure that at the youth's present rate of manoeuvre all day might not be what they would need. But there was nothing he could do about it now, for there was already a muddy farm Land Rover and a couple of boys on bicycles stacked up behind him – he could see them in his rear-view mirror – and peasants were the same the whole world over; whatever they said they liked nothing better than not to give way for men in suits driving gleaming cars.

Resigning himself to delay he started to settle back more comfortably into his seat, looking round casually into the field beside him –

It took every bit of his accumulated experience not to jerk upright again, but instead rather to hold the casual glance just long enough for ordinary unconcern, and then to continue slumping down as he would have done if he had never before seen the man striding across the field towards him.

There was no mistake –

He returned his gaze to the youth on the tractor for a moment, and then tipped back his head against the head-rest to study the roof of the car, as though surrendering to boredom.

In fact, he never had seen the man before, not in the flesh. But there was no mistake from the photographs, close-up front full-faced, side- and quarter-face, and long-shots snapped craftily to set him in the context of ordinary men – no mistake, even though he was here before he had been anticipated, dressed like any labourer too . . . creased open-necked shirt, stained khaki trousers stuffed into rubber boots – English 'Wellingtons', although the great aristocratic Iron Duke with whom mad old Blücher had kept faith at Waterloo had surely never worn anything so bucolic –

No mistake – the face and the size of the man, even the

36

solid, inexorable stride of the man across the rough pasture of the field – *like a tank*, thought Benedikt subjectively, out of the printed record – *tank-commander, Normandy 1944* . . . and that had been before he had ever been born, before Mother had met Papa even . . . even – unthinkably – when Mother and Father had been enemies, before they had been victor and vanquished –

He felt something touch the car, and twisted sideways towards the sound.

'Sorry, Mister – ' one of the boy-cyclists, a snub-nosed, cheeky-faced fourteen-year-old, alongside him now while squeezing past, addressed him briefly ' – I ain't scratched it – got rubber grips, see – ?' He indicated the handle-bars of his cycle with one momentarily-free hand before pushing down on the pedals to accelerate away.

'You get on out of 'ere, Benje, an' get off the bloody road!' shouted the farm labourer. 'An' you, Darren – your mum's been lookin' for you – '

The second cyclist whipped past Benedikt, in desperate pursuit of the departing Benje, who had swerved skilfully past the front wheels of the tractor.

'Little buggers!' The farm labourer shook his fist at them as Darren made a rude two-fingered signal backwards at him before swerving in Benje's wake.

'Problems, Cecil?' David Audley rested for a moment, grasping the top railing at the labourer's side, and then leaned on it, observing the road up and down.

'No problems, Doctor Audley.'

Cecil? Benedikt's concentration was side-tracked against his will away from David Audley by the incongruous name. *Benje* and *Darren* were bad enough – they were both English Christian names he didn't know . . . But *Cecil* . . . that was an exclusively aristocratic English name – wasn't there a renowned English lord, whom Mother had mentioned, who had lectured to her at Oxford – Lord David *Cecil* –

'Bobby's never going to get that trailer out,' said

Audley. 'Not if you want to keep those gate-posts, anyway.' He looked straight at Benedikt, before turning back to Cecil. 'I bet you a pint of best bitter.'

'Ahh . . . That's where you're wrong, Doctor.' Cecil didn't turn round. *'Right 'and down, lad – a bit more – steady! STEADY!'* He drew a deep breath. 'Bobby's goin' to learn – make it a pint of that Low-en-brow, right?'

'You're on. Low-en-brow it is.' Audley came back to Benedikt. 'I trust your business is not urgent, sir?'

Benedikt blinked at him through the thick lenses, playing for time. 'Please?'

Audley considered him for a moment. 'You . . . you-are-going-to-Duntisbury-Royal?' He spoke with exaggerated clarity, paused for an instant, then smiled helpfully. 'That's-all-there-is-down-this-road – ' he pointed ' – Duntisbury Royal?'

Benedikt nodded like a half-wit. 'Duntisbury Royal . . . yes.' He let his attention stray away from Audley, back to Cecil, who was shouting and gesticulating at the unfortunate youth on the tractor.

'Left 'and down – not too much – STEADY – '

The tractor roared and jerked.

'STOP!'

'Duntisbury Royal?' repeated Audley, catching a pause in the youth's agony.

Benedikt came back to him. 'So!' The man was some years younger than Papa, but the years had also been kinder to him, increasing the gap: he was not so much beginning to run to fat as to bulk, which his height and build minimized. When young, with those prize-fighter's features . . . features contradicted by the fierce hawkish eyes . . . he would have been a nasty customer to meet on a dark night lurking in a side-street, with that brawn moderated by the brains behind those eyes.

'So!' He nodded again, and tried to hide his thoughts behind the thick lenses. 'There is – ' he gestured uncertainly, as though searching for words ' – there is at

38

Duntisbury Royal an hotel . . . a public house?' He blinked. 'With rooms?'

'With – ' Audley's mouth opened, but the renewed roar of the tractor's engine cut him off.

'STEADY! AHH – !' Cecil's voice graduated from warning, through anger to despair, summoning both of them.

Benedikt watched, fascinated, as the tractor twisted the trailer out of the field. It was strange how the tractor was all noise and speed, its huge rear-wheels spinning madly, while the trailer appeared to follow more slowly in what seemed like its own silence, to catch the gate-post with the last metre of its frame. The post shuddered, then bent forwards and sideways, distorting and buckling the rails which met it, as the trailer scraped its way to freedom.

'*Jeesus-kee-rist-God-damn-and-blast-it-to-hell* – ' Cecil snatched the cloth-cap from his head and slapped it against his leg in rage. For a moment Benedikt thought he was going to dash the cap to the ground and stamp on it.

'I think I've just won a pint,' murmured Audley. Then, without taking his eyes off Cecil, he bent down to Benedikt's level. 'Your best bet is the *Eight Bells*, just beyond the church on the left when you get to the village. They don't really have rooms, but if you tell the landlord I sent you they might put you up – ' He straightened as Cecil turned towards them, and spread his hands eloquently.

Cecil stared at them darkly for a second or two, then jammed the cap back on his head and set off after the trailer, which was already hull-down in the next undulation of the road in the distance.

Benedikt watched him for another second or two, and then found to his surprise that Audley was no longer beside the car, but was back inside the field again, striking across it with long strides, as though he had urgent business elsewhere.

39

He stuck his head out of the window hastily. 'Sir – if you please, sir – !'

Almost without checking, Audley half-twisted in mid-stride. '*The-Eight-Bells* . . . just-past-the-church – ' he waved cheerily ' – you-can't-miss-it.'

After Audley had disappeared into the dead ground of the same slope which had swallowed up the trailer and tractor, Cecil stamping behind, Benedikt sat unmoving for a while. He had encountered David Audley, the legendary David Audley, unexpectedly. But he could *not* have avoided the encounter – and Audley, on the other hand, *could* have avoided it, very easily. Therefore . . . although Audley, equally, could not have expected *him*, but was expecting *someone* . . . ?

No. Alternatively, he was not expecting anyone, but he wanted to take a good, close-up look at anyone – any unaccountable stranger – who did appear in Duntisbury Chase . . . ?

Or . . . had it been pure accident? And how, indeed, could it be anything else, to combine Audley, appearing from nowhere in the thirty square miles of the Chase, which contained nowhere of importance – nowhere of human importance, anyway – except Duntisbury Royal itself, and its few isolated farmsteads . . . to combine Audley with Cecil and the youth on the tractor, to detain Thomas Wiesehöfer at this precise point in nowhere?

It could hardly be anything else but pure accident, however curious and inconvenient. Yet all the same, logic notwithstanding, such a pure, curious and inconvenient accident disturbed him when he set Audley's vast experience and known eccentricity against his own much shorter service. It was not simply that the man was a foreigner – the British, and especially the English, were not all that different, and the differences had been studied and codified – but rather that the man was in some sense a foreigner among his own people, a wild card in his own pack. So, knowing that, he must take nothing for granted.

So . . . taking nothing for granted as he shifted the gear change into drive . . . he took one keen look round in the rural emptiness of Duntisbury Chase.

There was nothing on the high naked ridge to his right, with its grass as close-cropped as an American pilot's head; while on his left the undulations he had already noted were broken only by those carefully placed individual trees, some tall and well-spread with age, some mature but still youthful, with here and there newly-planted saplings, until the ridge fell away finally into the bed of the stream itself.

Across the stream the pattern repeated itself. And what it was, what it all added up to, partly by its own topography, partly by what man had made of it, and finally by the descriptive noun attached to it, was marvellous hunting country: a *chase* not for pursuing game on foot, in the more popular European manner, but in the glorious English style, in the red coats which they so oddly (and typically) characterized as 'pink' – he could almost hear the hounds baying, and the sound of the horn, and the huntsman's *view-halloo* as the quarry broke cover –

A loud horn-sound, unmelodious and angry, startled him half out of his seat, hitting him from behind, reminding him even before he could look in his mirror of the farm Land Rover at his back, which he had quite forgotten.

His foot automatically depressed the accelerator, and the big car surged away, leaving the sound echoing behind him. Down . . . down and up – the trees and the empty pastures and the ridge flashed past on each side – down and up, and down and up . . .

There was a horseman on his left, galloping parallel to the road at full speed, ducking down under the branches of a tree and then emerging, with the clods flying from the horse's hooves. For a moment the horseman was ahead – not a man, but a boy . . . or a man, but jockey-size – then horse and rider vanished behind another tree, and the superior horse-power of the Mercedes left both behind effortlessly, and he was alone again.

The trees thickened suddenly on each side of the road, closing in on him, but he caught a glimpse of a squat church tower, grey-green with age, in a gap up in front, on his left.

And now there was a straggle of houses – little dwellings in weathered brick, hidden behind thick hedges under the trees –

But there was no road-sign . . . he frowned and peered into the overgrown verges, and saw no indication that this was Duntisbury Royal at last. And yet it must be Duntisbury Royal, because it could be nothing else – there *was* nothing else for it to be.

The church came into view, back from the road in its churchyard full of gravestones, some of them upright and some canted over; and further on, separated from the churchyard wall by a square of gravel, a low building with roof coming down to the ground floor, little bigger than an ordinary house but with a hanging sign on one gable-end which bore a representation of bells – eight bells, Benedikt guessed.

He pulled into the empty square of gravel, alongside a tall stone cross, which had a sword in high relief superimposed on it, on a plinth beside the churchyard entrance.

Benedikt stepped out of the car. There were words engraved on the plinth, cut deep, as the English always did cut their inscriptions, but he didn't need to read them, for he had read them on other similar crosses already.

Lest we forget . . . and somewhere, round the other sides, cut just as deep, would be *1914-18* and *1939-45*, each with its list of names even in this tiny place, which was so peaceful and far-removed from the quarrels of the great and powerful.

For the real Thomas Wiesehöfer it might have been a bad omen, he thought, closing the car door without locking it. But for the real Benedikt Schneider there could be no bad thoughts here: if they didn't want to forget, there was half of Benedikt Schneider which had a right to remember with them, as Mother had once reminded him, for his dead uncles and great-uncles on her side, who would anyway and at this length of time be unlikely to hold anything against his other dead uncles and great-uncles, who had been their enemies.

And, besides, who was he here for now, if not for *their* Elizabeth Regina, *D.G., Fid. Def.?*

He chose the Saloon Bar, because that was the bar Thomas Wiesehöfer would have chosen.

It was a dark little room, all the colder for its big empty fireplace, smelling of furniture polish and slightly of damp, and quite empty.

Eventually someone came to the bar, which was partly in this room, and partly in the adjoining Public Bar, which (so far as he could see through) looked lighter and more friendly.

The someone was a tall, slightly-built young man, who brought the Public Bar's friendly look with him.

'Please . . . do you have rooms, with bed-and-breakfast?' It took an effort to emphasize each *s*, and to roll each *r* gutturally, as he would ordinarily have prided himself in not doing, so as to be able to surprise the landlord later.

'Oh, no – I'm sorry – ' the young man sounded quite genuinely sorry, too ' – we don't have guests . . . we don't really have room – I'm sorry.'

'Ach – so!' Benedikt pretended disappointment. It ought to have been real disappointment, but suddenly he was glad that he wasn't going to be trapped in Duntisbury Royal, or Duntisbury Chase, tonight. And although his orders prompted him to mention now that a large ugly man who had omitted to give his name had sent him to the *Eight Bells*, those orders were not absolutely precise and instinct had just cancelled them.

'The nearest place, if you're looking for a bed, is the

Golden Cross at Fyfield St John, on the main road . . .' The landlord's face indicated some doubts about the *Golden Cross's* beds. 'Or, you could go back to Salisbury – if you've come from Salisbury, that is . . . there are lots of hotels there. It's not far, really.'

Benedikt nodded. The landlord was assuming from his speech, and perhaps from the big car outside, that he was a foreigner who had strayed off the beaten track. But, although there was no room at the inn, that was something which needed contradicting.

'Thank you.' He nodded again. 'But this is . . . Duntisbury Royal – yes?'

'Yes – ' The landlord began to polish an already well-polished glass ' – that's right.'

'And . . . there is here a *Rrr*oman villa? The Duntisbury *Rrr*oman villa?'

'Yes.' The landlord stopped polishing the glass. 'It's just behind the church, down towards the stream.' He blinked at Benedikt suddenly. 'But . . . it's on private land . . . I mean . . . they're not excavating it at the moment – they were in the middle of excavating it, but they've stopped for the time being.'

Benedikt nodded. 'The Wessex Archaeological Society – yes, I know. But I may look at it from the churchyard, perhaps?'

'Yes . . .' Mention of the Wessex Archaeological Society threw the landlord for a moment, and they both knew that churchyards were public land, in practice if not in law.

'So!' Benedikt nodded again. Nodding was standard practice for foreigners. Then, as though he had just remembered, he felt in his breast-pocket and produced his bit of paper. He adjusted his spectacles, which made the words difficult to read. 'Miss Rebecca Maxwell-Smith – ' he looked up at the landlord ' – it is Miss Rebecca Maxwell-Smith, of the Duntisbury Manor, Duntisbury Royal, to whom I am addressed. Could you direct me to her, please?'

If he had asked to be directed to Her Majesty Queen

Elizabeth, *D.G.*, *Fid. Def.*, at Buckingham Palace, he could hardly have disconcerted the young landlord more. Or . . . perhaps if he had asked for *David Audley* – ?

'Yes.' Now the landlord was nodding. 'Miss Becky . . . but she may not be in. I could phone her from here, if you like?'

'That would be most kind.' If he nodded again, his head would fall off. But he must remember where he was. 'I may have a drink, meanwhile?' He looked over the range of bottles behind the bar, and then at the beer pump-handles. 'Löwenbräu – a halfpint, please.'

As he watched the landlord draw the beer he realized suddenly what it was that Audley had won from Cecil. 'You will join me, please?' He put a £5 note on the bar.

'Thank you, but no.' The landlord set the glass down. 'It's only just gone twelve – too early for me. I'll go and phone for you, though.'

Benedikt drank some of the beer. He realized that Audley had been right – this was Low-en-brow, not Löwenbräu.

A very pretty girl appeared from a door behind the bar, and smiled at him. 'Are you being served?' she inquired.

Benedikt lifted his Low-en-brow. 'Thank you, yes. Do you serve lunch, please?'

'Bar snacks – what would you like?' She handed him a menu.

The bar snacks were very reasonably priced. And the Low-en-brow wasn't at all bad, really. And the girl was pretty, and the landlord was being helpful – come to that, even Dr David Audley had been helpful in his equivocal way, just as Cecil had been polite after his fashion. And here he was, an innocent German scholar, abroad on a summer's day in a tranquil English village of the sort that few mere tourists ever discovered, since there wasn't a single sign-post to direct them to it.

'Thank you, but no.' He looked at his watch. 'It is only ten minutes after twelve – that is too early for me.'

The pretty girl gave him another sunny smile, and turned away to start re-arranging the glasses behind the bar.

It was only instinct, of course . . . that prickling at the nape of the neck which came even against reason from some undiscovered part of the brain, although it always seemed to travel up the spine from the small of his back . . . or, if not instinct, then more simply his subjective reaction to the oil-and-water mixture of so much innocence here with what he knew about Audley and what lay somewhere in that quiet, tree-shaded churchyard.

Then the landlord came back, and as Benedikt rose from the bench on which he had seated himself he thought the man exchanged a glance with the girl. But he also thought he might have imagined what he thought, for she was the sort of girl with whom glances must often be exchanged.

'I'm sorry, but Miss Becky isn't at home.' The landlord shook his head apologetically. 'But I could phone again – they say she could be back any time . . . if you like to wait . . .' He shrugged. 'Or . . . I'm sure it *would* be all right for you to look at the Roman villa – I can't imagine Miss Becky minding . . . It's just that we're not very used to strangers.' He smiled again, and pointed to a pile of coins and notes on the bar. 'And I see that you're not very used to the price of beer in England, sir.'

'Thank you.' Benedikt was pleased to have established his foreignness. 'But you will take for the telephone calls, please . . . So I will go to the villa, and then return – yes?'

Outside, he first felt so absurdly and irrationally glad to be in the fresh air again, away from the claustrophobic little bar-room, that he concluded he was being frightened by shadows of his imagination. In the sunlight, with the green leaves everywhere, and the birds singing and fluttering in the trees, there was nothing to fear.

Not the small boy sitting on the churchyard wall, anyway: it was the same snub-nosed Benje who had pushed past the car, with his racing-cycle now propped up beside him.

He gave the boy a nod of recognition as he pushed open the wicket-gate into the churchyard.

It was an English churchyard like any other, with its scatter of newer gravestones among older ones on which the inscriptions ranged from the barely decipherable to mere lichen-covered indentation which only God could read. There was a neat little gravel path meandering between the stones and the occasional yew-tree, to divide just short of the porch, one branch leading directly to the door, the other curving round the building.

Under other circumstances Benedikt would have entered the church, as he had always been taught to do, to say a prayer. But the sun was warm on his face, and in these circumstances, in this place at this time, he judged that Mother would forgive him for breaking her rule, and would allow him to say the words of her old Englishman under the sky, as they had originally been prayed –

Lord, Thou knowest that I must be very busy this day. If I forget Thee, do not Thou forget me.

Instead, he followed the curving path along the side of the church, to the newest grave of all, which had instantly caught his eye.

HERBERT GEORGE MAXWELL
CBE, DSO, MC, RA
1912–1982

The inscription was cut deep into the new headstone: it would take centuries of wind and weather to erase it.

Under the date, but less deeply incised because of its complexity, was a military badge consisting of an antique cannon surmounted by a crown, standing upon the single Latin word "Ubique".

Below the stone, on the freshly-turned chalky soil, there was a plastic wreath of red poppies and laurel

47

leaves, with a ribbon identifying 'The Royal British Legion' across it, and an unmarked posy of fresh flowers and greenery.

Benedikt marked the difference between the two tributes: on closer scrutiny, the soil was no longer quite freshly turned, for there were already tiny green things sprouting from it – the delicate spears of young grass and the minute broad-leaved weeds which would eventually reduce General Herbert George Maxwell's last resting place to uniformity with all his neighbours in Duntisbury Royal churchyard and all his old comrades in dozens of far-flung military cemeteries (that was what 'Ubique' meant, after all, wasn't it?).

But, where the Royal British Legion wreath dated from the original burial judging by the rain-spotted dust which covered it, the posy had been cut and carefully put together only a few hours before.

So there was somebody in Duntisbury Royal who still loved *General Herbert George Maxwell, CBE, DSO, MC, RA,* aged 70 . . . *CBE* was some great honour, and *DSO* and *MC* were gallantry medals, and that crowned cannon could only mean *Royal Artillery,* not *Royal Academician*!

So here was the fuse . . . buried two metres deep, and impervious to any mischance now, but still as live and dangerous as any of the thousands of shells he had once fired, so it seemed.

But what shell, of all those thousands, had he fired which had killed him all those years after, so explosively?

They didn't know, they said.

And who had killed him, anyway?

They said they didn't know that, either.

Half-blurred, on the edge of his vision through the spectacles, he noticed another stone, but with the same name.

He turned his head towards it: *Edith Mary Maxwell, 1890–1960* . . . he peered further to the left, and then to the right . . . they were all Maxwells here – *Victoria Mary Maxwell* – all Maxwell women, anyway –

And there was something else – someone else – on that blurred no-man's-land –

Benje, the snub-nosed cyclist, was almost at his back, complete with his racing-bike.

'That's the Old General, the Squire,' said the boy, nodding at the new grave. 'We had a big funeral for him, with soldiers – gunners, they were.'

Benedikt nodded gravely.

'The IRA killed him,' said the boy. 'Blew him up, they did. Dad says they're a lot of bastards.'

'Yes?' said Benedikt.

But that was one thing they did *not* say: the IRA had not blown up General Herbert George Maxwell. If they were agreed on nothing else, British Intelligence and the IRA were both agreed on that.

2

It might be useful, thought Benedikt. And even if it was not useful, it would be instructive.

But most of all it might be useful.

'You knew the old general?'

The boy Benje started to nod, and then a sound behind him diverted his attention.

The other – the boy who had given Mr Cecil the rude signal – shot out from behind a nearby yew-tree on his bicycle, and came to a racing halt beside Benje in a spray of gravel.

Benedikt studied them both. They were two very different types, the boy Benje extrovert and cheekily-aggressive, and the other boy . . . What was his name? He had heard it, but it had escaped him . . . the other boy was black-haired and fine-boned, and altogether more withdrawn. The only thing they had in common was their transport: the low-handlebarred, multi-geared racing cycles were identical.

And he had a better introduction to them both there. 'Those look good bikes – BSA, are they?' He eased his accent, the better to communicate with them. 'You are brothers?'

'Me and him?' Benje threw the question back contemptuously. 'You must be joking!'

'You do not look like brothers – no.' He searched for an opening. 'But you bought the same machines.'

Benje shook his head. 'We didn't buy 'em.'

'Of course! You were given them.' He knew that wasn't what the boy had meant.

'No. We won them.' Benje couldn't let the mistake pass uncorrected.

'In a competition?'

Benje looked at him. 'Sort of.' He paused for an instant, then nodded at the tombstone. 'We got them from him.'

'From the General? He gave them to you?'

'No – not *gave*.' Benje frowned, suddenly tongue-tied.

'We both won places at King Edward's School.' The other boy filled the silence coolly. 'Everyone who wins a place at King Edward's – everyone from here – gets a bicycle from the Old General.' He put a capital letter on the title.

'Ah!' And with Duntisbury Royal's inaccessibility to public transport, that was an act of practical generosity, thought Benedikt. 'So you are able to cycle to school!'

'No.' Benje shook his head again. 'There's a taxi comes for us – collects us in the morning, an' brings us back after first prep.'

The other boy nodded. 'And the Old General pays for that as well.'

It was strange how they both held him in the living present, here of all places. But presumably the benefaction was endowed to outlast the benefactor.

''Sright,' agreed Benje. 'An' it's Blackie Nabb's old taxi, too – my dad reckons it's worth a fortune to him, picking us up. Says he wouldn't be able to run it if it wasn't for us, and Sandra Brown and Mary Hobbs – they go to the High.' He cocked his head at Benedikt. 'They got bikes, too.'

So the Old General was both directly and indirectly the village's benefactor – but not 'was', rather 'had been' . . . he was falling into their confusion of tenses.

He looked at them sadly. 'But now he is dead, the Old General . . .'

'Miss Becky is paying now,' said the other boy, mistaking his sadness with the cold logic of youth.

'Well, she would, wouldn't she! Becky's all right – she used to go to the High in Blackie's old rattle-trap too,

51

didn't she!' Benje's view of the Old General's successor was less deferential than his friend's, and so was the face he now presented to Benedikt, even though he could not yet quite nerve himself to ask the questions his curiosity had printed clearly on it.

'Miss Becky is the Old General's grand-daughter?' He prodded Benje towards those questions without scruple. It would not do to underestimate either of these children – it never did to underestimate any children, but these two particularly. For a start, they were perhaps older than he had at first thought, and in spite of their peasant accents they were scholarship boys as well, so it seemed. Exactly what that meant, he wasn't sure, in the present confused state of English education, which the English themselves had not standardized and didn't seem to understand, let alone agree on. But it was still probably true that when English education was good it was very good, and these were fledgling products of it.

'Yes.' Suspicion, rather than curiosity, was dominant in the other boy.

Darren, he remembered suddenly. The outlandish name.

'You're not English.' The first of Benje's questions came in the guise of a statement.

'No, I am not.' It nettled him slightly that the boy's first thrust had penetrated his almost faultless accent. 'So what am I, then?'

'German,' said Benje unhesitatingly.

'Or Swedish,' said Darren. 'Remember those two who came through last year, who stayed at the *Eight Bells*? The chap who played rugger – '

'German,' repeated Benje. 'Betcha 10p.'

So the *Eight Bells* did have rooms. 'What makes you so sure, Benje?' It was time to counter-attack just a little, to assert equality rather than any adult superiority.

'How d'you know my name?'

Benedikt smiled. 'Benje and Darren.'

'On the road below Caesar's Camp,' Darren jogged his friend's memory. 'When Old Cecil balled us out – remember?'

'Huh!' Benje didn't like being jogged, especially in front of the stranger whose car he had touched, and most especially when that stranger was a foreigner too, that sound suggested.

'But you are quite right.' Benedikt invested the admission with a touch of admiration: more than equality, he wanted their friendship, because with these two little mobile spies on his side he could have a mine of information open to him about Duntisbury Royal, past and present. Precious little that happened in the Chase would escape them, and David Audley was a stranger there also.

Benje thawed slightly.

'You are quite right,' he repeated himself, grinning now. 'Wiesehöfer – Thomas Wiesehöfer, from West Germany.' And since he judged it time to be honestly foreign he extended his hand to each of them in turn.

For a moment the handshaking unsettled them. But they accepted the alien custom manfully, like the well-brought-up lads he had also judged them to be under their brashness, and his heart twisted between approval of them and disapproval for his own disingenuousness.

Benje rallied first, predictably on his mettle after the debacle of the names. 'You've come to see . . . Miss Becky, have you?'

'Miss Becky?' That was a disconcertingly sharp little assumption, but having admitted it in the Eight Bells public house ten minutes ago he could not deny it now. 'Miss . . . Rebecca Maxwell-Smith is that?'

''Sright.' The boy folded his arms and appraised him with a customs officer's eye, as though waiting to hear what he had to declare.

'Yes.' He would dearly have liked to ask how Benje had reached that conclusion.But he had to bind them to him with trust before he started asking questions, so that the settlement of their curiosity took priority over his own. 'That is to say . . . I had thought to speak with General Maxwell – with the Old General. But it is with Miss Rebecca Maxwell-Smith that I must speak now, it seems.'

'Why d'you want to see her?' Darren continued the interrogation with all the delicacy of a GDR border guard.

'It is not her I wish to see, not really.' He nodded at them, as though revealing a confidence. 'It is the Roman villa – the Duntisbury Roman villa . . . it is on her land, yes?'

'The Roman villa?' Darren frowned at him.

'It is on her land, I believe – yes?'

'Yes.' Benje nodded at him. 'All the land round here's hers – it was the Old General's, but it's hers now – from Caesar's Camp to Woodbury Rings on the top, and along the stream down here, both sides – she owns the lot.' He paused. 'Why d'you want to see the Roman villa? There isn't much to see, you know.' He shook his head. 'Until they started digging it up there wasn't *anything* to see. It was just a field, that was all it was.'

'My Gran knew there was something there long before they dug anything up.' Darren wasn't going to let Benje do all the talking. 'She says, when she was a girl there were lots of rabbits down there, an' there was always lots of stuff – bits of brick an' such like – where they dug their holes – ' He stopped suddenly. 'Why d'you want to see the old Roman villa?'

Benedikt was ready for that one. 'Because I am a student of such things.'

Benje stared at him in disbelief. 'A student?'

Darren gave his friend a sidelong glance. 'Schoolmaster,' he murmured.

'No.' That would never do! 'I am not a schoolmaster. Looking at Roman things is my interest – my hobby – like stamp-collecting.' He grinned at them. 'We had Romans in Germany too – did you know that?'

'Huh!' Benje scowled.

Benedikt looked at him questioningly. 'Did you not know that?'

Darren's face split into a wicked grin. 'Oh, he knows it! *Germani multum,* Benje – eh?'

'*Germani multum* – huh!' Benje's freckled features twisted. '*Germani* flipping *multum . . . ab hac consuetudine differunt; nam neque druides habent, qui rebus divinis praesint, neque* flipping *sacrificiis student.*'

The contrast of the impeccable Latin – or it sounded impeccable, anyway – with the boy's accented English took Benedikt aback almost as much as the words themselves. He struggled for a moment with their meaning, rusty memories grating on each other – it was something about the Germans being different . . . not having Druids or making sacrifices – and then cut his losses.

'You are a Latin scholar – ' He cut off the statement as it doubled Darren up with laughter.

'Ha-ha-very-funny,' said Benje to his friend. Then he sniffed and turned to Benedikt. 'He thinks it's a joke that I had to learn a whole flipping page of Caesar – King Edward's is a very old-fashioned school – everyone says so.' He blinked suddenly. 'If you want to see the villa I can show you the way. It's just the other side of the church.'

'Thank you.' Benedikt leaned forward slightly towards the boy. 'I went to an old-fashioned school too – I had the same trouble.'

'With Latin?' Benje pointed the way.

'With English, actually,' Benedikt lied.

'You speak it jolly well now.'

Benedikt shrugged. 'So . . . one day you will speak Latin very well.'

''Cept there's no one to speak it to –

> *Latin is a language*
> *As dead as dead can be.*
> *It killed the Ancient Romans –*
> *And now it's killing me!'*

They rounded the end of the church.

'But it will help you speak your own language.' Benedikt summoned up Mother's view on the subject. 'To learn a foreign language, you have to learn your own.'

'That's what David says. Actually, I don't mind Latin. But I'd rather learn French – or German, of course.' Benje amended his opinion hastily, out of consideration for his new companion, Benedikt suspected.

'German is a not-so-difficult language, I think.' Benedikt nodded, man-to-man. 'But David is right – he is your schoolmaster?'

'No. David Aud – ' Benje caught himself. 'He's just someone I know, that's all.'

'Well, I agree with him.' That was interesting: David Audley was here, in the midst of them in the little village, and known to them – known to Mr Cecil, and known to Benje, and certainly known to Miss Becky . . . But someone had told Benje not to broadcast the fact of his being there.

They were approaching a stile set in the churchyard wall.

'We go over here . . . What's your job then – what do you do, if you're not a schoolmaster?' Benje gestured towards the stile. 'Were you ever in the army?'

'No.' He set his hand on the wall. It was odd how much the lie cost him – how much he would have liked to have won Benje's good regard, as he surely could have done with the truth, boys being what they were the world over, whatever they might think later in their student days. 'My eye-sight is not good, unfortunately. And I have flat feet.' He swung himself up, over the stile. 'They would not have me.'

'Hard luck.' Benje commiserated with him. 'We've got a boy like that in our form – he can't play cricket.' He looked over his shoulder. 'But Darren can't play cricket either – he can see perfectly well, but he can't hit a ball to save his life.'

'Cricket's a boring game,' said Darren dismissively from behind them. 'You were lucky – I don't expect they tried to make you play it, Mr – Mr . . .'

'Thomas,' said Benedikt. If they called David Audley 'David', they must learn to call him 'Thomas'. He was more than half-way to getting through to them now, and if he could get on Christian name terms he would be all the way.

'There's the villa,' said Benje, pointing.

The field sloped gently away from them, down to a belt of trees which must mark the course of the stream which ran the length of the valley between the ridges on each side.

It was a typical Roman site – that was what had been said of it – sheltered and watered, just the sort of place the Romanized Britons, if not the Romans themselves, would have been encouraged to choose in all the confidence of Roman peace, with no thought for defence behind the shield of the legions.

He looked round, to try and get his bearings. Somewhere on his left, up the valley, ran the line of the Roman road from the coast, and 'Caesar's Camp' might well be its marker, if the name meant anything more than peasant legend.

He came back to the excavation itself, on the furthest side of the field away from him, almost under the trees. Clearly, it was not far beyond the exploratory phase of the trial trenches to establish its general shape – even the two temporary huts, erected presumably to house finds and equipment respectively, had a brand-new, unweathered look; nor was much work in progress, with only a man and a youth in sight, squatting beside a grid cut in the turf which was partially covered by a great sheet of yellow plastic.

'Come on,' said Benje. 'They won't mind as long as you're with us.'

They were half-way across the field before the man stood up, and became instantly recognizable.

'Who is that?' asked Benedikt innocently. 'One of the archaeologists, is he?'

'Mmm . . .' Benje nodded.

'Yes,' said Darren, coming up on his other side. 'But you didn't tell us what you do. You're not a schoolmaster – ?'

'I am a civil servant.' The youth was standing up now. 'I work for the government.'

'Are you on holiday?' Darren was really becoming rather tiresomely inquisitive.

'Yes.' But it was the youth who was coming to meet him, not David Audley. 'I am with the embassy in London – or, I will be from next Monday. I am just starting a tour of duty in England, you see – '

It was not a youth – it was a girl – a young woman –

Miss Becky

A heavy thumping sound diverted his attention momentarily, coming from the margin of the trees beside the huts, just to his right: the front half of a horse appeared through the foliage – it tossed its head at him, and then swung round on its tether, stamping the ground with its hind legs and flicking its tail at him.

'Can I help you?'

Cool, educated voice, too full of confidence and self-assurance to allow any other emotion room in it: Miss Becky for sure – Miss Rebecca Maxwell-Smith, only twenty years old, but already very much the Lady of the Manor on her own land, the undisputed mistress of Duntisbury Chase.

'His name's Thomas – Thomas Wise – *Vise* – *Veese* – *Veesehoff* – ' Benje gave up the attempt in despair.

'Wiesehöfer.' Benedikt met her gaze directly, and the sympathetic half-smile he had conjured up on Benje's behalf almost died on his lips, because the look in those pale blue-grey eyes – more grey than blue – transfixed him: where that voice was neutral upper-class English, those eyes had the duellist's look in them, of pistols-at-twelve-paces and then the churchyard behind him. 'Thomas Wiesehöfer.'

'He's German,' said Darren.

'He's come to see the villa,' said Benje.

'He's a civil servant,' said Darren. 'He's on holiday.'

'He's an expert on Roman villas,' said Benje. 'They're his hobby – like stamp-collecting, Becky.'

Her eyes left Benedikt, softening suddenly into more-blue-than-grey as they switched to each of his defenders in turn. 'Oh, yes?' She smiled. 'And he drives a Mercedes with CD plates?'

Benedikt glanced sideways, at Benje, and made an oddly moving discovery: just as there was an emotion described as hero-worship, which he had seen on very rare occasions in the faces of men and boys for other men and other boys, so there was also one of *heroine*-worship, quite devoid of any sexual undertones, which a boy at least (if not a man) could have for someone of the other sex . . . Or which – he glanced quickly at Darren, and found no such look there – or which, anyway, this boy Benje had for this young woman, Miss Becky.

'You know about him?' Benje didn't sound put out by his heroine's omniscience, it merely confirmed what he already believed, Benedikt guessed.

'I am not . . . most regrettably, I must admit that I am *not* an expert on Roman villas.' He would have to beware of Benje's loyalty – it might be safer to cultivate Darren; but meanwhile he must head off that misapprehension. 'Roman roads are more my . . . my speciality.' He smiled shyly at Miss Becky, and was relieved to find the remains of her softened expression still visible. 'Miss Maxwell-Smith?'

'Yes.' Without that coldness behind the eyes, and even with her hair severely pulled back into a pony-tail, she was quite a pretty girl, though she fell well short of beauty – it was a face with character bred into it, but at first sight he could not decide whether the jaw-line betrayed self-will and obstinacy, or determination and constancy.

'I am passing by . . . on holiday, as my friends here

have said, before I take up my post in our embassy in London.' He paused, and blinked at her as though taking time to sort out his English. 'I am going to Maiden Castle, near Dorchester . . . and to see the country of Thomas Hardy.' Another pause. 'But in London I was told of your villa, Miss Maxwell-Smith, by . . . by Professor Handforth-Jones, of the Society for the Advancement of Romano-British Studies.'

He had not intended producing Professor Handforth-Jones, like a rabbit out of the magician's hat, so early in his introduction. But Audley had come up behind her as he spoke.

'Tony Handforth-Jones?' Audley rose to the name.

Rebecca Maxwell-Smith half-turned, half looked up to the big man. 'You've heard of him?'

'I know him. He's a good friend of mine – and a damn good archaeologist too. But he's more into military sites in Scotland at the moment – Agricola's line-of-march, and the location of Mons Graupius, and that sort of thing.' He nodded at her. 'But he'll have heard of your Fighting Man, for sure.' He gave Benedikt a nod. 'Hullo again.'

Rebecca Maxwell-Smith looked from one to the other of them. 'You've already met?'

'We've met.' Another nod. 'But we haven't actually been introduced. The Mercedes with the CD plates – I told you.'

'Oh!' She caught her mistake skilfully. 'How silly of me! Yes . . . well . . . Mr Wiesehöfer – this is Dr David Audley, who is helping us with our excavations.'

'"Helping" is hardly the word.' Audley shook his head. 'I'm no archaeologist – and Roman Britain isn't my field . . . The truth is, I'm a wheelbarrow-wheeler, and a cook-and-bottle washer, and a hewer-of-wood and drawer-of-water, is what I am, Mr Wiesehöfer. Not a professional.'

He had the build for manual work, thought Benedikt, smiling back at the disclaimer. But he was also a professional in another field, who wasn't prepared to compromise his cover by lying about his qualifications for being here in Duntisbury Chase, even for the benefit of an innocent foreigner.

'Dr Audley.' He nodded again. It would be interesting to probe that cover further, to find out how Audley accounted for his presence. But it wasn't in Thomas Wiesehöfer's own cover to show such curiosity yet.

'If you want to see the villa – here it is.' Rebecca Maxwell-Smith gestured around her. 'We haven't got very far with it, but of course you're welcome to see what there is of it.'

'This is the end of the preliminary reconnaissance operations,' explained Audley. 'The big effort starts next spring.'

'Ah, yes.' What Audley had not added was that the reconnaissance had ended prematurely, somewhat to the archaeologists' irritation. At first, after the General's death, they had been allowed to carry on, with only the loss of a single day for the funeral. But then Miss Rebecca Maxwell-Smith had very recently indicated her wish that operations should cease for the time being, with the promise of generous financial aid the following year when she had full control of her inheritance. And with the estate trustees already obedient to her strong will, there was nothing the archaeologists had been able to do about it except to register their disappointment publicly – and their mystification at her change of heart privately. But Thomas Wiesehöfer ought not to know any of that.

He looked around. 'But you have made discoveries, so I have been told.'

'Oh yes.' The girl nodded. 'They have a fair idea of the extent of the buildings, as far as the trees.'

'They've uncovered the edge of a pavement over there – ' Audley pointed ' – and it just may be an Orpheus one, too.' He watched Benedikt covertly as he spoke.

'An Orpheus pavement?' Benedikt obliged him

61

quickly. 'I have seen fragments of such a pavement not far from my home, near Münster-Sarmsheim, also discovered recently – not as large as your great pavement at Woodchester, of course . . . But there are many villas in the territories of the Treveri, so there is always hope.' He smiled at Audley. 'I may see this find, perhaps?'

'I'm sorry – it's been covered up again,' the girl apologized. 'To protect it from the frost during the winter.'

'Ah yes!' He transferred the smile to her.

'And I'm afraid our Fighting Man isn't on view, either.' She shook her head sadly. 'They've taken him away for detailed study – they didn't want to risk leaving him, once they'd found him. Did your friend in London tell you about him?'

'Professor Handforth-Jones? Yes . . . that is, he spoke of a warrior. I did not quite understand . . . but a warrior, yes.'

'We call him our Fighting Man.' She pointed to a larger area of excavation. 'He was found there, in what may have been a barn. They think he was a Saxon, judging by his equipment.'

'A burial?' He nodded. 'It was the custom sometimes, was it not . . . of the Saxon invaders . . . to bury dead persons in such ruins?' That was what Handforth-Jones had said, anyway.

'No.' She frowned for an instant. 'I mean, it may have been their custom – I'm not a historian. But, what I mean is, they don't think *he* was buried – deliberately buried.'

'It was pure luck, really,' said Audley. 'They were digging one of their trial trenches, and they hit the remains of this chap straight away, under the fallen debris of the roof – and just the way he'd fallen, too – sword in hand – *literally* sword in hand.' He paused for a moment, staring not at Benedikt, but across the field towards the area of excavation which the girl had indicated. 'Or . . . what remained of the sword and the hand, anyway . . .

and everything else he died with, so they think – helmet of some sort, and a belt with a dagger, and maybe some sort of crude cuirass even . . . Right, Becky?'

The girl nodded. 'They're not sure about that. They said it was much too early to be certain. But they did get very excited about him, and they were tremendously careful about lifting him out – in the end they undercut him, and raised him in one piece . . . What they think – well, they don't go as far as saying that they think it, but it's one theory – is that the barn caught fire, and fell on him . . . when the villa was sacked. Because they found evidence of fire, both there and in another trench, over on the other side.' She pointed. 'And the way they thought it might have happened is that he was killed in the barn *here*, but in all the confusion no one saw that – or no one lived to tell the tale, anyway . . . And the barn caught fire, and fell down, but maybe it was empty, so no one picked over the ruins, like they would have done with the main buildings – or, it could have been at night that the villa was sacked . . . But they didn't see what happened to him, one way or another, anyway. He just disappeared.'

'"Missing, presumed killed in action",' murmured Audley. 'Or maybe even "AWOL", as we used to record more uncharitably in some cases.'

'It's how he was when they found him, you see,' explained the girl. 'He had his arms flung out wide, with all his equipment and his sword still in his hand, like David says. And what Dr Johns says is that if his own side had buried him they might have left his weapons with him, but they'd have laid him out properly at the very least. But if his side had lost, then the other side would have stripped him – they wouldn't have let perfectly good weapons go to waste.'

Benedikt looked around him. The gently sloping meadow betrayed no tell-tale signs of what lay beneath it, except where the trial excavations had been dug. It was just a field, with trees on three sides of it, the roofs of Duntisbury Royal peeping through them on one side, bounded on the fourth by the churchyard wall and the tree-shaded church itself. And it looked as though it had been just a field since the beginning of time.

You must rebuild in your imagination, was what Papa always said about sites such as this. But it required an immense effort of will to raise up a great mansion in this grassy emptiness – a house with colonnades, and many rooms, and gracious pavements on which Orpheus had tamed his wild beasts in the lamplight, where generations of people had lived.

And then one day . . . one night . . . this dream of a great house had turned into a nightmare, with the red flower of the raiders' fires bursting out of the thatch of the out-buildings as the house died, signalling the end of civilization –

But it probably hadn't been anything like that, he disciplined himself: the end would more likely have come much more slowly and ignominiously, with the original owners of the Orpheus pavement long gone, and their uncouth inheritors squabbling in the decayed ruins with invaders who were almost indistinguishable from them, but more virile.

The bleakness of that conclusion roused him. Whatever way the Duntisbury Roman villa had gone down into the dark, it was of no importance to him.

He blinked at Audley through the thick lenses of the spectacles. 'That is a most interesting theory, Dr – Dr Audley.'

Audley smiled. 'Not mine, Mr Wiesehöfer. And not the most interesting thing about the Fighting Man either, to my way of thinking.'

Benedikt looked at him questioningly.

'He was killed close to the door – almost in the doorway. They know that because of the position of the post-holes left by the door-posts.'

'So?' He thought there was something curiously mischievous in Audley's smile.

64

'So . . . how was he killed? And who killed him?'
Audley paused. 'Supposing the barn didn't fall on him and
kill him . . . and if it was just about to collapse he would
hardly have gone into it . . . did some poor frightened
little Briton stab him from behind as he went in – someone
lurking just inside the door, say? Or did some hulking
great German – I beg your pardon! – some hulking great
Saxon or *Jutish* warrior spear him from the front, while he
was defending the doorway like Horatius on the bridge?'

Benedikt frowned. 'But did you not say – or was it not
Miss Maxwell-Smith who said . . . that he was a Saxon
warrior?'

The smile was almost evil now. 'That's what the experts
think, yes. But apparently there were people called
'*foederati*' in those days, Mr Wiesehöfer.'

'*Foedus*,' piped up Benje suddenly. '*Foedus – foederis*
. . . "a league between states or an agreement or covenant
between individuals" – that's the noun . . . But there's an
adjective *foedus* which means "foul, filthy and horrible" –
like *foedi oculi* means "bloodshot eyes", like Blackie
Nabb's got on Sunday mornings – '

'Benje!' snapped Miss Maxwell-Smith, suddenly much
older than her years. 'You mustn't say that about
Blackie.'

'Well, it's true, isn't it?' Benje was not overawed by his
heroine. 'Dad says if it wasn't for the Old General,
Blackie 'ud 'ave been disqualified from driving years ago – '
he caught himself too late as he realized he had mentioned
someone the memory of whom would pain her. 'Sorry,
Becky!'

'My fault – ' interposed Audley quickly ' – I told young
Benjamin about *foedus* and the *foederati* . . . We were
having a discussion about the Latin language, and we
decided the Roman-Britons must have made a joke of it –
how their new Foreign Legion of great hairy beer-swilling
Ger – *Saxon* – mercenary bodyguards were a filthy lot,
with bloodshot eyes, like – '

'David!' Miss Maxwell-Smith treated Dr Audley with the same disapproval as Benje.

'Sorry, Becky.' Audley accepted the rebuke meekly, as though accepting also that Mr Blackie Nabb's drinking habits were now under Miss Maxwell-Smith's special protection. 'The point is, Mr Wiesehöfer, that there were these Saxon *foederati* who were hired, and eventually given land to settle on, in return for protecting the Britons against their own Saxon folk who came raiding.' He stared at Benedikt for a moment. 'So . . . was our Fighting Man one of the *foederati* being true to his salt, to the death, like a good mercenary? Or was he a raider who came up the valley from the east, or over the hill from the south, to get his comeuppance and his just deserts, eh? Only time will tell!'

So that was it, thought Benedikt: Audley could hardly have made it plainer if he had inscribed it in deeply-chiselled stone for his benefit.

'So! Yes . . .' He met the big man's stare with obstinate innocence, refusing to be overborne by it. 'That is something which only your experts will be able to tell – and perhaps not even they will be able to provide an answer to satisfy you.'

'Were there *foederati* in Germany?' Benje's eyes were bright with intelligence. 'The Romans had German provinces, didn't they? They must have had German soldiers – they had British soldiers in their army, you know.'

It was impossible not to meet a boy like Benje more than half-way. 'There have been German soldiers in the British Army, young man. Our Hanoverian Corps in my grandfather's time carried the name "Gibraltar" among the battle honours on the flags of its regiments – "*Mit Eliot zu Ruhm und Sieg*" was written on their standards: "*With Eliot to Glory and Victory*" – we helped to defend your rock once upon a time, under a General Eliot . . . And we fought in Spain, for your Duke of Wellington –'

'Garcia Hernandez,' said Audley suddenly. 'The King's

German Legion broke a French square there – the 1st and 2nd Dragoons, under Major-General von Bock . . . He'd already been wounded – it was after the battle of Salamanca – and he was extremely short-sighted, like you, Mr Wiesehöfer . . . But he was a splendid chap, and those KGL regiments were by far the best cavalry Wellington had – the best ones on either side, in fact . . . the British were the best horsemen, but as soldiers they were undisciplined rubbish, most of them   Garcia Hernandez was the finest cavalry action of the whole campaign. Rommel would have been proud of them.'

Benedikt looked at Audley in total surprise. The man had been in a British armoured regiment in 1944, of course, so he was a cavalry man of sorts – the *dossier* said as much. But it had also stated quite clearly that he was a medievalist when not an eccentric ornament of British Intelligence.

Audley registered his surprise. 'I had an ancestor there –at Salamanca . . . an idiot officer in *our* dragoons. He was killed earlier the same day, when they smashed the French in Le Marchant's charge,' he explained almost shyly. 'Family history, you might say . . . my mother's family, Mr Wiesehöfer.' Then he nodded. 'But you're quite right about the Germans in the British service – Hessians in America, but most of all Hanoverians against Napoleon, whom they didn't like at all . . . They used to slip across the Channel and enlist in a depot not far from here, at Weymouth – the 1st and 2nd eventually became the Kaiser's 13th and 14th Uhlans . . . "*Tapfer und Treu*" was the 1st's motto at Salamanca and Garcia Hernandez – ' he looked down at Benje ' – *Fortis et Fidelis* to you, young Benjamin. Not a bad motto for anyone, *foederati* or native.'

'*Brave and faithful*,' translated Benedikt.

'So what was our Fighting Man?' Audley considered him, unsmiling this time. 'We may never know – you may be right. All we do know for sure is that he came into Duntisbury Chase alive, and he stayed for fifteen hundred years – dead.'

3

'A fascinating old mechanism.' The priest nodded towards the contraption of cog-wheels and weights and ropes which Benedikt had been dutifully studying for the last five minutes. 'They say that it is the oldest clock in England still in working order. But that is not strictly true, of course, for it was silent for many years, and it has been extensively restored.'

As though it had been listening for its cue, the mechanism jerked suddenly, and the ropes on the wall quivered, and somewhere far away and high up a bell rang in answer to the movement, joining the other bells which had been calling the faithful to prayer. In God's world it must be time for evensong, to give thanks for the day's blessings and to pray for safety during the hours of darkness to come.

The priest plucked nervously at the folds of his long black cassock. 'Mr Wiesehöfer?' He smiled tentatively at Benedikt.

A priest? But a priest, of course! Who better, in a cathedral, than a priest?

Benedikt nodded. 'Good evening, Father. I am Thomas Wiesehöfer, yes.'

'Mr Wiesehöfer.' The priest looked half relieved, half fearful. Perhaps he really was a priest. 'If you would follow me, please.'

Benedikt crossed the nave silently in the wake of the black cassock, pausing only to pay his duty in the central aisle in conformity with his guide. There was a small gathering of evening worshippers far down the rows of chairs towards the high altar, he observed. It would have been pleasant to have been able to join them – it would have been something to tell Mother in his next letter, the reading of which would have pleased her. But he had other gods to worship now, the unforgiving old earth-bound gods of man's world.

The priest waited for him by a doorway, flanked by an elderly black-gowned verger who regarded him with a mixture of disapproval and slight suspicion as he squeezed through the half-closed door into the gloom beyond.

It was a cloister. He turned, expecting the priest to follow him, but the man remained in the gap, unmoving.

'Down to your right, Mr Wiesehöfer – you will see a light.'

Benedikt looked to his right. On one side the cloister was open, but the evening had come prematurely for the time of year under a canopy of low clouds and the passage ahead of him was full of shadows. Far down it he could see a faint yellow light diffusing out of a gap in the wall.

He turned back to the priest. 'Thank you, Father.'

To his surprise, he saw the priest's hand, pale against the cassock, sign the cross for him. 'God bless you, and keep you always in His mercy, Mr Wiesehöfer.'

Then the door closed with a thud which echoed down the cloisters ahead, towards where the light waited.

Amen to that – his own thought mingled with the blessing.

But why all the precautions? The blessing was fair enough, and better than fair, and any man far from home might feel the better for it. And it had been a good contact. But this was *their* territory, where *their* writ ran on *their* terms. So . . . why all the precautions?

The wall on his left was rich with memorial tablets, all probably dedicated to the departed faithful of the diocese but which he could not read in the half-light. Then, of course, the English loved their memorials: they had a Roman weakness for cutting words into stone, as he had observed in the body of the cathedral, not merely to recall its past servants, but also the servants of the state who had died in their imperial wars and lay in faraway graves. Their 'Fighting Men', indeed!

The opening out of which the pale yellow light came was a doorway: a tiny arched doorway, so low that he had to duck his head to pass beneath it.

'Mind the step, Captain Schneider,' said a voice which he had never heard before – which was certainly not the voice of the Special Branch man Herzner had introduced to him.

Outside, the light had been pale, but inside it was bright enough to make him blink at the single unshaded bulb which hung low in the little room, surrounded by the smell of old stone and damp, slightly flavoured with furniture polish.

Polish – polished shoes – *highly* polished shoes, glistening ox-blood red-brown ... then trousers with old-fashioned turn-ups in them, immaculately creased in expensive British tweed, lifting his eyes up, past the matching jacket, and the Old School or regimental striped tie –

'Captain Schneider – ' Above the tie, the face was fierce, almost brick-red, to match the receding pepper-and-salt hair, and unmistakable from its photographs ' – I'm Colonel Butler ... and Chief Inspector Andrew you already know.'

Benedikt snapped into top gear. Chief Inspector Andrew, slender and sharp-faced, and sharp-witted, he did already know, and had expected; but Colonel Butler he also knew, but had never met, and had certainly not expected to meet here – *now*. And Colonel Butler changed all his points of reference.

He straightened up. 'Sir ... Chief Inspector ...'

The thing to remember – Herzner on the Chief Inspector, and the Kommissar print-out from Wiesbaden on Colonel Butler – was that neither of them was a quite typical specimen of the breed he represented: the system had worked on them both, moulding them to its traditions, but they were also both meritocrats who had risen from the ranks, each therefore with his own element of unpredictability. And that wasn't an altogether comforting thing to have to remember.

'Captain.' The Chief Inspector acknowledged him with a nod of recognition. 'You found Duntisbury Chase, then?'

'Yes.' Benedikt had expected the Colonel to conduct the meeting, but the Colonel studied him in silence. 'I have been there – I have looked around it, as you asked me to do, Chief Inspector.'

'Interesting place, is it?'

'Most interesting.' If the Chief Inspector was going to ask the questions, then he would ignore the Colonel until the Colonel chose not to be ignored. 'Duntisbury Royal is the name of the village. I arrived there just before midday. I went to the public house, which is named the *Eight Bells*. I drank a glass of Löwenbräu there, but I was unsuccessful in booking a room for the night. The landlord directed me to the Roman villa which is being excavated nearby. On the site I met Miss Rebecca Maxwell-Smith, who is the owner of most of the land around the village. She introduced me to Dr David Audley, who is presently staying at Duntisbury Manor, where she lives. I returned to the public house, where I had lunch. After lunch I walked round the village, and then on up to Duntisbury Rings, which is an Iron Age earthwork on the ridge to the south. From there I walked along the ridge, westwards, until I reached another earthwork, which is known as Caesar's Camp, but which is certainly not a Roman construction – it is more likely a tribal fort, like the other earthwork, only much later in date. I then spent the rest of the afternoon ostensibly searching for the line of the Roman road which crosses the valley from south-west to north-east. I left the Chase at 1730 hours, and came directly here, as arranged with you yesterday.'

Chief Inspector Andrew nodded. About half-way

through the recital he had flicked one quick look at Colonel Butler, after the mention of Audley. 'What did Audley say to you?'

'We discussed the antiquities of Duntisbury Royal . . . briefly.'

'Oh aye? You know something about antiquities, do you? Iron Age earthworks and Roman villas?'

'I know little about earthworks. I know a Roman fort when I see one. But more about Roman roads, as it happens.' Benedikt understood that, while he was re-plying to the Special Branch man's questions, he was actually speaking to the Colonel, and being assessed on his answers. 'You warned me that Dr Audley was in Duntisbury Chase, Chief Inspector. You did not tell me why *I* might be there, however . . . and it is not a place to which strangers are likely to come by accident – or perhaps it is only by accident that they may come there, when they wish to be somewhere else, so that they would not wish to remain there, as I had to do. So I needed a reason.'

They waited for him to continue.

'The Press Attaché obtained for me photo-copies of newspaper cuttings in which Duntisbury Chase – or Dun-tisbury Royal – was mentioned.' He shrugged. 'Mostly they concerned the death of General Herbert Maxwell . . . or, so far as Duntisbury Royal was concerned, his funeral . . . But I could not think of any sufficient reason for Thomas Wiesehöfer to be interested in a victim of terrorism – nor did I judge it prudent to display such an interest, even if I had thought of a reason . . . However, there was a report of an archaeological discovery there, and of excavations in progress . . . And, you see, Chief Inspector, my father was for many years a professor of Roman Archaeology in Germany. As a boy I used to accompany him on his journeys, during the holidays . . . Later on, when I was at university, I used to drive him – he lost an arm during the war, in Africa. Tracing Roman roads was one of his hobbies, so I am not unacquainted with the terms used – with the metalling and the alignments, and so on . . . Even, Chief Inspector, I believe I may have identified a terraced *agger* this afternoon, on the slopes of the ridge near Caesar's Camp, though on chalk downland it may be difficult to prove, since such terraces were often unmetalled, and it may be only a pre-Roman tribal trackway, you see – eh?'

The Special Branch man gave him a thin smile. 'You mean . . . you think you can bullshit David Audley, eh?'

'He's not an archaeologist,' said Benedikt mildly. 'I believe he is a medievalist . . . among other things. Is that not so?'

The smile compressed into an unsmiling line. 'What you want to ask yourself, Captain – or, let's say, what's more important – is . . . whatever he is . . . *did* you bullshit him?'

Benedikt shook his head. 'That is impossible to say, Chief Inspector. I am not aware of having made any mistakes . . . But . . . it is true that he warned me off – '

'Warned you off?' That made the Special Branch man frown. 'How?'

Benedikt smiled. 'He told me what happened – or what might have happened – to another German who strayed into Duntisbury Chase.'

'What German?' Chief Inspector Andrew obviously didn't know about the Fighting Man. 'What happened to him?'

'He died there.' Benedikt raised his hand. 'It was a very long time ago, Chief Inspector – in the last days of the Romans.' He didn't want to antagonize the man. 'They dug up the bones of an Anglo-Saxon warrior – a Germanic soldier . . . He told me about it in some detail. But it was gently done; for me, if it concerned me, in whichever way it concerned me – something of interest to an archaeologist, but a warning to someone who wasn't.'

Colonel Butler stirred. 'Aye – that would be Audley!' He spoke with feeling. 'That would be Audley to the life!'

Benedikt turned to him. 'But he could hardly have known what I was doing there.' The curiosity which had been consuming him drove him on now. 'Or, if he did, he knows more than I know, anyway.'

'Aye.' The candid expression on Colonel Butler's face suggested depressingly that such might well be the case. 'Happen he does, Captain . . . happen he does.'

The English construction 'happen' threw Benedikt for a moment, until he concluded it must be a dialect word, meaning 'perhaps'. 'But not from me, sir.'

'No.' Butler's harsh features softened. 'You've done very well, Captain Schneider. I'm grateful to you.'

Now was the time, when the Colonel had spoken to him, but evidently thought that his brief and unimaginative report, plus the Fighting Man episode, was all that he had to tell: *now the Colonel was ready for him.*

'I don't mean just from me – from what I said.' The final lesson of the seminar on de-briefing surfaced in his memory: and this, a de-briefing by a foreigner unwilling to press him too hard, was an exemplar of that lesson, *that the correct delivery of information could be almost as important as the information itself, if it was to convince the listener!*

'Go on, Captain.' Colonel Butler knew there was more.

'Yes, sir.' He could feel the Colonel's attention concentrate on him. 'The brief which was given to me, with Major Herzner's agreement, was that I should go down to Duntisbury Chase and have a look round it, to see what was there – to see *who* was there . . . to see if there was anything to be seen – if there was anything out of place. A reconnaissance, in fact.'

'A reconnaissance – aye, Captain.'

'Yes. I was told only that Dr David Audley was there, which might otherwise have surprised me – taken me by surprise, I mean.'

Colonel Butler said nothing to that.

'From that I chose to assume that . . . *first* . . . you were using me on unofficial attachment because – '

'*Official* attachment, Captain Schneider,' snapped Butler. 'Your transfer to London is to liaise with the appropriate British intelligence agencies.'

'Yes, sir. But not for another ten days – and because I'm not known over here – because I have no experience of British operations *and* I'm not known over here . . . no more than Dr Wiesehöfer is known, as it happens – '

'All right, Captain. So you're not known.' Butler lifted his chin belligerently. 'Or . . . let us say . . . what you did in Sonnenstrand, and what you've been doing in Yugoslavia since then, isn't known – to those who don't need to know it – right?'

Benedikt swallowed. It was as Herzner had said: *Don't be deceived into thinking that his bite won't be as bad as his bark just because he looks like one of their sergeant-majors . . .*

But he had to go on now, even though he didn't fancy moving from *first* to *second*. 'Yes, sir. So . . .'

'So I didn't have anyone else to use at short notice, who wouldn't be known to David Audley?' Butler brushed his hesitation aside. 'Very well – you can assume that, too – just so long as you *also* assume . . . no, not assume – so long as you also *rely* on the certainty that Dr Audley is a senior officer of unimpeachable reliability, on whose loyalty I would bet my life as well as yours – that will save us all time . . . and it may even save you from a certain amount of worry and embarrassment, according to how accurate the print-out from your Wiesbaden computer has been. Right, Captain?'

Right, Captain? Audley was a specialist – and very nearly an exclusive specialist, too – on Soviet intentions. And that *had* been worrying – no question about that! But . . . so where had the Kommissar got it wrong? That was worrying, too.

But he still had to go on, jumping some of his clever assumptions which had maybe not been so clever.

'A reconnaissance, Captain.' Butler exercised the

senior officer's prerogative of mercy. 'We'll come back to Audley later . . . A reconnaissance, you were saying?'

The correct response to mercy, when there was no other alternative, was confession.

'You are quite right. There is something wrong with Duntisbury Chase.' The pressure on him suddenly crystallized all Benedikt's impressions. 'I've never been in a place like it – not even on the other side.' The crystallization left him with an extraordinary and frightening near-certainty which up until this moment had been a subjective theory he would only have dared to advance tentatively. Even . . . even though he believed it himself, now, as all the pieces of it slotted into the places which had been made to fit them, it seemed quite outrageous for a stretch of peaceful English countryside.

'Trust Audley.' Chief Inspector Andrew nodded at Colonel Butler. 'Jesus Christ!'

'Ssh!' Colonel Butler raised his hand and nodded encouragingly at Benedikt. 'Tell us, Captain. And don't be put off just because of anything I've said.'

That was the final incentive Benedikt needed.

'If you wanted me to look at them, I thought they might want to look at me, Colonel. So I prepared my belongings for them.'

'Fair enough.'

'They opened the car – and they opened all my baggage. They went through everything.'

Andrew frowned. 'But you came straight here – ?'

'I'm in a multi-storey car-park. And it only took a minute to check, Chief Inspector. Because I set it up to be checked – and it had been searched – '

Butler gestured to stop him. 'Professionally?'

This time Benedikt frowned. 'They did not leave obvious traces – there were no marks on the locks, or anything crude . . . But they had plenty of time, while I was going round the Chase – '

'Not Audley.' Colonel Butler nodded to Andrew, then

76

came back to Benedikt. 'Opening things up delicately is not one of his skills – it's a skill he has always been at pains not to acquire. So he had someone else with him who could do it, that's all.'

Benedikt stared at him. If it had not been Audley . . . it had never occurred to him that it had not been Audley. But . . . Rebecca Maxwell-Smith would not possess that sort of expertise, and neither Old Cecil nor young Bobby fitted the bill, any better than did the friendly landlord of the *Eight Bells,* or his nubile assistant –

'What else?' The Colonel prodded him.

What else, indeed!

Yet it still required an effort. 'There are no signs to Duntisbury Royal, Colonel. Would you believe that?'

'Signs?'

'Signposts . . . On the main road there are many little side-roads, all with signs naming villages – even naming farms. But there is no sign "Duntisbury Royal" on the signpost on the main road.'

'So how did you get there?'

'I asked the way. There is a petrol-station near the turning – it is the only such place for several miles, and therefore the obvious place at which to inquire.' Benedikt paused. 'But later on, when I returned, I examined the signpost. There was an arm on the post, but it has been cut off with a wood-saw.'

Butler nodded slowly. 'So you asked the way.'

'So I asked the way. So I was expected.'

'Expected?'

'Along the way, perhaps ten minutes, I was delayed by a farm tractor, manoeuvring on to the road a trailer. And behind me there came a Land Rover, boxing me in.' He paused again.

'You mean, the petrol-station attendant warned them that you were coming?' Butler cocked his head. 'Why should he do that?'

'So that I could be examined . . . scrutinized.'

'By whom?'

'There were two men in the Land Rover. Their windscreen was so dirty I could not make them out, but they could have studied me easily enough. But also by David Audley, certainly.'

'Audley was there?'

'He arrived there. And he came up to the car to look at me closely – to hear me speak, perhaps.'

Chief Inspector Andrew shook his head. 'But you said you met him . . . at the Roman place?'

'I was introduced to him there. I was directed to him there, the second time. But the first time . . . we were not introduced.'

'So he wanted to know more about you?'

'By then he knew more about me, I think. At the public house I explained why I had come to Duntisbury Royal. But he wanted to know more than that – yes.'

Colonel Butler rubbed his chin, and in the silence of the little stone cell Benedikt could hear the slight rasping sound of the blunt fingers on the invisible stubble.

'And what did he make of you, Captain Schneider? You said you made no mistakes?'

'I do not believe I did. Also, at least he would not have taken me for a soldier, Colonel. And if he telephones the embassy they will tell him about Dr Wiesehöfer – they will confirm what I told him. Major Herzner will have seen to that.'

The two men exchanged glances.

'He has phoned the embassy?' Benedikt looked from one to the other, and the Colonel nodded to the Special Branch man.

'Somebody phoned the embassy.' Andrew nodded. 'Not from there – we're monitoring all the calls from Duntisbury Royal. And not Audley either.' He studied Benedikt for a moment. 'What did you say Herr – Dr – Wiesehöfer did for a living?'

'I said he was a civil servant, Chief Inspector.'

'And what does he do?'

'He is a civil servant.' They would know, of course. 'He is a procurement advisor on the NATO standardization committee.'

Andrew half-smiled. 'Yes . . . well, it was from the export director of Anglo-American Electronics, the call was. They specialize in micro-systems for missiles for NATO.'

But why the half-smile? 'So it was a genuine call?'

Chief Inspector Andrew shrugged. 'Could be.'

'The trouble with David Audley . . . is that he knows a lot of people, Captain,' said Butler.

'Like the managing director of AAE, for one,' said Andrew. 'So, if he was going to check up on you, this is exactly the way he might do it – on the old boy network. But there's no way we can check up on *that* without spooking him, because the MD there owes him a big favour, and we can't rely on patriotism being thicker than gratitude in his case, because he's an American.'

The contradictions of the situation were beginning to confuse Benedikt. In Germany the managing director of a company specializing in NATO missile-systems would be no problem, he would know where his duty lay, and his best interests too. But then in Germany, when Colonel Butler's opposite number trusted a senior officer to the extent that Colonel Butler trusted Dr David Audley, there would have been no problem to resolve in the first place. It was all very confusing.

Butler had stopped stroking his chin. 'Why would he not take you for a soldier?'

That, at least, was easy. He extracted the spectacle-case from his pocket, and the spectacles from the case.

'Soldiers are not half-blind.' He perched the appalling things on his nose. His eyes hurt and the faces of the two men swam in an opaque sea, and he took the spectacles off quickly. 'I use them with contact lenses – I became used to them several years ago – ' He smiled at Colonel

Butler, remembering Sonnenstrand ' – in Bulgaria. With contact lenses, it is a matter of growing accustomed to them. Then the glasses by themselves are no problem. Also, with contact lenses and the necessary preparations which go with them, no one questions that I should have all that in my baggage too – they cannot know that the lenses correct the glasses, not the eye-sight, you see.'

'Huh!' Colonel Butler sniffed. 'A gimmick.'

'But a convincing one, sir. And not inappropriate for a student of Roman roads.'

Butler remained unconvinced. 'But Audley's no fool. And I didn't expect him to surface so quickly. I was expecting him to keep in the background.' He shook his head. 'So I wouldn't bet on it – and that gives us less time, I'm afraid . . . Always supposing that we have any time.'

'The Roman roads weren't bad, sir,' demurred the Chief Inspector. 'He can hardly have been expecting that, for God's sake! Not in the time we had – '

'Huh!' This time it was more like a growl. 'He once passed *me* off as an expert on Roman fortification – or on Byzantine fortification, anyway, which is a damn sight more obscure than Roman roads – and in a damn sight less time, too!' He grimaced reminiscently. 'But you couldn't know that – I doubt whether even Captain Schneider's computer in Wiesbaden knows it!'

The Colonel was plainly worried about his unimpeachably reliable subordinate, notwithstanding that loyalty-to-the-death. And although that added to Benedikt's confusion, so far as that was possible, it also fed his instinctive liking for the man: Colonel Butler was a leader out of the same mould as Papa's idols.

'I don't know what he made of me, sir.' He came back to the original question. 'But I was not the man he was waiting for – that I know.'

'The man?' Colonel Butler forgot his worries. 'The man?'

'It could not have been a woman. He would not have

come to look at me if I had been the wrong sex.' He stretched what he believed to its limits. 'At the worst . . . he was not sure of me – that I was not doing what I was actually doing . . . Looking over the place, that is.'

'What makes you think that?'

'I was never alone, sir. From the moment I entered the Chase, there was always someone, I think, who was watching me.' He struggled with the concept. 'At the road-block . . . and in the public house . . . But there was a man on the hillside – on the ridge – before that . . . And in the village, when I walked round it, there was this woman on a bicycle who seemed to follow us – '

'Us?'

Benedikt smiled. 'There were these two little boys I met, on their racing bicycles – they showed me round . . . Before lunch they took me to the Roman villa, and afterwards they led me through the village, to the footpath which leads to the Duntisbury Rings – '

Benje had been dismissive: *'She's just an old nosey-parker – you don't want to take any notice of her.'*

She had been tall and thin, riding a tall and thin bicycle unbalanced by an immense wicker basket resting on her front mudguard. But she had been there behind them, off and on, until the second man had appeared.

' – and after her there was another man – '

The man with the gun couched under his arm, on the skyline.

'That's Old Levi – from the Almshouses. He lives on boiled sausages, Mum says – and boiled rabbits, when he can bag one, 'cause there're not many of them around . . . An' he sleeps in his gumboots, Mum says . . . Because when they took him into the cottage hospital, when he had 'flu, they had to cut them off his feet, to get him into bed – yrrch!'

But Old Levi – (who didn't look particularly old, from the way he kept up with them; but everyone who wasn't obviously young was old to Benje and Darren) but Old

Levi had paced them, on the skyline and off it, all the way from Duntisbury Rings to Caesar's Camp, and then down along the possible terrace of the Roman *agger* into the valley, to the sun-dappled pools where the stream idled between the trees –

Another thought struck him, which dove-tailed beautifully with everything else he had said, like the good work of a master carpenter slotting together, yet much more frightening, and much more humiliatingly –

'What's the matter?' It was the Chief Inspector who had read his face more quickly.

The little boys! thought Benedikt. The little *clever* boys, with their clever and insistent questions – ?

But he had clued himself to the answer, with his own remembrance of that village near Leipzig two years ago, when because of his stupidity the Russians and the East Germans had both been close behind him – inescapably close – with the women carrying their sheets off the line, done by another stream, and the children coming back from school, staring at him with huge eyes until the women had sent them about their business as he had slipped away into the trees –

All he had to do was to reverse the situation – he had said as much himself: *I've never been in a place like it, not even on the other side* – to become an enemy, not a friend!

But here in England – ?

Here in England, too! Yes!

He looked at Chief Inspector Andrew, then at Colonel Butler. 'I think I have been stupid, you know.'

They both waited for the end-product of that conclusion.

'It is not that I have given anything away. Perhaps quite the contrary . . . But I have nevertheless been stupid.'

Suddenly he saw the little girl beside the water-splash, sitting on the footbridge in her grubby dress, and then ducking behind the phone-box. And *then into it* –

'Yes . . . these two small boys, who accompanied me . . . not so little, but not big boys . . .'

'Little boys?' Butler regarded him incredulously.

'They attached themselves to me.' There had been no escape from them then, and there was no escape from them now. 'I . . . I have experience with boys. I have nephews . . . and I help to run a youth club for the church, in the place where I live, when I am there.' The need for honesty outweighed the burden of his humiliation: in a de-briefing honesty was essential, anything less than the truth mediated against security. 'I thought to use them – to ask questions which I could not so easily ask their elders.'

'Yes?' The Special Branch man was there.

'I thought I was cultivating *them*. But now I'm not sure that it wasn't the other way round – that they were questioning *me* . . . And that they were watching me more closely than their elders could have done – that the woman, and the second man . . . they were the back-up, watching over the boys, rather than watching me.'

'Yeah – *yeah*!' Chief Inspector Andrew at least didn't find it outrageous. 'I've seen little kids look out for their elder brothers, on a job . . . Nothing like this, of course. But if you've got a bright kid . . .' He nodded at Butler.

'God bless my soul!' The Colonel took a moment to adjust to the idea. 'Children?'

'These were clever children, sir.' Benedikt himself still couldn't quite accept the little girl at the water-splash. 'They were at . . . is it "secondary school", you call it?'

'Comprehensive? Grammar?' hazarded Andrew. 'Public?'

'It was named after a king of England. And they both learnt Latin.'

'They still learn Latin at comprehensive schools, or some of them do,' said Andrew. 'Thank God!'

'They had scholarships – '

'Never mind!' snapped Butler. 'What you're saying . . . what you are saying is . . . the whole village?' The adjustment still taxed him, too. 'The children . . . the tractor driver – and the Land Rover driver . . . the woman on the bicycle, and the man with the shot-gun . . . ?'

'The petrol-station attendant at the garage,' supplemented Andrew. 'Him too. And the publican.'

'And Miss Rebecca Maxwell-Smith.' The Colonel added to the roll-call. 'And Audley.'

Benedikt began to feel foolish. Behind the Iron Curtain was one thing, from the Elbe to the Vistula and along the Danube . . . But not in England, surely! Or . . . if in Toxteth and Brixton, maybe . . . not in Duntisbury Royal, anyway –

Yet Colonel Butler was nodding at his Chief Inspector. 'That could be it. Remember how she said "we"? "*We* really have a chance"?'

Benedikt stopped feeling foolish. 'A chance of what, sir?'

Butler came back to him. 'Let us get this absolutely straight, Captain. You believe, having been to Duntisbury Royal, that they are waiting for a man to arrive there?'

'A man – or men, perhaps.' Benedikt nodded. 'Or someone.'

'With hostile intent?'

He could only shrug. 'I cannot tell that. But they had no flags out – no garlands of welcome. They wished to be warned of the approach of strangers, and they were concerned to identify such strangers.' In the end he had to commit himself. 'What I am saying is . . . subjective, of course. Since you asked me to look there, I went there looking for something. And there was Audley . . .'

'And there was Audley.' A corner of the Colonel's mouth twitched. 'And you would know that where Audley goes there is trouble – that would be on your computer.'

'Yes.' No point in denying that, even though Audley had not operated in Germany for many years. He stared at the Colonel. 'Hostile intent . . . yes. Or the intent may be with the stranger. So perhaps defensive intent, sir.'

'And the whole village is involved in this . . . defensive intent?'

That was still the sticking point. 'I did not meet the whole village. It seems . . . unlikely.'

'Unlikely?'

'In England unlikely. There are places where it would not be unlikely – places where the government of the country is hated, and where strangers are feared and distrusted – where the laws are unjust and oppressive . . . And also in peasant communities, where there is still traditional leadership and strong feelings of local solidarity. In such places it is the objective of the regime to cut off such leadership and undermine such feelings, but sometimes such efforts have the opposite effect. But . . .'

'But?'

'But I do not think I am describing England in the last quarter of the twentieth century, Colonel. That is the difficulty.'

Colonel Butler nodded. 'Yes. So it is possible that you have imagined all this?' He smiled suddenly. 'Not altogether unreasonably . . . on the basis of your instructions, and the presence of David Audley . . . and also perhaps because of your own experiences elsewhere, eh?'

'I did not imagine the searching of my baggage.'

'No. But that could have been an ordinary thief – ordinary, but skilful – on the look-out for money and a good German camera. There's a lot of that about in England in the last quarter of the twentieth century, I'm afraid, Captain.'

Well: there was the challenge. And all the rest of what they had said could have been merely leading him on.

'My car was parked very publicly, outside the public house, beside what passes for the main street in Duntisbury Royal. It would have had to have been a very skilful thief.' Benedikt played for time.

'Oh, we've got a few of them.' Chief Inspector Andrew cocked his head ruefully. 'They just don't go around in cloth caps and striped jerseys any more, carrying bags labelled "Swag".'

No more time.

He looked the Colonel in the eye. 'No. Duntisbury Royal is different. There is something very wrong there. I cannot prove it, but I *feel* it.' His confidence strengthened as he spoke. 'It is . . . what I feel is . . . it is a most beautiful and peaceful valley, where the people are kind and helpful – *and I was glad to get out of it in one piece, Colonel.*'

They stared at each other for one more moment, then the Colonel turned to his colleague. 'Aye . . . Well, show him the papers, Andrew. Sheet by sheet, if you please. He's ready for them now.'

The Special Branch man half-turned, to pick up a grey folder which had been hidden behind him within the jumble of stacked ecclesiastical furniture half-filling the cell. From the folder he passed a single sheet of closely-typed paper to Benedikt.

Herbert George Maxwell was born in 1912, the son of Lieutenant-Colonel Julian Robert Maxwell MC, Grenadier Guards, who was killed in action in 1917 shortly after succeeding to command the 2nd/21st West Yorks at Ypres, and who as 'Robert Julian' was widely recognized as one of the most lyrical of the war poets while his military identity remained a close secret shared only with a few close friends.

The Maxwell family has lived at Duntisbury Manor, in Duntisbury Chase, Dorset, since the Reformation. From the time of Marlborough the first-born son of the house without exception has served the sovereign as a soldier, invariably rising to command a distinguished regiment of cavalry or battalion of infantry, and often retiring from a higher command still.

'Robert Julian's' poems were nothing exceptional in the Maxwells; most of the soldiers among them were considered by their colleagues to be 'brainy', and army gossip and gaps in their recorded service indicate a remarkable range of interests, from the collection of antiquities in Italy and Greece to friendship with Darwin and Huxley. At the same time, the Maxwells traditionally devoted much of their lives to the service of the family estate, of which the Manor was the centre and the surrounding farms of Duntisbury Chase the greater part, which pursuit was not in those days incompatible with a military career.

Herbert Maxwell differed from his ancestors only in joining the Royal Artillery. After his father's death he was brought up by his mother, but with help from her brother, Major William James Lonsdale, who had lost an arm commanding a troop of field-guns at Mons in 1914, and who looked after the estate at his brother-in-law's request until 1917 and thereafter until his nephew's majority, retiring to Bournemouth then, where he died in 1934. Herbert was educated, as his father had been, at Wellington, and, as his uncle had been, at the Royal Military Academy, Woolwich. He was commissioned in 1932, serving subsequently with pack-guns on the North-West Frontier and later with the Home Forces, latterly as an instructor in Gunnery at the School of Artillery, Larkhill, not far from his beloved Duntisbury Chase. He was a devoted –

The sheet ended there, and Benedikt looked up, to receive the next one.

Husband? There had been no mention of wife and children yet –

– student of symphonic music of the eighteenth and nineteenth centuries, and officers who served with him remember his books on musicology, his portable radiogramophone apparatus dismantled for carrying in steel cartridge-boxes, and his box of gramophone records.

On the outbreak of war in 1939 Maxwell left the School of Artillery – the Commandant later remarked that he all but cut his way out of Larkhill – and returned to take command of a troop in his old regiment, which was one of the first artillery formations to go to France in that autumn, and one of the last to leave, via Dunkirk in June 1940. Awarded the Military Cross for gallant and above all effective conduct as one of his regiment's Observation Post officers in actions from near Brussels all the way back to Ypres and then to Nieuport, he remarked of this period long afterwards that if there were a military manoeuvre more difficult to do well than a fighting retreat, he had yet to see it; and that while it was not a test he would choose, nothing revealed the quality of units and formations more clearly than did a lost battle – not even the debilitating stalemate they had endured between September and May.

Soon after returning to England with the remnants of his troop, Maxwell was appointed General Staff Officer Grade III Liaison at Divisional Headquarters. He said of this period afterwards that it was his most entertaining and unrewarding military job: all he had to do was stand about pretending that he knew what was going on, until called upon to dash off on a powerful motor-cycle to talk to some senior officer who knew even less than he did.

By the end of 1940 the division of which Maxwell's regiment formed a part was back to full strength. But for many months the war was conducted without the help of what its officers and men considered to be the best regiment in the best division in the British Army. Early in 1943 the command of Maxwell's troop fell vacant and he returned to it, however – which was correctly recognized

*by members of the regiment as a sure sign that their long
wait would soon be over.*

The second sheet ended on that note of high expectation,
but Benedikt was beginning to become confused again.
This was all very interesting, the ancient history of the
Maxwells – or, at least, it would have been very interesting
to Papa, whose guns had been the best ones in his beloved
Division Afrika zur besondern Verfügung – the immortal
90th Light – and who, come to that, knew exactly how
Major William James Lonsdale had felt at Mons, and
afterwards. But where did it all fit into the modern history
of Miss Rebecca Maxwell-Smith and Duntisbury Chase?

*In March the division sailed to Algeria, to join the First
Army in its assault on Tunisia. Herbert Maxwell promptly
fell ill with a bad case of dysentery, and so missed the
spoiling attack by the Germans across the Goubellat Plain
south-west of Tunis. The attack was launched with their
customary élan and professionalism in an area where the
British forces were not well deployed for defence.
However, when the German armour made contact south of
Medjez-el-Bab it had the misfortune not only of encounter-
ing two of the most capable of the British divisions (one
arriving and the other about to depart), in a sector where a
single brigade might have been expected, and there were
not only more British regular officers per square mile than
anywhere else in North Africa, but also the new British 17-
pdr anti-tank guns which matched the fearsome and much
admired German 88s –*

Papa *would* like this – to be characterized as 'fearsome and
much-admired' would make his day – his month – his year –

* * *

89

– fearsome and much admired 88s. Even so, the Germans inflicted casualties, and when the uproar died down there were promotions. Herbert Maxwell thus returned afterwards to the command of a battery in another regiment.

After the inevitable end in North Africa, where the struggle had become unequal, there was another distressing period of inaction for Major Maxwell, during which the division was called on to reinforce other formations, and when trained and experienced units seemed on the verge of disintegration. Maxwell nevertheless held his battery together, and was rewarded by transfer, sailing to Italy in February 1944 as Second-in-Command of his original regiment.

The Italian front was static for a while, and the guns were in the comparatively quiet Garigliano sector. But in May the regiment formed part of the great concentration of artillery supporting the Eighth Army's third and final attack across the Rapido, past the dominating height of the Montecassino Abbey. The crossing was difficult and casualties heavy among all ranks, but particularly among officers. More than one Commanding Officer of an artillery regiment was disabled by nebelwerfer fire on brigade headquarters –

There had been a slow change in the narrative, Benedikt noted, as he reached for the next sheet. It had moved gradually from the generalized second-hand, with memories recalled 'long afterwards', to exact recollection which could only come from first-hand experience: the narrator had not been in Larkhill or Dunkirk, but he had crossed the Rapido under that nebelwerfer barrage –

– at this time. Maxwell was promoted and transferred again, this time taking command of a regiment.

The family record was unblemished, though with guns this time, rather than horsemen or sweating infantrymen. But what command was there for little fierce Becky, in her turn?

This was when I knew him –

The confirmation of his guess so quickly warmed Benedikt, rousing his confidence and his interest –

This was when I knew him, as far as a subaltern officer in action on his gun-position ever gets to know his Commanding Officer, whose place is either at Regimental Headquarters or with the infantry most of the time; we never had a regimental officers' mess within range of the enemy; and as far as a temporary officer in a regular regiment of artillery dared to know his superiors –

This hadn't been written, either: it had been taped or taken down in shorthand from someone long afterwards . . . someone highly literate and discerning, with a trained mind and memory, recollecting not only his memories of long ago, but also the facts and impressions which a young and inquiring mind had soaked up in combat, to fit him for his 'temporary' career.

Papa had been just like that.

He looked up at Colonel Butler. 'Who wrote this, Colonel? Or can't you tell me?'

Butler gazed at him with a hint of approval, as though he understood what lay behind the question. 'I don't suppose it matters if you know, Captain. At least . . . let's say it's one of our most distinguished and enlightened

High Court judges. Somebody I'd like to come up before if I was innocent – and not if I was guilty. Okay?'

He was a fine-looking man, and dressed well in a horsey sort of way. In wet weather in action he wore breeches and riding-boots with his battledress blouse. His nickname . . . though not to anybody as junior as I . . . was 'Squire' – he had served once, sometime, with the son of one of his tenants, who called him that instead of 'sir', and the name stayed with him. In fact, they said that between Dunkirk and the Tunisian campaign he spent every leave down on his estate in Duntisbury Chase, so it wasn't inappropriate . . . But I know that all the regular officers, who in our regiment occupied all the captaincies and above at the beginning of the Italian campaign . . . they all thought very well of him, as a horseman and a gentleman, as well as professionally – the old-fashioned order, if you like – and the other ranks worshipped him. As for the subalterns . . . and by now they were entirely temporary officers . . . they trusted his calm competence, and responded to him as . . . as an elder brother, perhaps – quite terrifyingly exacting in the line but always friendly . . . It isn't true to say that we would have died for him, because you don't think of it like that – you may have to die, it's always a possibility, because that's the nature of war, but no one wants to. But he was the closest one I came to who might have made me think like that, if the choice had been put to me. Which it wasn't, thank God! Where was I, though? It's the facts you want – Montecassino, yes . . . Well, the regiment performed quite adequately there, and when they gave him his DSO we were all well-pleased for him, even though some of us had been a bit miffed in the past because all the gongs went to the regulars, by custom, because they needed them professionally, and we were going back to civilian life afterwards, and wouldn't need such things . . . But when he got it we were perfectly content – and he made it plain, of

*course, that he regarded it as a form of congratulations to
the regiment for doing its job properly.*

The last sheet came to him.

*But he didn't get any more promotion during the war, as I
recall – because he was already quite young for his rank,
the way the army conducts its arcane affairs . . . But there
were the divisional reunions, and I used to see him there,
off and on, and from below the salt we all watched his
progress, the way one does . . . I think he was a brigade
major in one of the few undisbanded divisions in '46, and
then he was a half-colonel again, as GSO I in the British
Army of the Rhine – we cracked a bottle of champagne
over that, I do remember . . . In fact, that's when we
realized where he'd been at one stage, between campaigns
– on one of the short war-time courses at the Staff College
. . . Which shows that they'd got some sense – and that
legged him up to Brigadier General Staff eventually, and
finally Major-General as Second-in-Command, BAOR –
missiles, and things, which he was quite bright enough to
handle . . . But that would have been when Duntisbury
Chase was pulling him away, with his retirement coming
up – CBE, naturally . . . though we would have voted
for a K – a knighthood . . . But then that never was
Maxwell style: do your duty and keep a gentlemanly
profile – 'fear God and honour the King' – and make sure
everyone below you is all right, that was his style . . . Also
there was some family trouble – daughter and son-in-law
killed in a smash somewhere . . . never met his wife, bit of
an invalid – blissfully happy marriage though, they say
. . . But there was this little grand-daughter they were
bringing up – something like that, anyway . . . That's all –
I'm not going to pronounce on the manner of his passing,
because that may conceivably become my business one*

day, and I shall reserve my views on that until then, just in case.

He handed back the full collection to the Special Branch man – or, as he noticed when the man replaced them in the folder, perhaps not the full collection.

'Yes, there is more.' Colonel Butler had observed his glance at the folder. 'There is the recollection from an aged general, whose GSO III he was, and a letter from a headmaster, on whose board of governors he served, who knew him well more recently, and a conversation in the *Eight Bells* which was taped ten days ago surreptitiously by a plain-clothes detective, not long after his death – the local taxi-man talking to the local ne'er-do-well, with occasional mumblings from his retired groom, who could think back as far as his father and his uncle. But they all simply confirm what the judge said in their own different ways.'

Benedikt nodded. 'He was a well-respected man.'

'More than that. Perhaps a glance at the first page of what the Vicar said at the funeral might help you. Andrew?' The Colonel paused. 'Did you meet the Vicar on your tour, Captain?'

'No sir.'

'Aye . . . well, it's too small to maintain a clergyman of its own now, the village. But it's a Maxwell living, and the old General paid out of his own pocket for a retired priest to look after the parish.'

Most of you, who today fill this little church which he loved, in this place which he loved and shared with us, will have known our dear Squire too well for any words of mine to be necessary. Some of you grew up with him, and knew him as a boy and a young man; some of you served with him in the war, and afterwards; some of you, the younger

*members of this congregation, were privileged to be his
friends in his later years.*

*There are, however, a few who are here today in our
midst in their official capacities, discharging their duties, to
whom our Squire can only be a name, albeit an honoured
one. It is to them that I say . . . that we who knew him are
not here to mourn, but to give thanks for his life, which
enriched ours, and to pray not only for him, but also – as
he would have wished – for God's mercy and forgiveness
on those who must one day stand before the Judgement
Seat to account for their actions –*

'You don't need any more. Except to know that he went
on for another page about the perfection of God's justice,
and the imperfection of man's, and the uselessness of
bitterness and anger. He's a sharp old bird, is the Vicar, I
rather suspect.'

Benedikt looked at him questioningly.

'He's not in on it, but he might have sniffed trouble, is
my guess,' said Colonel Butler simply. 'Because what they
plan to do is to get the man who put the bomb in the old
General's car to Duntisbury Chase, and then deliver him
to that Judgement Seat themselves.'

'You know this?' Benedikt felt a small twinge of anger.
'You have known this all along – since the beginning?'

'I first heard about some of it a very short time ago. I
learnt a bit more about it yesterday. Enough to go to your
Major Herzner, who owes me a favour.' If the Colonel
had noticed his anger, it didn't bother him. 'But I haven't
been rock-hard certain until this evening, if that's what
you want to know, Captain.'

Suddenly there was no room for anger, there were too
many questions in his head for that.

'Aye – ' The Colonel forestalled him ' – and now you'll
be asking why I didn't go straight down to Duntisbury and
ask Dr David Audley what the hell he's playing at, eh?'

That – among other things –

'Instead of which I let you take your chance?' Butler shook his head. 'I tell you one thing, Captain Schneider – whatever David Audley's playing at, it won't be murder. And it certainly won't be acting as an accessory to a teenage slip of a girl and a bunch of farm labourers – least of all when he's given someone his private promise that he'll look after her. He's a tricky blighter, if there ever was one, but that isn't *his* style' The grizzled head shook again. 'You weren't in any danger.'

Benedikt recalled the Wiesbaden Kommissar's print-out on Audley: whatever his failings the man had an intuition for mischief like a bomb-sniffing dog for explosives.

'But *someone* is in danger, Colonel.' Obviously the Colonel trusted the man up to a point, but only up to a point. 'Who was it who set the bomb under General Maxwell's car?'

For a moment the Colonel looked at him in silence. 'They haven't the slightest idea. They don't know *who* – and they don't know *why*.'

'They?'

'The Anti-Terrorist Squad,' said Andrew. 'Their inquiries are proceeding – officially. But the truth is, they're at a dead standstill.'

'And your inquiries?'

Andrew looked at the Colonel, and not too happily, Benedikt thought.

'Do not exist – for anyone else's consumption. Not yet.' The Colonel's features hardened. 'And we know no more than they do. As yet.'

It was easy to see why the Chief Inspector wasn't altogether happy. 'Except that Dr Audley is in Duntisbury Chase?'

'Dr Audley is on leave, Captain.'

'Writing another book,' murmured Andrew. 'He writes books.'

On feudalism, remembered Benedikt. And perhaps Duntisbury Chase was at present not such an inappropriate place for him to be, in which to study a text-book example of its survival in the 1980s. But that was not why he was there.

He had come to the real question at last. 'But in Duntisbury Chase they know – they know *who* and *why*. That must be so, Colonel.'

'Happen they do. Or someone in there does – aye.'

But perhaps . . . but *happen* . . . that was really not so surprising, thought Benedikt. Peasants the world over kept their own counsel, close-mouthed, rejecting outside interference in their affairs; and if there was a secret in the Chase, the people of the Chase would be more likely to know it than any outsiders, even outsiders with all the resources of the British intelligence and police agencies.

It was not what they knew, but what they proposed to do about it, and what that signified, which was so startling.

'And . . . whoever it was . . . they know he's coming to them – '

'*Right!*' Colonel Butler pounced on him before he could finish. 'They know he's coming to them! And the Vicar preached to deaf ears: it's good, old-fashioned Old Testament vengeance for them, and no messing around. But that won't do for David Audley, Captain – do you see?'

Knowing the man was everything – in this case, reflected Benedikt. Colonel Butler was known to be a stickler for the book, army-trained, which was the antithesis of everything that was known about Dr David Audley. But each was an intelligent and successful officer, and if the Colonel was now consciously and deliberately breaking every rule in his own book there had to be an over-riding reason for it.

'Looking after the girl – that's what he promised to do, so that'll be what he'll be doing. But there's got to be more to it than that.'

Not knowing the man was the problem. Benedikt ran

the film of his memory, marrying it to the print-out: Audley striding away across the field, super-confident – over-confident? – in his old clothes . . . the scholar built like a boxer: in good shape, but physically past his prime – too old for the ring, too old for field-work . . . for guarding a girl – or a secret – from a professional, with a village of unprofessional peasants at his back?

Then he knew what was coming.

'I don't want to spoil whatever he's doing. Because it's my guess that he's seen something that they haven't seen – it depends how far he is into their confidence, but acting as a bodyguard doesn't suit him any better than acting as an accessory to murder. I don't want to spoil it – but I don't want to leave it to chance, Captain. I need to know what's really happening in there.'

He knew exactly what was coming. And it would be better to meet it as a volunteer than to wait for the order which would be couched as a request, from one ally to another.

He shrugged. 'Major Herzner has lent me to you for a week, Colonel. I could go back . . . But if Dr Audley has contacts of his own . . . I do not resemble Dr Wiesehöfer very closely. So I do not think my cover will last so long – always supposing that it has survived this afternoon.'

'Forty-eight hours, at most – if you go back,' said Chief Inspector Andrew. 'He'll have to get back to Germany. Herzner's got it buttoned up here.'

'No.' Butler shook his head. 'Forty-eight hours is too much – it's making pictures we'd like to see. And with Audley you don't make pictures. We'll go for another cover.'

'Another cover?' Benedikt couldn't conceal his disappointment. It wasn't that Colonel Butler's lack of confidence in his Roman roads disappointed him – it was good that the Colonel preferred to plan for the worst, rather than the best. But anything which reminded him of Papa had its own special virtue, and the gentle study of small irregularities in the ground for signs of the passing of mighty Caesar's legions had recalled happy memories of the old man's boyish enthusiasm, and his own happiest days.

'Don't worry, Captain! I have a cover much closer to your real skin in mind.' The Colonel misread his face. 'But I won't send you naked back into Duntisbury Chase. And I won't forget what you are doing for Her Majesty's peace, either.'

It was an old-fashioned way of expressing gratitude, thought Benedikt – it was like granting him a *Mit Eliot zu Ruhm und Sieg* battle-honour of his own. Indeed, it was almost embarrassing . . . except that it gave him an insight into Colonel Butler which the Kommissar had not printed out.

'And I'll give you something better than that.' The Colonel became matter-of-fact again. 'I'll tell you what I particularly want to know which shouldn't be too difficult to find out.'

He was almost diverted from his concentration on what Butler was saying by the change in Chief Inspector Andrew's expression, which graduated in that instant from proper subordinate interest to equal concentration.

'Yes, sir?' What the Colonel was giving him now was something new to the Chief Inspector also.

'I told you no lie when I said that we don't know much more than what the Anti-Terrorist Squad knows – other than what we know about Audley being there, of course.' The Colonel bridged the huge gap effortlessly. 'But what you've told me – the fact that you confirm what we've suspected . . . that helps me to see it through Audley's eyes. And because of that I can see a lot more than I saw before.'

The Chief Inspector's face confirmed his impression: he was in on a new picture of what was happening in Duntisbury Chase.

'Unfinished business. That's the only thing which could

bring back the bomber to Duntisbury. So the bomb didn't do the job . . . and he's dealt with bombers before – and bombs – Audley has. I should have thought of that before, too!' Butler castigated himself for his error.

Bombs –

Benedikt had dealt with bombs, too: bombs were the dirtiest killing method, because no matter what the bombers said – and even when they said it honestly in their hearts – bombs were in the end indiscriminate, counting the risk to the innocent passer-by as incidental to hitting the target; and while that might have to be a harsh necessity in war, in peace – in Her Majesty's peace –

'Unfinished business,' repeated Colonel Butler.

In peace, bombers were the dirtiest killers, never taking the face-to-face risks – killing the bomb-disposal men when they failed to hit their targets –

The chasm opened up at Benedikt's feet, which he was trained to avoid: *Why shouldn't the bastards be killed like mad dogs? What was so wrong with what the 'slip of a girl' and the peasants of Duntisbury Chase planned to do?*

'What unfinished business?' Andrew addressed his superior more sharply than he had done before.

'Kelly, of course. Gunner Kelly, man!' Butler snapped back at him.

'*Kelly –* ?'

'He should have gone up with the car – with the General.' Butler reacted to the snap harshly. 'You've been telling me that from the start, damn it! Loyal Gunner Kelly – wasn't he distraught when they tried to talk to him? Wasn't he so sick that he couldn't even go to the funeral? Maybe he thought someone was going to take another shot at him! Or maybe he was busy doing something else, perhaps.'

'But – '

'But he was with the General in the war? And he's been back with him for the last four years?' Butler stabbed a finger at Andrew. 'But where was he in between? And what's more to the point . . . where is he *now*?'

100

The Chief Inspector said nothing, and the Colonel encompassed them both. 'If you think about what *we* know, that the Squad doesn't know – Audley maybe knows . . . is that it isn't finished, what happened in Bournemouth – and Gunner Kelly *should* have been finished there, with the General.'

Pause.

'So what I want to know – from *you*, Andrew – is the life-story of Gunner Kelly, from Connemara or wherever, until the day he didn't drive the General's car a fortnight ago.'

Pause.

'And what I want to know from *you*, Captain Schneider, is whether Gunner Kelly is in Duntisbury Chase now – because he's supposed to have gone away for a holiday somewhere, but I think he is there . . . And if he is there, I want to know what he's doing there.'

4

The furniture removal van lurched abruptly left and then right in quick succession, following the driver's scripted indecision, and then suddenly juddered to a stop.

Benedikt stood up in the darkness and applied his eye to the narrow opening which had been left for him in the little sliding hatch in the partition which separated the cargo space from the driver's cab. The headlights blazed ahead undipped, out across the darkly rippling water of the ford, illuminating the road ahead, and the telephone box, and the overhanging trees.

'You there?' The driver didn't turn round.

'Yes.' He divided the gap between eye and ear.

'We're at the water's edge. I'm going to switch on the cab light so I can look at the map. Then I'll get the torch, and get out and look for a signpost. Okay?'

'Yes.' The repetition of orders was unnecessary, but it was reassuringly exact. It wasn't Checkpoint Charlie they were going through, but there was still no room for error.

He ducked down into his own darkness again, and looked at his watch. It was 2242 exactly – three minutes to the police car.

The engine noise ceased suddenly, and a thin bar of yellow light filled the gap. For a few moments the map rustled on the other side of the partition, and then the light went out.

'There's someone out there – ' The driver hissed the words ' – I can see a torch . . . I'm getting out.'

The cabin-door clicked, and there was a scrape of boots on metal as the driver swung himself out. The van shuddered slightly.

'Aw – *fuck*!' exclaimed the driver angrily.

Benedikt raised his ear to the edge of the gap, and was rewarded with the sound of a splash. The driver swore again. Cautiously Benedikt turned his head, just in time to catch the lancing beam of a torch directed from the other side of the water towards the side of the van.

'Are you *arl-roight* there?' The question came across the water from the source of the torch-beam, in a rich peasant accent.

'No, I'm fucking not, mate!' The driver answered irritably, in his own townsman's accent. 'I'm up to my fucking knees in fucking water – that's what I am!'

'Arrr . . . You didn't ought to 'ave stopped there.' The voice was unsympathetic. 'You want to get out of there – you're in the water there, you are.'

The driver didn't swear in answer to that, but emitted a throaty sound of exasperation. There came another splashing sound, and then a stamping of boots on tarmac.

'Where you goin', then?' the voice challenged.

The stamping stopped. 'Where the fuck am I, mate?'

'Where d'you want to be?'

The driver swore. 'Not bloody 'ere, I don't think. 'Old on a mo' an' I'll tell yer . . . Norton somethin' . . . 'old on . . . Norton Down – The Old Vicarage, Norton Down – name of Winterbotham . . . Major E. H. Winterbotham, The Old Vicarage, Norton Down.'

'Norton Down?' The voice echoed the name incredulously.

'Yeah. Major Winterbotham – you know 'im?'

'This aren't the way to Norton Down.' Scorn had replaced incredulity.

Benedikt looked at his watch again. The police were due any second.

'Fourth turning, they told me. Down the hill till the road forks, an' it's signposted there, to the right.' There was a pause. 'Left goes to Cucklesford St Mary an' right to Norton Down – bloody stupid names!' Another pause. 'But I can't see any bloody sign!'

'Arr . . . nor you can! Because there ain't none.' The peasant belittled the townsman. 'You took the wrong road – that's what you done. Cucklesford St Mary an' Norton Down's on t'other side.'

The driver grunted helplessly. 'Can I get through from 'ere? Where am I?'

'Na . . . If I was goin' to Norton Down from wherever you come from I wouldn't start from 'ere. What you want t'do is to turn round an' go back where you come from . . . an' then – '

The fierce headlights of the police car and the sound of its engine arrived almost simultaneously, to cut off these extraordinary directions in mid-flow. They must have coasted down the ridge from the main road to arrive so silently, with the kink in the final approach, and the trees themselves, cutting off the warning of their arrival until the final bend.

But now the speaker on the other side of the water, who had been hidden behind his own torch-beam outside the van's headlights, was suddenly caught in the glare as the police car pulled alongside the van, outside Benedikt's vision.

He heard a car door slam.

'What's this, then?' It was strange how the official voice was the same the world over – confidently suspicious and suspiciously confident. 'Is that you over there, Blackie Nabb? What are you doing here?'

'Arr . . . Mr Russell?' The voice parried the question. 'Is that Mr Russell?'

'You know me, Blackie. Why aren't you in the *Eight Bells*?'

'The *Eight Bells*?'

Now, *there was a difference*, from the world over, thought Benedikt: there might be suspicion both ways here, between *Mr* Russell and the man over the water . . . but there was no fear in either of them – and – what was a greater difference – there was no hatred either!

'The *Eight Bells*, Mr Russell?' False incomprehension filled the question. 'But it's gone closing time – an' I've been over to my sister's, at Cassell's, anyway . . . So what would I be doin' at the *Bells*, then?'

The other police-car door slammed.

'What's this, Russell?' A senior-officer voice, not so much confident as super-confident, and alien for that reason, cut in. 'Who is this?'

'I don't know, sir.' Mr Russell answered his officer evenly, also without fear. 'But that's Mr Nabb over there, who runs the taxi-service in the village.'

'Oh, yes?' The senior officer sounded as though he had heard of 'Mr Nabb'. 'And where's his taxi?'

No answer came from over the water, and Benedikt began at last to understand the dimensions of the drama to which he was a witness, which Chief Inspector Andrew had enlisted to serve Colonel Butler's purpose.

'I don't think he's on duty tonight, sir. It looks like he's visiting his sister, Mrs Tanner . . . She's married to Mr Tanner, who's manager at Cassell's Farm, sir.'

'Oh, yes?'

Benedikt's dislike of the officer voice – the inspector voice – blossomed with his understanding: it had suited Colonel Butler's plan that the local police were busy in this part of Dorset, leaning on after-hours drinking in public houses, which was in contravention of Britain's archaic licensing laws – it had suited him that the *Eight Bells* in Duntisbury Royal, although not a primary target, had been one of the subsidiary targets to which Chief Inspector Andrew with his special contacts could divert one particular attack at short notice.

What he had not understood until now was that, while the inspector wanted to catch the *Eight Bells* regulars drinking happily after hours, the local constable – *Mr* Russell – had no such ambition . . . Because *Mr* Russell, at the very first opportunity, had warned *Mr* Nabb what he was about, and close to a convenient phone-box.

'Oh, yes?' The Inspector had made some of those same connections, if not all of them, by the sound of his voice. 'And who are you, then?'

He had come back to the van-driver, realized Benedikt.

'Eh?' The van-driver sounded not one bit abashed by the question. 'What the fuck is that meant to mean – who am I?'

He had to adjust, thought Benedikt: the Inspector must know what he was doing, and this was all for Mr Nabb's benefit – 'Blackie' Nabb's benefit – if he was on duty at the ford, as they had expected someone to be on duty here, as the first trip-wire in Duntisbury Chase's defence system.

But the corollary of that was that the Inspector must behave as he would have behaved in real life – so that 'Blackie' Nabb should react in the same way, to warn the Chase of the arrival of the police within that same defence system.

But . . . in the meantime . . . the van-driver had to react also – and this was England – rural England in the 1980s – and that in itself was educational.

'What are you doing here?'

'Doing?' the van-driver echoed the verb insolently. 'I wish to fuck I knew, mate!'

'There's no need to use that sort of language with me – not if you want to stay out of a cell tonight.' The Inspector remained coolly unmoved by the insolence, he merely pitched his voice so that it could be heard on the other side of the water. 'I've got a warrant-card in my pocket . . . and we've had enough burglaries round here for me to inquire what you're doing in these parts at this hour of the night. So you can argue the toss with me, and I can put the constable here behind the wheel of your vehicle and take you back to the nearest police station – if you like . . . And we can sort you out there.' Pause. 'Or you can answer the question. Take your pick.'

Two seconds – five seconds –

'Well?'

One second –

'All right, guv'!'

'Well?' The repetition was lazy with dominance.

'Worsdale, guv – Jack Worsdale . . . Easy Removals – you can ring my gaffer, Mr Page, if you don't believe me – straight up!' This pause, thought Benedikt, covered a pointing finger at the phone-box, to support the surrender. 'Takin' an upright grand – a grand pi*aner* – to Major Sidebotham – *Winter*botham . . . at Norton – Norton *Down* – The Old Vicarage, Norton Down.'

'At this hour of night?'

'There was an 'old-up on the M3 – on the Alton junction – wiv' a tail-back . . .'

Pause.

'There was a crash on the M3, sir. Junction 5,' said Constable Russell, almost apologetically. 'Early this evening. The road was blocked for nearly two hours.'

'An' I 'ad a blow-out near Stockbridge.' The van-driver achieved a genuine whine. 'Took me another hour – *and* they gave me the wrong direction then – '

'All right!' The Inspector cut short the explanation. 'Is the back locked?'

'Locked, guv ? Naow. There's only the pianer in there – '

'Russell. Go round the back and have a look inside . . . You stay here, where I can see you . . . and you over there – Mr Nabb, is it? – *you* stay where I can see you, too! I have business in Duntisbury Royal when I've dealt with this man and his vehicle.'

Benedikt started to move.

'What are you doing?' shouted the Inspector.

Benedikt continued to move, past the blanket-covered, lashed-down object in the centre of the cargo-space.

'Keep yer 'air on – I ain't goin' anywhere. I'm jest goin' to phone the missus to tell 'er I'll be late 'ome.'

Benedikt smiled to himself in the darkness. Whether he was on guard duty or not, Blackie Nabb had put two and two together satisfactorily, and was about to warn the *Eight Bells* of the impending after-hours raid.

But meanwhile, the business of the night was beginning at last, because from outside, at the back of the van, there came the sound of the scrape and clunk of the locking-bar which secured the doors. He sank on to one knee beside the piano – it probably was a piano, and maybe Jack Worsdale was a van-driver, and the police really had intended to raid Duntisbury Royal to catch after-hours drinkers.

His finger touched and ran along the rough bark – it felt like genuine tree-bark – which covered the Special Air Service's cylinder, past the false branches – genuine plastic – until they felt the cord at the end, with its wrist-loop.

One of the doors banged open and a bright torch-beam transfixed him.

'Nothing in here, sir,' called the policeman. 'Just the piano, it looks like – like he said. It's all clear.'

The policeman moved away, leaving the door open, sweeping the bushes with his torch.

Now it had to be done quickly. It was all clear, and the policeman would have scouted round with his torch to make sure of that, in so far as it was possible. And Blackie Nabb was in the phone-box, and it was unlikely that they'd have more than one guard this far from the village.

The cylinder was unnaturally heavy – heavy not because of its contents, but because it had to float correctly and unobtrusively, like a water-logged tree-trunk. But he was ready for its weight, and the van's position – front wheels already in the water, within a metre of the footbridge alongside it – cut the distance he had to move to a minimum. Half a dozen noiseless steps took him into the water, and if he made any splash it was covered by the extra banging the policeman made as he closed up the van. Even before that had finished he had ducked down under the footbridge into the darkness and deeper water downstream, cradling the cylinder in his arms.

The immediate need was to put distance between himself and the vicinity of the ford, in case Mr Nabb strayed round to the footbridge, for the reflected light from the headlights of the furniture van illuminated the pool that was scoured below the bridge by the flow from off the hard surface of the ford. But the action wasn't as easy as the thought, for though the water took the weight of the cylinder from him, the thick mud of the river-bed sucked down his feet, holding him back.

River – R. Addle – River Addle – the map had called the blue line which straggled along the margin of Duntisbury Chase. But a river it was not; perhaps in mid-winter, or when the spring floods rose, it might aspire to that description; but here, even in this deeper pool in the middle of a damp English summer, its mud and water between them could only submerge him to chest-height.

His feet came free at last, and he was able to push forward, half-swimming, half-walking, in the wake of the cylinder, which had already begun to drift away on the sluggish current.

At least the distances were miniature, though: a dozen noiseless strokes and trailing branches brushed his head as he reached the exit from the pool; and then, as utter darkness closed around him, he could already see a paler area ahead of him, like the night outside a tunnel, which marked the end of the woods surrounding the ford, and the beginning of the open fields through which the River Addle flowed, with only occasional willow-trees on its banks, until it reached the trees of the Roman villa site on the edge of the village.

River, indeed! thought Benedikt contemptuously, as his feet sank into another shallow part of the bed of the 'river', and one of his hands touched the SAS cylinder, which had snagged on a tree-root –

What am I doing here, encased in a wet-suit, crawling up a muddy English ditch like this towards an English village, for all the world as though I'm penetrating a high-risk

Comecon installation, somewhere east of the line? It's ridiculous!

He pushed the cylinder aside and waded out into the open, beyond the last straggle of undergrowth. An image of the air photograph Colonel Butler had shown him reproduced itself in his brain: from this point he had perhaps a mile of river to negotiate, little more, along the valley bottom, although the road he had travelled a few hours before – the rolling English drunkard's road – had meandered for twice that distance.

What am I doing here?

Herzner's voice answered him: *Whatever it is he wants you to do, within reason – do it. This has the smell of one of their domestic scandals, so it may be tricky . . . But Colonel Butler is a man of honour, as well as influence in high places. If we assist him he will not forget it . . . And Audley . . . Audley will either go to the very top or into the outer darkness – perhaps Audley and Butler together . . . one more Intelligence failure over here, and they are well-placed to pick up the pieces and take over. So you are in the nature of an investment, Schneider – a professional and political investment –*

Benedikt did not much like being *an investment*, the more so if there were politics involved, and most of all when someone as equivocal as Dr David Audley was involved in them. It would be better – or, at least, it would be simpler – to scc himself as a loyal ally of an ancient comrade-in-arms . . . in the mud of the Addle stream now, but once in the mud of the Lasne, where the road to the field of Waterloo crossed it, straining to get von Bülow's guns across to save Wellington's army, with old Blücher's challenge in his ears: *Come on, lads! Would you have me break my word!*

Treading mud, he could see just above the banks of the Addle, across the fields on each side.

Well, at least there was one thing he could do, which had nothing to do with being a loyal ally, even: he could see – literally see – how good the British image intensifiers were, courtesy of the SAS, as supplied to the Falklands reconnaissance groups!

Well . . . they were good – they were really quite good, and almost as good as those on which he had trained –

Good enough, anyway, to observe the herd of cows munching peacefully far away across the field to his right . . . and no hazards or obstacles in prospect except those designed to give the fox-hunters good practice, with not one yard of barbed-wire, which the riders hated as much as any infantryman.

He pushed forward, keeping to the deepest centre of the stream, where he could almost swim. After a few strokes, the cord on his wrist tugged at his stroke, but a second tug freed the cylinder – that was how the plastic branches were designed: to look real, but to bend and give way as soon as extra pressure was exerted on them, to allow the *ersatz* tree-trunk to follow its master –

It was easy. With the weak current behind him, and the water holding him up and taking the weight of the cylinder, he could make something like walking pace, with his head below the bank. At intervals, he stood up – always between the clumps of willows to which any inexperienced sentry would inevitably gravitate – but each sweep identified only animals . . . first cows, which took no notice of him, and later sheep, which bleated weakly and uneasily, as though they couldn't quite remember the nights when the wolves had hunted their remote ancestors, but nevertheless hadn't lost some dim frightening memory of long-extinct enemies, from which their loving guardians, the good shepherds, protected them all the way to the slaughter-house. But their warning protests were quickly silenced when he sank down into the stream and let himself drift by their wallows, careful only not to sample any of the fouled water.

The River *Addle* –

Addled eggs his English vocabulary had given him, but

Mother's dictionary had warningly added the definition of *addle* as 'stinking urine or liquid filth'; which he could believe now, after having traversed several trampled-down gaps in the Addle's banks where its fauna drank and defecated, so that he didn't even like to wipe his sweaty face with Addle-water, let alone quench his thirst with it.

But it was easy. If there were night-guards out in Duntisbury Chase, they were not here, along the Addle – Colonel Butler had calculated correctly . . . Maybe there were no such guards maybe they had imagined the whole thing, between them, and this was all for nothing; the only obstacles to his passage were the wires stretched across the stream at field boundaries – not barbed-wires of course (not barbed-wire in the Chase!), but inoffensive strands under which he could duck with no fear of snagging himself even if he had touched them –

It was easy –

And now the wolf – or this fox, anyway – was almost within the fold – *this* fold – on the edge of the belt of trees which marked the beginning of the Roman villa-site on the outskirts of Duntisbury Royal itself, where he planned to come ashore.

It was easy –

He caught hold of a tree-root eroded out of the bank with his free hand, and jerked the cord which attached him to the cylinder trailing five metres behind him. This was the ideal landfall –

Then, suddenly, *it was not so easy!*

The bright red tip of a cigarette flared briefly, like a fire-fly in the dark, downstream not twenty metres from him, freezing him into immobility in that instant, with half his body out of the water.

The flare died down, then disappeared altogether – there was the thick trunk of an old willow-tree curving out over the stream where it had disappeared – then the fire-fly flew in an arc, out over and into the stream, to be instantly extinguished.

Not *easy* – but *too easy*: now it was his own undeserved good luck which froze him, congealing the sweat on his face as he sank back noiselessly into the stream, crouching down in it.

He had been foolish; he had not accorded Colonel Butler his absolute confidence – and, even worse, not backing his own judgement of Duntisbury Chase, because it had seemed to him over-imaginative: *Audley's not trained to set up anything like this . . . But don't underrate him for that reason: if there is anything there, waiting for you, it'll be maybe amateurish . . . But, if he had anything to do with it, it won't be predictably amateurish. So we'll take precautions –*

He swore silently under his breath, easing himself closer to a tall growth of water-weeds on the edge of the stream. The damnable truth was that this *was* both predictable and amateurish, and he had still nearly been caught by it: predictable, because the air photos had shown a narrow footbridge across the Addle not far downstream from here, so that this was where he ought to have expected a hazard . . . and amateurish . . . God! If Audley hadn't had to make do with an unskilled sentry who smoked on guard-duty he himself would be in no position now to criticize that!

Just in time, he remembered the ersatz tree-trunk –

Or *not* just in time – it was already floating past him down-stream, fatally out of reach, and the slimy cord eluded his grip long enough to make it behave – damn it, almost level with the sentry! – as no ordinary drifting log ought to behave. He would have to let the line play out –

'Dad!'

The unexpected sound caught him with his senses at full stretch: dry mouth, although it wasn't a Kalashnikov waiting for him in the dark – could the cigarette-smoker see the log? – and the sweet-rotten smell of the stream, of growing and summer-flowering things, and dead things,

113

and wet mud in his nostrils, and all the small night sounds of the countryside in his ears.

'Dad?'

This time it was a much louder whisper, urgent inquiry edged with apprehension.

'Ssssh! Over here, boy!'

The soft crunch-and-swish marked the movement of the boy towards the man through the river-bank vegetation.

'Ouch!'

'Ssssh!'

'I stung meself, Dad. Dad – '

'What you doin' 'ere? Does your Mum know – ?' The sentry began accusingly, cutting off the boy with his first question angrily, then amending his anger with doubt in the second question.

'Yes, Dad. She said for me to come.'

Benedikt recognized the speaker. But of course – if it was anyone, it would be he!

'She – what?'

'She said I could come. She didn't send me. Mr Kelly sent me – she said I could come, though – '

Kelly!

'Kelly?'

Mr Kelly sent me! With those four words the greater part of his mission was accomplished: *Kelly was in Duntisbury Chase.*

'The police are in the village, Dad,' Benje came to the point breathlessly.

'What?'

'The police, Dad. Mr Russell an' another one – an inspector, Mr Kelly told Mum . . . They went to the *Bells.*'

Benedikt began to play out the line, to let the log drift past the point of danger.

'The *Bells*?' The father didn't sound as intelligent as the son.

'It's okay – they didn't catch 'em. The till was open an'

114

the door locked . . . But Mr Kelly says for me to tell you to stay here – 'cause Old Joapey can't come yet, because he was in the *Bells* when the police came – '

The line tautened to full stretch. The log must be well beyond Dad by now, and there would never be a better moment to follow it, while the man was digesting this news of the police raid.

'Mr Kelly got out the back though – ' continued Benje ' – an' he came straight to Mum – '

Benedikt took a deep breath and sank into the water. It was hardly a metre deep, and he was forced to propel himself downstream like some blind and primitive amphibious creature, half swimming and half crawling: it was like nothing he had ever done before, but the need for absolute silence made further analysis impossible. All he could do was to count his strokes, allowing for the fact that some of them were hardly strokes at all, when his fingers sank into the mud or encountered harder objects – all the waterlogged and sunken detritus from the world outside and above the stream . . . fallen branches and tangled lumps of river-weed roots and the submerged stems of the reeds.

He counted almost to the limit before anchoring one hand in a tangle and letting himself surface, pulling sideways on his anchor as he did so, so that he came up close alongside the reeds and away from open water.

For a moment he could hear nothing. Then the soft murmur of voices came through. He had not travelled very far by the sound of them . . . not much further downstream from Dad than he had been upstream of the man before he had started. But the reeds were protectively tall, and the continuing murmur reassured him that his passage had gone unnoticed.

For another moment he was torn between the temptation to stay where he was, to listen to whatever father and son had to say to each other, or to put more distance between himself and them while he had the best chance.

But the temptation to stay was a weak one: the boy's job would have been simply to have warned his father to stay on guard, or out of the village, because his relief – 'Old Joapey', presumably – was otherwise engaged. It was unlikely that Kelly . . . or, more likely, Audley himself . . . would have confided more to a mere child, however intelligent.

Audley . . . or Kelly . . . or both: that was the second and last part of what Colonel Butler wanted to know. And the best way to that was to move now, while he had the opportunity, while the presence of the police would inhibit movement within the village.

He pushed out into the stream again, keeping as close to the reeds as possible, without bothering to use the image intensifier. Either the night was less dark now or his own night sight had improved: the loom of the footbridge ahead quickly became the bridge itself, a low structure similar to that beside the ford which he had already negotiated. Beyond it the trees thickened on both sides of the stream and the sun-loving reeds ended. The sky above him became patches of blue-black against a tracery of interlocking branches as he approached the planned landfall.

Everything was all right now: he was in the right place at just about the right time. He had been careless, but he had also been lucky, and the one cancelled out the other to leave him feeling slightly ridiculous. This was England, not the Other Side – and this was the altogether ridiculous River Addle, a tributary of the negligible River Avon (which was confusingly just one of the many English River Avons), not of the Elbe or the Oder or the Danube or the Vistula . . . And that had been Benje's Dad smoking on the bank back there, not some double-trusted Communist border guard armed with the latest lethal technology and keen to try it out on anyone crossing his line from either side of it.

Ridiculous indeed!

There was an area of not-quite-darkness just ahead,

116

beneath a break in the canopy of leaves, where the spring floods had undercut the bank to create an overhang. That would be a good place to moor the log after he had swopped the wet-suit for its contents, where if it was seen it would be thought to have snagged itself naturally among the exposed tree-roots.

He hauled in the line, bringing the log to his landing place, and eased himself silently on to the bank. For a moment nothing stirred, then suddenly a bird squawked in panic just above his head and flapped noisily from its roost, away down the course of the stream, to find some safer refuge.

He hugged the ground, waiting for silence to gather round him again, listening to it thicken until all he could hear came from far away: among the distant night noises he could even distinguish the faint hum of a vehicle on the main road on the ridge, two or three kilometres in a straight line across country from the valley.

Perhaps not quite ridiculous: perhaps practice of a sort . . . or, if not practice, at least a reminder of the risks and discomforts which his successors in the field must endure on his orders – successors who could not depend on luck cancelling carelessness.

Well . . . the silence around him was absolute again, and the fox was in the fold undetected, with a job to do . . . so whether that job was ridiculous, or a little gentle practice, or a timely reminder of harsher realities . . . all of that hardly mattered.

He sighed, and lifted the log out of the water on to dry land, feeling along it in the dark for the concealed catches which opened it.

Out of the wet-suit, and dry, and properly dressed again like an innocent tourist – an innocent Thomas Wiesehöfer – he felt much better.

Of course, he was still an intruder, and if challenged

and identified he had only his story of an evening walk on the downland which had been overtaken by darkness and had ended with his becoming hopelessly lost. Even as he rehearsed it to himself while crossing the Roman villa field from the stream, it sounded thin and unconvincing to him. But what could they do but believe him?

And, anyway, thin and unconvincing or not, it was better than being caught in a wet-suit: a stranger in slightly crumpled slacks and wind-cheater might or might not be up to no good. But a stranger abroad in a wet-suit after dark could only be either a lunatic or a villain.

But . . . beneath *what could they do*? that other question still plagued him, as it plagued Colonel Butler: *What was Audley doing?*

It was extraordinary that the inhabitants of a peaceful English village should conspire together to revenge themselves on a terrorist. And yet, supposing that they had found some way of luring the killer to them, it was not unbelievable.

Even Colonel Butler had admitted that: '*We don't have the death penalty, Captain Schneider – every time it comes up in Parliament on a free vote it's thrown out. But if you put it to a referendum . . . which God forbid! . . . we'd have it back – and probably public executions as well. What they'd say is . . . killing children and coppers on the beat . . . "String 'em up". And rapists who kill, and traitors, and terrorists – "Hanging's too good for them", they'd say – the majority would . . . terrorists – and particularly terrorists with bombs . . .*'

He could see the churchyard wall ahead, and the stile which he had crossed and recrossed a few hours earlier.

The age of direct action: The Greens and Ban the Bomb, Ban Nuclear Power, Ban War itself . . . And here they had, if not the Greens, something like them in England – CND and other peace movements . . . and Greenpeace, and all the animal-lovers, who raided the laboratories and disrupted the hunting of animals.

118

Hunting humans, now – maybe that wasn't so wicked!

He climbed the stile, avoiding the gravel path in preference for the noiseless grass between the gravestones.

Colonel Butler: *'They've got longer memories in the country . . . Not that they needed them for the Old General. He was something rather special, so it seems – something out of the past, just as Duntisbury Chase and Duntisbury Royal are also out of the past, and rather special . . . I think we have to accept that they conceive they have a duty – that they loved him and that therefore they have the obligation and the right to avenge him, Captain.'*

That was the motive-power behind direct action, and what made it so dangerous: it had the powerful fuels of love and duty and self-righteousness in the engine-room, which gave ordinary decent men and women the resolution to act and to endure.

He could see the tall cross of the War Memorial ahead of him now, between two of the ancient yew-trees which the English habitually planted in their churchyards –

The question was not where the true power came from – here, in this churchyard, approaching *that* cross, which was the symbol of the Saviour of both the English and the Germans in their last hour, commemorating the fallen on both sides – which had been Papa's cross and Mother's cross simultaneously . . . the question was *who was on the bridge here, at the controls, in the driving seat, directing that power to what ends*?

He came to the churchyard's wicket-gate, close by the memorial and with the loom of the *Eight Bells* on his left. There was a single light in the public house, but in a dormer window in the roof, not at ground level; yet there was no police car in the car park – there were no cars at all . . . And Colonel Butler had promised that the police would stay in the village, prowling around, until after midnight.

He looked at his watch.

The question was . . . but the question divided itself as he approached it . . .

Rebecca Maxwell-Smith and the inhabitants of Duntisbury Royal might have desired vengeance, but they would
not have known how to encompass it.

Mr Kelly – *Gunner* Kelly, from long ago – would have
desired that same vengeance . . . and if Colonel Butler's
guess was correct Kelly was the extra ingredient in the
Duntisbury Chase conspiracy.

But it was Dr David Audley who gave that conspiracy a
dimension of importance to the security of the state –
who, if the Colonel was right, would not be interested in
vengeance, and who would not connive in murder, least of
all a murder by Miss Rebecca Maxwell-Smith, whose
welfare he had promised to safeguard.

But now the more important question was . . . how long
after midnight would the police prowl around Duntisbury
Royal? And that relegated all the other questions to
temporary obscurity.

Through the wicket-gate – it had been well-oiled at
midday, so it would not betray him now – and quickly
across the road to the grass verge on the other side: at
least he possessed the enormous advantage of having
walked through the village this afternoon in Benje's
company, even if he had been steered away from the
lodge gates, and the lodge, and the manor house itself.

And another thing was for sure: he could not approach
the lodge, where Gunner Kelly lived, directly from the
road. If there had been someone on watch at the ford and
near the footbridge, there would surely be someone in the
tangle of shrubbery on each side keeping an eye on those
iron gates. But that presented no special problem, because where the grounds of the manor fronted the village
there was a thick belt of trees held back by a stone wall;
and the wall, neither too high nor (so far as he had
observed) topped with spikes or broken glass, he could
scale at any point (spikes and lacerating points of glass
would not be the Maxwell family style: the esteem in
which they were held suggested to Benedikt that they

would fight their intruders fairly, without such unpleasantness).

Where to cross the wall, though . . . that had to be an arbitrary decision: not too close to the lodge entrance, but it was a long wall, undulating with the rise and fall of the land itself, so not too far away either.

When he was half-way to the gates, approaching headlights drove him down into the shelter of the convenient gateway of a darkened cottage: he shrank close to a thick hedge until the vehicle cruised past slowly, its lights searching out the road ahead of it; but, with relief, he saw that it was Mr Russell's police car, unmistakable with its broad red-stripe-against-white as it rolled by, even though its illuminated *Police* sign was not switched on. And with Mr Russell still in Duntisbury Royal now he could reasonably depend on a few undisturbed minutes.

Darkness and silence settled back in its wake, and this piece of wall was as good as any other.

Over the wall, under the trees, it was darker still, and he would dearly have liked the help of the torch with which the SAS cylinder had supplied him. But although it was impossible now to move in total silence, the thick carpet of leaves, soft and springy under his feet, blanked out all but the occasional sound.

Also, the trees were not so thick that he couldn't make out the obstacles ahead of him: separate tangles of branches and thickets of vegetation in clearings routed him through the woods along an obvious path, with no real alternative. And he knew, estimating distance half by experience from the afternoon and half by his sixth directional sense, that he was making progress to where he wanted to go, safely inside the manor grounds at the rear of the house itself.

Then his next step sank deeper into the leaves –
And deeper –

And deeper – *and suddenly too deep* –

Too late, he tried to throw his weight back, as his foot sank down past ankle, past knee – suddenly he had no foot, no ankle, no knee, no leg, *and he was trying to fall back, but he was falling forwards into ground which was opening up underneath him* –

5

The pit, on a quick estimate, was something more than three metres deep – nearer four even – and at least two metres square at the bottom. And its walls were sheer.

Not to panic, Benedikt admonished himself.

He switched off his torch and extended his arms on each side of him, adjusting his position until he lost contact with the side closest to where he had landed. Even with the torch as an extension to one hand he couldn't touch both walls simultaneously, and the same applied when he swivelled through ninety degrees.

More than two metres wide each way, then. And probably three metres deep. And sheer-walled.

He stood absolutely still, counting off his heart-beats until he was sure he could hear no sound but the thump in his own chest. He had seemed to descend with a great crashing noise, yet most of that must have been in his own ears, and if there was no sentry near the pit his fall might yet be unnoticed.

Not to panic, then!

He shifted his feet. At least he had fallen soft, into what felt underfoot like a mixture of wet broken earth and leaves; and now he was standing almost knee deep in the wreckage of the false floor of the wood above him, through which he had plunged.

Damn it to hell! It was anger, not panic, which momentarily clogged his throat and his thinking: *To be caught like this, in the oldest, simplest trap of all – like an animal!*

With an effort of will he swallowed his anger and cleared his head. Wasting time on that foolish emotion only compounded his difficulties. And, given time, there

123

there was no trap from which a thinking animal could not escape –

He risked the torch again. Down here, at least, it would not betray him far and wide, as it would have done up above, so long as he kept the beam down –

The walls were pale and chalky: this was ideal ground for digging without revetment, like that into which Grandpapa must have dug in France all those years ago, for his Siegfried Stellung –

Above him, almost within reach – perhaps within reach, the remains of the lattice of woven branches which had supported the deceptive roof of the trap gaped downwards: it had been so well-fabricated that he had not dislodged the whole construction in his fall –

If he could reach up and pull the whole of it down . . . would that raise him high enough . . . or provide him with anything he could use – ?

He studied the lattice, shading the beam of his torch with his hand. A single leaf, detaching itself from the thick layer which had concealed the trap, floated down on to him, brushing past his cheek. With a spasm of despair he saw that it was too far above him, undeniably built by someone who knew his business – someone who had calculated a structure just strong enough to bear that treacherous carpet of leaves, which had at first yielded under him like the rest of the forest floor, and then had welcomed him into the pit when it was too late.

He fought back the despair as it edged him again towards that other trap of panic from which he had already forced himself back.

This was not on the Other Side: he was not Benedikt Schneider, whose print-out and voice-print and finger-prints and photograph were all on the A10 KGB Red Code –

This was Thomas Wiesehöfer, and this was England – and if that was also Dr David Audley's England it was Colonel Butler's England too –

So . . . what could they do to him, anyway – Dr David

124

So . . . what could they do to him, anyway – Dr David Audley – and Miss Rebecca Maxwell-Smith, and Gunner Kelly, and Benje's Dad smoking on the river-bank – ? What could they do to him?

So . . . perhaps what he ought to do, as Thomas Wiesehöfer – as innocent Thomas Wiesehöfer – was to shout *'Help'* at the top of his voice, and *be* Thomas Wiesehöfer thereafter –

What he did do was to uncover the full beam of his torch, as Thomas Wiesehöfer might have done, to examine the unexpected man-trap into which he had fallen.

Another leaf, and then a whole handful of leaves, descended from above with a dry scraping sound, as though dislodged by the light itself. And there, high up and half-hidden amongst the sagging lattice-work on the edge of the pit in the nearest corner to where he had fallen, was the end of a rope-ladder!

Benedikt cursed himself for not noticing it immediately, as an innocent Thomas Wiesehöfer would surely have done once he had collected his wits after plunging into the pit. In the direct beam of the torch there was no doubt about it: it was a genuine and undoubted rope-ladder, its rungs stretched and mud-stained with previous use by the diggers of the pit!

It was hardly believable, even for amateurs . . . but someone had been careless again, failing to draw up the rope-ladder which the diggers had used – failing to draw it up that last half-metre, to the lip of the pit – ?

Unless – he frowned to himself as an alternative possibility, even more unbelievable, intruded into his mind – unless this wasn't a man-trap at all – ?

An *animal*-trap? If it was a man-trap then that rope-ladder had no place in it. But an *animal*-trap –

Yet what sort of animal was there in Duntisbury Chase that they might want to trap – if everything which he and Colonel Butler had imagined was no more than an illusion of a fevered sense of insecurity? There were no wild boar

125

in England, there were only foxes and deer . . . But was this how the English trapped those creatures out of season?

He shook his head. Man or animal, it didn't matter. All that mattered was getting out of the pit while there was still time to do so: Thomas and Benedikt were both agreed on that!

He turned the torch to the debris in which he stood, foraging among the branches of the fallen part of the lattice. With the right extension to his arm the rope-ladder was well within reach, and after that everything depended on whether it was firmly anchored above, sufficiently to bear his weight, or merely piled for removal with that careless end enticing him to disappointment.

He hooked the end of the branch over the rung and pulled gently. The rope bowed, and then tautened as he increased the pressure. A quantity of leaves and assorted duff from the forest floor above descended on him, together with small hard fragments of chalk from the lip of the pit. For a moment the rope-ladder resisted him while it sorted itself out, then it came free with a sudden rush-and-slither, bringing down a miniature deluge of the same mixture with it, including a larger lump of chalk which struck him sharply and painfully on the cheek-bone. The noise of it all, confined within the almost-enclosed space of the pit, seemed as deafening as his original fall, so that when the silence came back once more and lengthened again into safety he marvelled at his continued good fortune.

Then reason asserted itself. Man-trap or animal-trap, there must be others like it in other likely places: traps sited like this one, which used the natural forest obstacles to funnel the quarry along convenient routes into them. But the village's manpower available over every twenty-four hours of light and darkness must be strictly limited, and most of it would have to be used to cover the open country which could not be man-trapped, so that the traps would only be checked at intervals. Not for Duntisbury Royal the vicious anti-personnel mines, and voracious dogs, and merciless heat-seeking sensors of the Other Side's frontier, thank God!

And, once again, he had been lucky nevertheless, to fall into this trap between checks, with time to spare (or perhaps the police raid had dislocated the schedule?) – and luckiest of all to fall into this particular trap, of all others, in which their carelessness had again cancelled out their ingenuity.

But now there was no more time to lose if he was to capitalize on that good fortune: he had to cut his losses and run with what he had –

He stuffed the torch back into his pocket and reached for the rope-ladder, fumbling in the dark over the rough chalk wall of the pit until his fingers closed on it.

Already his mind was ranging freely above him, mapping out his route to safety: straight up the nearest ridge to the south was the shortest way, but he no longer trusted any part of Duntisbury Royal along which he hadn't travelled this night, so back along the path by which he had come was the way he intended to leave, wading the River Addle below the footbridge. The SAS cylinder with his wet-suit inside it was safely moored out of sight and could be left to Colonel Butler to recover at his leisure as his problem: the rule now was the same rule for any operation which had gone sour, with the priority on getting the human material out, regardless of loss of equipment. And this time *he* was the human material –

Get out quickly, or go to ground if you can't get out!

He grasped the vertical of the rope ladder firmly, at full stretch, and felt for the lowest rung with his left foot – *by God, he had gone to ground literally already, but it was out of ground and away that he wanted to go now!*

The rope-ladder stretched under his weight, tapering and twisting as all rope-ladders did, but he was ready for its distortion from his training – compared with that these few metres would be a piece of cake –

His left shoulder banged against the hard wall of the pit – this was the crucial moment when he would really find out whether the damn thing was properly anchored, as he raised his right foot to find the next rung.

It was holding – his foot found the rung –

He was going to get out of the pit –

More of the debris from above cascaded down on him. But one more stretch, and he would be at ground-level again – out of the man-trap at last.

The rope-ladder gave way not quite in the same instant of time when the tremendous concussive *bang* exploded above him: he was already in mid-air, falling backwards, when the sound of it enveloped him, so that in the moment he had no understanding of where the sound came from – above, or below, or inside –

Then he was on his back, bouncing off the wreckage which cushioned his fall for half another instant, until his head hit the chalk wall behind him, starting another explosion inside his head to mingle with the echoes of the explosion outside –

He came back to full consciousness in a matter of seconds, but into total confusion: he was aware only that he had threshed about wildly, half-stunned and enmeshed equally in panic and the rope-ladder, which had followed him down into the pit, twining round him like a living thing in the darkness.

Yet it was the awareness – the understanding that he was still alive – which created the confusion. His head hurt, but it hurt high up at the back, where it had struck the wall of the pit: it didn't hurt because it had been blown to pieces by that shot from above. *That shot* – ?

But, anyway, there was no sound from above now. The echoes of the explosion and the ringing in his ears had both died away into an unnatural silence.

Yet he wasn't dead – he could move his legs and his arms and his hands and his fingers – he could feel the leaves and branches beneath him, and he could hear them rasp and crunch beneath him . . . against that other silence –

God damn! It hadn't been a shot at all – there was no one up there, above him. *God damn*!

He shook the blasphemy from his head and sat up, fumbling in his pocket for his torch.

Of course there were other pits like this – other man-traps waiting for their quarry. But they couldn't cover all of them, so they had rigged up a trap-within-a-trap: the convenient rope-ladder offering its help to any thinking animal which might fall into the pit by day or night . . . Only the other end of the ladder wasn't anchored at all – it was simply attached to some sort of explosive device, set in the same fashion as a trip-flare, but attached in this case to a warning maroon which would betray the intelligent prisoner as soon as he put his full weight on it.

Benedikt ground his teeth in anger with himself – and with Audley – Colonel Butler had warned him that Audley would be *tricky* – and then with Colonel Butler, and everyone from Herzner at the Embassy – *just a little job for Colonel Butler, Captain Schneider* – to Miss Rebecca Maxwell-Smith and Benje's Dad . . . and even Thomas Wiesehöfer –

Thomas Wiesehöfer –

* * *

Now they would be coming, summoned by that ear-splitting warning – and coming quickly –

Still no sound from above.

He brushed the dirt from his face. There was an egg on the back of his head which was tender to the touch of his finger-tips – and . . . and a slightly raised contusion of his cheek-bone, where the lump of chalk had hit him: it even boasted a sticky crater where the chalk had cut into his flesh –

But there was no more time for thought: someone was coming – he could hear voices –

'*Help!*' shouted Thomas Wiesehöfer, lost on his evening stroll in a foreign country and trapped in an incomprehensible pit.

And now there was light as well as sound above – and he must get rid of his own tell-tale torch –

'Help!' He stuffed the torch under the debris beneath him, and stood up on top of it, steadying himself on the nearest wall. '*Help!*' He achieved a note of desperation which was too close to the truth for comfortable analysis.

The light intensified, finally shining down directly into his eyes.

'Grüss Gott!' exclaimed Thomas Wiesehöfer fervently. 'Please! I haff fallen into – into this place – this hole in the ground! Please to help me – I am wounded and bleeding.'

The beam of the torch explored him.

'Please to help me!' appealed Thomas Wiesehöfer.

There was a pause above.

'Please – '

'It's that bloody Jerry.' The voice ignored his appeal.

'What?' Another voice.

'That Jerry – from this afternoon . . . the one that was nosing around . . . the one that was in the *Bells*.'

'What?' A second light entered the pit, fixing itself on Thomas Wiesehöfer. 'You'm right.'

'Please!' Thomas Wiesehöfer was running out of steam.

'What'll us do with 'im, then?' The rich country voice behind the second torch also ignored his appeal.

'Knock the bugger on the 'ead an' fill in the bloody 'ole, I would, if I 'ad my way,' said the first speaker uncompromisingly.

'Looks like someone's already given 'im one for starters. See 'is face there?'

'Ah, I see'd it. Must 'a done that when 'e went in. Serve 'im right!' The first speaker was clearly unmoved by the state of their captive's appearance. 'Serve the bugger right!'

Thomas Wiesehöfer decided to get angry. 'You up there – do you hear me? I haff fallen in this hole – you will help me out at once, please!'

'Arr! So you fell into the 'ole, did you now, Mister?' The first speaker echoed him unsympathetically. 'An' what was you doin' out 'ere in the first place, eh?'

'Poachin' on the Old Squire's land, that's Miss Becky's now, mebbe?' The second speaker chuckled grimly. 'Bloody foreigner – poachin' on Miss Becky's land! This'll learn 'im, then!'

'What?' They were playing with him, the swine! 'I do not understand – ?'

'Arr? Nor you don't, don't you?' The first speaker chipped in. 'Well then . . . you just bide where you are, Mister – you just bide there – see?' The torch flashed out. 'Keep clear of anyone we catches, is what they said – just make sure they stays where they are 'til we can cast an eye on 'em – so that's what us'll do.'

They? *Damn them*!

'You down there – ' the words descended through the darkness, which was once again complete ' – I got a 12-bore an' I knows how to use it. So you stay quiet then . . . understand?'

Benedikt suddenly understood all too well. If the situation in the Chase was as Colonel Butler had believed it to be . . . and everything which had happened to him confirmed that now beyond all doubt . . . then this trap had been built for a very dangerous animal, and the night-guards would have been warned to take no chances with it. Of course, being the amateurs they were, they had forgotten half their instructions immediately and had taken a careless look at their catch, chattering like monkeys; but now native caution had reasserted itself, edged with apprehension.

So . . . however Thomas Wiesehöfer might have reacted to that threat in all his injured innocence, Benedikt Schneider wasn't about to argue with a shot-gun in the hands of a nervous peasant. Even the prospect of crossing swords at a disadvantage with Audley was to be preferred to that: here in England, with Colonel Butler as his last resort (however humiliating that might be, and more so than his present predicament), he could survive failure there. But a shot-gun was something else, and there would be no surviving that.

So . . . better to use what time he had to compose himself, and to rehearse the Wiesehöfer story, weak though it was.

Audley wouldn't believe it, of course. But that didn't mean that he wouldn't accept it, if he judged the risk of turning the mysterious Wiesehöfer loose more acceptable than detaining him, which carried the equal risk of alerting whoever had sent him to –

No. That was wishful thinking, because the risks weren't equal – because he already knew too much about the Chase's defences.

So Audley *must* detain him . . . at least so long as he stuck to his Wiesehöfer cover . . . until the real target came into sight.

Therefore, at the right moment, he would have to abandon Wiesehöfer for Schneider, in the rôle Colonel Butler had prepared for just such an emergency –

Benedikt frowned in the darkness as the thought struck

him that Colonel Butler might have reckoned all along that his tricky Dr David Audley *would* catch him. In which case –

His ears, attuned to the slightest variation in the pattern of occasional sounds from above, caught something different, diverting him from further contemplation of the idea that Colonel Butler might have been playing a deeper game: someone else was whispering up there – but stretching his hearing to its limits he still couldn't make out individual words, only the contrast of the new sound with the gravelly undertones of the two countrymen – it was softer, almost liquid . . . it was a sound which, if amplified, would become a clear, high-pitched cry, where theirs would become an Anglo-Saxon bellow.

'Well now, let's be seeing you then!'

A light shone into Benedikt's face, blinding him again. But it came from a different direction – the light came from one side of the pit, the voice from the other.

'Easy now!' The voice tightened as Benedikt raised one hand to shade his eyes. 'Let's be seeing the other hand then, if you please! Because there's a gun on you – *slowly now* – and I wouldn't like for it to go off.'

Benedikt raised his other hand automatically.

Kelly –

The Irish voice was overlaid with years of English-speaking, but it was unmistakable.

Gunner Kelly –

'Please?' He packed the whole of Thomas Wiesehöfer into the appeal. 'What is happening? I do not understand – ?'

'Of course you don't.' Kelly agreed with him. 'Mr Wiesehöfer, is it? Or *Herr* Wiesehöfer – so it is!'

He hadn't bargained on Gunner Kelly. With Audley he would have known where he was, but the old Irishman was an unknown factor.

'Yes.' No – not quite an unknown factor, more an unexpected one at this stage of the confrontation; and he must not let mere surprise stampede him into error. The essential script still applied, subject only to appropriate amendment where necessary. 'Who are you?' He sharpened his voice.

Gunner Kelly – Michael Kelly, manservant to the late General Herbert George Maxwell –

'Who am I?' The question seemed to surprise the Irishman.

Who was he? Colonel Butler's Special Branch officer had answered that all too sketchily, with the sort of facts a routine police inquiry might have unearthed about any honest citizen who had never tangled with authority until pure bad luck had placed him near the scene of a crime.

Michael Kelly, born in Dublin 62 years ago, when Dublin had still been part of the still-mighty British Empire –

'Who am I, you're asking?' The note of surprise was edged with banter, as though it ought to be obvious to Thomas Wiesehöfer that such a question had no priority, coming from the bottom of a man-trap.

Michael Kelly, formerly of Kelly's Taxis in Yorkshire – but . . . *Kelly's Taxis was one broken-down Austin Cambridge until it ran off the road* . . . but, much more to the point – *formerly Royal Artillery, long-service enlistment –*

'Yes,' snapped Thomas Wiesehöfer stoutly, ignoring the reaction to his own question. 'Are you the Police?'

Silence.

'Are you the Police?' Thomas Wiesehöfer, encased in the inadequate armour of injured and angry innocence, might take enough courage from that silence to repeat the question even more stoutly.

'Am I the *Pol-iss*?' Incredulity. 'The *Pol-iss*?' Derision. 'Now, for why should I be the *Poliss*, in God's name?' Derisive incredulity.

What should Thomas Wiesehöfer do now – also in God's name? Most likely he would not know what to do! And all Benedikt himself could think of was to consult his memory of Colonel Butler's image of Gunner Kelly, based as it was more on the Colonel's old soldier's memory of old soldiers than on any precise and worthwhile intelligence about that man.

'*A long-service regular – twenty-one years . . . and the son of a soldier too . . . And mustered out in the same rank he started with.*' (A curious softening of the expression there, at odds with the harsh bark: Colonel Butler recalling other faces from happier times?) '*But don't make the mistake of thinking him stupid, if you come up against him, Captain Schneider. You must have come up against the same type in the Wehrmacht – the old sweats who knew more about the service than you did, and knew what they wanted – the ones you tried to promote, who knew exactly how to lose their stripes short of a court-martial . . . If you could ever beat one of them at his own game you'd get the finest non-commissioned material of all – better than the ones who hungered for promotion, even . . . the villains, if you like – but it was St Paul who spread the Gospel to the Gentiles, remember – the biggest villain of all – not St Peter . . . So don't you underestimate him, Captain . . . And an Irishman too – because with them it's the heart they give, not the head, when they make the break: you can't reason with them, and they're ready for the best and the worst then – they'll charge machine-guns head-on to save you, or they'll shoot you in the back – and you'll never know which until it happens, because they're what God made them, which is smarter than a cartload of monkeys, and not what you'd like them to be –*'

More silence. And then the movement of the man above, dislodging more of the surface above into the pit.

'The Poliss –' Gunner Kelly's voice lifted out of the hole as he delivered the words to those beside him ' – would you believe that, now!'

135

Benedikt began to believe Colonel Butler's theories absolutely. 'You are not the Police?' But then a nasty thought dissolved his satisfaction: for where was David Audley? He should have been here by now, after the roar of that maroon. But he wasn't – and this was therefore an unforeseen circumstance, in which Gunner Kelly might decide, heart over head, to 'knock 'im on the 'ead an' fill in the bloody 'ole', with no more questions asked – that might be the easiest heart-way with an intractable problem.

'Why should I be the Poliss, then?' The question came down to him challengingly, but reassuringly.

Benedikt thought quickly. 'You threaten me with guns – with firearms.' Only outraged innocence presented itself as a proper reaction. 'By what right? You have no right to threaten me so!'

'No right?' Kelly paused. 'Rights, is it then? Well then, Mister – *Mein Herr* – you tell me by what right ye are on private property at this hour of the night, when every Christian man should be in his bed, with his loving wife beside him? Can you be telling me that, and I will be telling you about my rights in the matter then!'

Anger for anger, he was being given. And how should poor Thomas Wiesehöfer react to that? He would be frightened, decided Benedikt instantly – he would be scared halfway to death, and not less so for being innocent.

'But . . . but I do not know – I am lost in the darkness upon the hillside, and I saw a light – I do not know where I am!' he protested desperately. 'What is this place?'

Again no answer came back directly down to him. And that might mean the beginning of doubt up above . . . but, for sure, Thomas Wiesehöfer in his confusion would not be computing any such blessing: rather, far more likely, fear would be sharpening his wits –

'Please – is this Duntisbury Royal?'

Again there was no immediate answer, though this time he caught the soft murmur of whispering.

'Is this Duntisbury Royal?' he repeated the question.

'Ah . . . now how would you be knowing that then – if you do not know where you are?'

'You know my name – you spoke my name . . . Please, if this is Duntisbury Royal, I wish to speak to Miss Rebecca Maxwell-Smith . . . or . . . to Mr – *Dr* . . . Dr David Audley – I am known to them, and they will speak for me.'

The sounds from above increased, and someone stepping on the edge of the pit dislodged more debris on top of Benedikt just as he opened his mouth to repeat the request.

He spluttered for a moment. 'Please – I wish – '

'Shut up and listen!' The Irishman cut him off. 'There's a ladder comin' down to you, Mister. But you come up easy now, an' don't try anythin' . . . Because there'll be a light on you, an' there'll be a gun on you, an' him as holds the light won't be him as holds the gun – do you take my meaning?'

Benedikt took the Irishman's meaning. 'Yes.'

The ladder came down with a slither and another miniature avalanche, but this time he was ready for the debris, with eyes and mouth closed. He fumbled in the dark for it, feeling quickly for the rungs with his foot before the Irishman could change his mind.

'Easy now!' The moment he stepped off the ladder a hand grasped his arm tightly, swinging him round until he sensed that he was facing the pit again. A second later a flashlight from the other side of the pit blinded him. 'Steady now!'

They weren't taking any chances: one push and he was back in the pit. He tensed against the pressure.

Hands ran up and down him – they certainly weren't taking any chances – practised hands, which knew where to look and how to look through questing fingertips – trained hands, which were never those of any Dorset countryman. But he should have known that even without the soft Irish voice in his ear: Gunner Kelly was British

137

Army-trained, and the British Army had kept up its skills over the years, searching black, brown and yellow as well as white for concealed weapons.

'He's clean.' Kelly completed his task by lifting Benedikt's wallet, passport and spectacle-case from the inside breast-pocket of the wind-cheater. 'You can turn round, Herr Wiesehöfer.'

There was something odd about the man's voice. It varied slightly, oscillating between its native Irish brogue and the classless English which had been superimposed on it over two-thirds of the man's lifetime: it was almost like listening to two different persons – the English-Irish soldier, trained and disciplined by his masters to automatic loyalty and obedience, and the soft-voice Irish boy who had crossed the sea all those years before, following his father in that hard service which had nevertheless consumed and conquered him at the last, turning him to vengeance.

'Come on, then – follow the red light,' the voice commanded him, English-Irish.

There were two lights: one, from a powerful flashlight, transfixed him; the other, a weaker blob of red, bobbed up and down ahead of him.

'Joapey – you and Blackie cover this sector until you're relieved. An' no lights, mind you!'

Growl. 'What we do that for? We got the bugger, 'aven't us?'

'We got *this* bugger, sure. But suppose he's just a scout – one of a matchin' pair of buggers?' The Irishman paused eloquently. 'You get it through your head, Joapey – we're not playin' games on this one, like with the Squire's keepers in the old days, an' you get a belt on the ear an' a kick up the arse if you lose. This one . . . you get careless, you lose like the rabbit loses – you get your bloody neck stretched.'

Growl. 'I knows that. But you said they warn't comin' yet, an' – '

'I said I didn't *reckon* on 'em comin' yet.' Curiously, the Irishman echoed the man's accent now, in a third voice unlike his other two. 'An', I also said there's nothin' cert'n in this life 'cept birth an' death an' taxes – ' the third voice graduated from scorn to gentle chiding ' – man, this is your ground an' you know it better than any stranger poachin' in it, but I don't want Miss Becky pipin' her eye for you . . . If you ain't got the guts for it, then just you say so.'

Growl. 'No! I never said that – now you'm puttin' words in my mouth what I never said!'

'A'right, then . . . Now, Mister – ' Discipline restored, the Irishman came back to Benedikt ' – let's not keep our betters waiting.'

'Betters' could only mean Audley and Miss Becky, and they were infinitely preferable to a shot-gun at his back. But the light blinded him, and he was still close to the pit.

He tried to shield his eyes. 'I cannot see where I am going.'

'Put the light on his feet,' snapped Kelly, and the beam instantly followed his order. In the absence of those 'betters' there was no question about who was in command in Duntisbury Chase.

Benedikt remembered Thomas Wiesehöfer. 'Where are you taking me?'

'Just follow the red light, an' maybe you'll find out.'

The red blob danced ahead like a firefly, and Benedikt stumbled after it. Captivity was a new and wholly disagreeable experience, but he must put this feeling of helpless anger out of his mind first, and at once –

A branch brushed his face, and he lifted his arm ahead of him to clear his way. *Follow the red light –*

Michael Kelly –

Michael Kelly was no simple Irish peasant – and no oafish unpromotable private soldier either, Colonel Butler was right: that handling of the recalcitrant sentry and the sure voice of command which went with it – more, those three voices which the man turned on and off at will – all of that marked him out as someone more formidable in the reckoning.

The red light and the path at his feet twisted and turned; then he caught a glimpse of other lights, pale yellow, flicking on and off through the intervening trees on his left – now ahead – now on his left again: they must be approaching the manor house –

Colonel Butler had been right, but his rightness had hitherto been no more than logic and the shrewd assessment of experience and possibilities: young Miss Rebecca Maxwell-Smith might have the desire for vengeance, and the will to match it, but she surely lacked the stomach for this kind of work, and the certain knowledge to make the work worthwhile –

The lights were brighter now, diffusing through the trees into light itself –

And Audley . . . *Dr David Audley* . . . he had the expertise, or the perverse trickiness, to devise such old-fashioned man-traps; but he had appeared on the scene too late to be their sole architect –

The trees ended abruptly. Simultaneously he was out of the wood and on to the well-kept lawn which ran down to the manor house, smooth springy turf underfoot, and no more trailing branches and bramble tendrils plucking at him in the dark.

And there was the manor itself, brightly lit –

He strove for a moment to hold his inner train of thought on its lines, but the impact of his first true vision of the building was too strong for him, wrenching him irresistibly off course against his will.

He knew already what it was like, with Colonel Butler's photographs and plans etched on his memory: the solid, rectangular three-storey mansion, its incongruous towers at each corner – half house and half castle. Yet now what had seemed to him unnatural and ugly – the towers were no higher than the house, and neither towers nor house were surmounted by roofs, as would have been the case with every such still-inhabited survival in his own country – it had its own reality, dramatically illuminated by lights on the terrace below and from the crenellated parapet above against the intense blackness which framed it: Duntisbury Manor, in Duntisbury Royal, in Duntisbury Chase in the county of Dorset, was where it had been for half a thousand years or more, grown out of its own ground – *and woe betide the invader*!

'Get on with you, then!' Kelly urged him from behind.

Benedikt stood firm, scrutinizing the manor in his own time. 'This is Duntisbury Manor – is it?' He let Thomas Wiesehöfer speak. For, after all, poor Thomas had never seen the Manor, lacking the benefit of Colonel Butler's researches and advice.

'And what else would it be – Buckingham Palace?' Kelly sniffed. 'Did ye not see it this afternoon – or 'twould be yesterday afternoon now – when ye were out and about, snoopin' round the village?'

'Please?' Benedikt decided that Thomas would be unfamiliar with 'snooping'. In their insularity, the English took it for granted that most foreigners could understand their language and were unconcerned about their own ignorance. 'What is . . . "snoopin"?'

'Don't turn round! Never mind – just get on – go on with you,' ordered Kelly.

There now! thought Benedikt, stepping forward again: Michael Kelly had recalled him to the consideration of what was important again – which was Michael Thomas Kelly himself.

There were three ingredients here, in Duntisbury Chase, which had come together like those in gunpowder to produce an explosive mixture – Miss Rebecca Maxwell-Smith and Dr David Audley and Gunner Kelly. And Colonel Butler had known about the first two of them, and had guessed about the third – and the Colonel had been right: there was a sulphurous smell about Gunner Kelly, he was sure of that now.

Gunner Kelly –

They were approaching the Manor. The flashlight at his feet picked out a gravel path which circled an immense ornamental pond on which the night sky was reflected like a black mirror.

Gunner Kelly – the other two were what they were – and the path, which had been crunching under his feet, ended with a flight of steps leading him downwards, on to a wide stone-flagged terrace on which the flashlight at his back lost itself in the great pool of light which filled the south frontage of the manor: the façade, which had seemed so much longer and lower from that first view, now towered above him, with the curve of the towers on each side embracing him –

Gunner Kelly, with his sharp words of command, and his chameleon voices, and the inner certainty of those voices matching the certainty of his searching fingertips – *Gunner Kelly* was something more than the faithful retainer the facts had made him, the Old General's loyal servant in life and the Old General's grand-daughter's obedient instrument now.

He paused, as though irresolute now that he had lost the guiding light at his feet. There were French windows cut into the thickness of the ground floor, with other windows similarly pierced on each side of them betrayed by chinks of light through drawn curtains. But the true entrance was there in the angle of the south-western tower, shadowed under a twisted canopy of branches and leaves.

Benedikt's adrenalin pumped. For Benedikt Schneider knew now that, if Miss Becky had supplied the will to this mischief, and if David Audley had fashioned the means to it, the spark must have come from outside them – the spark and the certainty –

'Go on, then!' Kelly circled to his right, carefully out of reach. 'What are ye waitin' for?'

And Benedikt Schneider knew that Gunner Kelly was the source of that spark – that Colonel Butler had been right. But he was playing Thomas Wiesehöfer now, and poor Thomas would not know – could not know – that the postern door of Duntisbury Manor was on his left, shrouded by the famous Duntisbury Magnolia, the seeds of which dated from the days when the Elector of Hanover had ruled American colonies as King of England.

'Please?' The more he suspected Kelly, the more determined he was to play Thomas as long as possible.

The postern door saved them both from more shadow-boxing by opening with a sharp metallic *clunk* of a heavy latch and an un-oiled whinny of iron hinges.

'Michael?' The door rattled on a chain. 'Have you got him?'

'Madam . . . safe as the Bank of England.' Where Miss Rebecca Maxwell-Smith's voice had a more nervous ring to it than Benedikt remembered from their first meeting, Kelly's was cheerfully deferential. 'Out of Number Two in the spinney. And 'tis that German gentleman from this afternoon – Herr Wiesehöfer . . . So Dr Audley was right, would you believe it?'

Damnation! Audley suspicious was one thing. But Audley *right* – Audley *certain* – *damnation!*

The chain rattled again, and the door opened wide.

'Was he alone – ' She stopped as she stared at him.

'That I can't say, Madam. Until we know how he got in . . . But there's a full alert, an' everyone's posted – '

'What have you done to him?' She cut Kelly off angrily.

'Done to him? We haven't laid a finger on him, Madam,' protested Kelly. 'Not a finger!'

'Then why is there blood on his face?' Her voice shook.

'Blood on his face?' Kelly paused. 'Oh, sure – so he fell into Number Two, didn't he? An' that's twelve foot if it's an inch – '

She gestured to silence him. 'Herr Wiesehöfer – are you all right?'

Benedikt put his hand to his face. Now . . . if there was blood, it would have dried by now . . . but in this fierce light he would look worse than he felt, and that might be to his advantage.

'Madam – ' began Kelly. 'Madam – '

'Be quiet, Michael!' The strain in her voice confirmed his thought: for all that she was the mistress of Duntisbury Chase she was still only twenty years old, and blood spilt in her service was something new to her.

'Madam!' said Kelly sharply, in his turn. 'No – '

'Hush, Michael! Herr Wiesehöfer – '

'No, Madam – I will not hush, begging your pardon!' The sharp note vanished into the calmness of obstinacy. 'We are standin' in the light, with all the dark hill above us – an' I have this old itch between my shoulder-blades . . . So, I would most respectfully urge you to go inside – for my sake, if not for yours, if you please.'

'Oh, Michael – ' As he had spoken she had switched from Benedikt to Kelly, and then from Kelly to the great darkness out of which they had come, and then back to Kelly again ' – I'm sorry! How stupid of me!' Finally she came back to Benedikt. 'If you would kindly come into the house, Herr Wiesehöfer – at once.'

Neither Benedikt nor Herr Wiesehöfer required any further order: they felt the same itch in that instant, of the crossed wires in the night-sight, telescopically enlarging each of them out of the dark, shifting from one to the other, looking for a target, making their flesh crawl: that was a memory shared by both of them from the past!

Only at the last moment, when Miss Becky seemed to want him to enter first, did Herr Wiesehöfer assert himself, who had no reason for being frightened of such nightmares, more than he was already terrified: he must let ladies go first, or betray himself.

'Go on, Miss Becky – lead the way!' Kelly resolved the impasse quickly. 'And now *you*, Herr Wiesehöfer – get on with you!'

Benedikt followed her thankfully from unsafe light to safety: stone staircase, with worn steps, on his left – arched doorway, low door closed – cellar door? – ahead . . . open door and passage on his right, leading into the house.

He followed her down the passage. The house was cold now – cold because they were into the chill hours beyond midnight, and with no fires lit these thick walls had repelled the inadequate warmth of yesterday's sunshine all too efficiently; but cold also because he was tired and frightened, Benedikt equally with Thomas.

'Hold on, there,' commanded Kelly from behind him. 'The door by you – you can see the wash-basin, and there's a hand-towel beside it . . . So you just make yourself presentable for the young lady, then – okay *mein Herr*?'

It wasn't solicitude for him, thought Benedikt: the sight of blood had been questioned by Miss Becky, so that blood was better washed off, that was all.

He moved to close the door without thinking, but Kelly kicked out with his foot to hold it open. 'Uh-uh! Easy now . . . Just the water and the towel, where I can see you.'

Benedikt studied himself in the small mirror above the wash-basin. He had not really bled very much – the cut was small, and not very deep – but he had spread what there had been quite artistically, to good effect.

'Michael!'

'Coming, Madam!' But in replying to her Kelly didn't take his eye off his prisoner. A careful man, was Gunner Kelly. A careful man . . .

He wiped his face slowly, taking his time to get his first proper view of the Irishman, and was repaid with similar scrutiny.

'Sure, and that's nothin' then, is it? I cut meself worse than that shavin' many a morning.' Kelly shook his head. 'Ye'll not be takin' an honourable scar home to the Fatherland with that little scratch . . . if you should be so lucky, eh?'

The man was disappointingly nondescript. With that

short unstylish haircut – almost cropped brush-like, iron-grey speckled with black – and the rounded blob of a nose in an expanse of leathery skin . . . skin not drawn tight enough to betray any memorable bone-structure beneath . . . it was any face in a crowd. In fact, he had seen it before, not just in the inadequate enlargement Colonel Butler had supplied, but now – now that he saw it in that flesh – from his childhood recollections: it was any face in any crowd of British soldiers in the Rhine Army, substituting age and stone-sober suspicion for youth and beer-swilled truculence.

Kelly pointed. 'That way, straight ahead . . . An' just so we understand each other, there's no way out of this house that's not locked or guarded – understand?'

Benedikt gave him Thomas Wiesehöfer's baffled frown, but with the sinking feeling that poor Thomas was already less than a skin-deep covering, with David Audley waiting for him.

But, to his surprise, there was only Miss Becky in the room beyond the door – a long, low-ceilinged room, bisected with a single huge beam which made him want to stoop, the girl standing alone with her back to a great empty fireplace.

'Herr Wiesehöfer – ' She looked at him, then past him. 'Michael?'

'Dr Audley not back then, Madam?' Kelly had experienced the same surprise, but without the need to conceal it.

'He should be here very soon.' She frowned uncertainly. 'You think we should wait?'

'Not at all – 'tis no matter. We don't need him to ask a simple question of the man.'

The expression on Miss Becky's face suggested that Audley was exactly what she needed most. 'I don't know, Michael. David understands this better than we do.'

It was time for Thomas Wiesehöfer to speak. 'Fräulein – Miss . . . Miss Maxwell-Smith – ' More in bafflement

146

than anger first, with anger in reserve: that was the right note ' – Fräulein – I also do not understand this! I do not – '

'No!' Kelly snapped into life. 'No – that's not goin' to be the way of it at all!'

Benedikt turned toward him. *Anger,* then – ?

'With your permission, Madam – ' Kelly was just too quick for him ' – we should ask this . . . gentleman . . . how he came to be night-walkin' in the spinney when honest folk are in their beds – for a start.'

Anger – outrage – forward, then!

'What? W-what?' He spluttered his sudden loss of control.

'Aye – what, indeed!' Kelly lifted a chin which was blue-grey with stubble. 'What the devil were ye trespassin' on the lady's land for? Answer me that now?'

'Trespassing?' Benedikt drew himself up to his full height, remembering the beam too late, but just missing it. 'I wish to speak to the Police! I *demand* to speak to the Police!'

'The Police?' exclaimed Miss Becky.

'The Police, Fräulein – yes!' It was a rotten story he had ready-prepared for them – Kelly, for one, would never believe it. But that was all he had for this moment. 'Yes.'

'Aaargh! Don't you believe him! He tried that one on me – "Is you the Poliss?" he says. But I wasn't havin' that one, by God!'

'But, Michael – '

'No, Madam! Leave this one to me.' Kelly's voice softened and he looked sidelong at Benedikt, half closing his eyes. 'Am I the Poliss, then? No, I am not the Poliss – nor would I ever be. But I'll tell you who I am, since ye ask.' He paused, reaching inside his jacket, to the waist-band. *'I'm the fella with the gun, is who I am.'*

Benedikt gaped at the pistol, as much for himself as for Thomas Wiesehöfer, without need for any acting ability. With what he knew they were planning perhaps it should

147

not surprise him so much, it was only one more straw in the wind. Yet in showing it to him now, the Irishman had proved his point dramatically, with no going back: shot-guns were no less lethal – probably more so in unskilled hands – but even in peaceful law-abiding England many thousands of ordinary citizens possessed shot-guns legiti-mately, especially in the country areas like this. But an automatic pistol was something altogether different.

'God in heaven!' he whispered hoarsely.

'Oh-aye, 'tis one of yours, surely.' The Irishman's voice was matter-of-fact, as though it was a screwdriver in his hand. He didn't point the pistol, he held it diagonally across his chest, the fingers of his free hand playing imaginary stops on its frame. 'A very fine weapon. But you'd be knowing that well enough, of course.'

It was an old Luger – an old long-barrelled Luger, of the sort which had served in half the world's armies at one time or another . . . and this one looked so worn that it could have served with most of them, starting even before Kelly himself was born, never mind Benedikt.

He measured the distance between them. Four metres and a long settee, high-backed and heavy-looking: that was too far and too much for any ambitious ideas. And sixty years might have slowed the man, but not sufficiently: age did not wither well-maintained weapons – *fine* well-maintained weapons . . . not enough, anyway, for him to try his luck with an old soldier.

'Yes.' Kelly nodded, eyeing him speculatively, almost slyly, as though he could read his prisoner's mind. 'It makes a difference, does a gun – like the Squire himself used to say, in the old days, even with our little pop-guns: "The gun, Michael," says he, "'tis the final argument of kings, which is the last argument of all" – an' this is a gun I have in my hand, an' although it's even smaller, it will serve for you and me . . . an' especially for you, because you're the target – aye, an' do you know what sort of target, now?' He paused only for effect, not for a reply. 'A "Mike Target" is what ye are.'

148

It was half in Benedikt's mind to dismiss the man as a garrulous old fool – were not Irishmen all notoriously garrulous? But there was nothing foolish about a 9-millimetre Luger, no matter in whose hands.

'A "Mike Target",' Kelly repeated the words, savouring them. 'Named after me, it was . . . but that's another story . . . "Mike Target" was a *regimental* target – something really worth having – twenty-four guns on one target . . . three batteries of eight guns, each of two troops of four guns, out of sight of one another . . . *aaargh,* but it was a sort of democratic form of gunnery, would ye know . . . The Germans – that's your lot, begod, an' a smart lot of fellas they were – *they* had the best gun of the war that I saw, that we called "the eighty-eight", an' a terrible murderous weapon it was . . . But we had the best *regiments* of guns – an' the Squire's the best of them, no question – for he invented ways of control and command, and different ways of applying fire . . . I thank my stars I was on the English side, an' not facing regiments like his, begod!'

Benedikt tried to make sense of what the man was driving at, but could only think irrelevantly *wouldn't Papa like to be here, instead of me, because those were his guns, those terrible murderous weapons!'*

'Aaargh! No twenty-four guns have I – just this one little gun – ' The Irishman caressed the Luger ' – but a Mike Target ye are all the same, the best I've had in range for many a year!' He nodded at Benedikt, like a friendly enemy. 'So I'll not be asking you again why you were trespassin' on the lady's land, for you'd only tell me black lies that you'd got all ready for me – later, maybe, but not now . . .'

There was something wrong, alarm bells in his mind warned Benedikt: if Kelly no longer rated *why* as of the first importance, what could be coming next, instead?

The Irishman's free hand released the Luger barrel and plunged into his coat-pocket.

'See here.' He brandished Thomas Wiesehöfer's spectacle case. 'And don't say ye don't see, for ye recognized my young mistress upon the terrace, with her under the leaves in the shadow, an' what's in my hand is plain enough, as *I* can see plain enough for meself, surely.'

A frisson of triumph excited Benedikt. They had been clever – how they had been so clever, he didn't know, but they had been clever, nevertheless. Only, they had not been clever enough.

'It is . . . the case for my spectacles . . . which you took from me – ' He feigned incomprehension.

'So it is! And thick as pebbles are your lenses – blind as a bat in sunlight, ye are, ye have said as much to the children . . . So how is it that ye see me now so clearly, with these in my hand, and no spectacles on your nose? Would you tell me that?'

More incomprehension. *Frown, and shake your head, Herr Wiesehöfer!*

'I do not understand.' He spread his hands. 'I am wearing my contact lenses . . . Do you not have contact lenses in England?' He had the man now.

'F-what?' For the first time Kelly was taken aback, and Benedikt blessed the ultimate insistence on detail – the final rule which he had obeyed automatically because it was laid down to be obeyed.

Benedikt pointed at his eyes, confident of the tiny plain lenses which only an expert could differentiate from the real thing, and which had once helped him to accustom himself to the false ones. 'I wear my spectacles . . . sometimes . . . and my lenses sometimes . . . If you wish to see them, I can oblige you. But . . . I do not understand – I do not understand *anything* that you are saying – or doing!' he looked at Miss Becky despairingly. ' – Fräulein, if you would tell me, please, what is happening?'

Miss Becky looked at Kelly. 'Michael – ?'

Perhaps it was time for the rotten excuse at last, thought Benedikt.

Kelly frowned at him, the lines round his mouth working deeper. 'We still don't know why he was in the spinney, Miss Becky.'

It *was* time. 'I was walking on the hills . . . I left my car at a village – I do not remember . . . it is Rockbourne, perhaps – or Wimbourne . . . or Wimbury or Rockbury, or Rockbury St Martin – I do not remember . . . But I walked upon the hills, and it grew dark, and I lost my way.' With the contact lenses in support, the rotten excuse wasn't so bad: they weren't the border police, and he wasn't behind the line on the Other Side, after all. 'I saw the light in the valley – '

There was a dull *boom* – the sound of a heavy door closing somewhere within the house – the echo of which both cut him off and roused them both out of their evident embarrassment.

Another *boom,* nearer now. Audley . . . if it was Audley, they were both glad now, he could see it in their expressions –

But should he be glad? After believing that he was beaten, now he knew he was winning? Except that . . . even if Audley accepted the plain contact lenses in support of his explanation . . . that illegal Luger pistol tied him to the illegality of whatever they were doing, making him too hot to let loose, after all that had happened to him, in the pit and afterwards –

The latch on the door behind Kelly snapped as sharp as a pistol-shot, so that it was a credit to the Irishman's nerves that he didn't move a muscle, except to drop the discredited spectacle-case quickly into his pocket, as Dr David Audley came through the doorway like the wrath of God.

'What the hell's happening?' Audley took in the three of them at a glance. 'What's he doing here?' The glance ranged back from Benedikt to Gunner Kelly, taking fire from what it observed. 'For Christ's sake – what's that bloody cannon out for?'

151

'Oh, David – ' began Miss Becky, and then stopped.

'We caught him in Number Two pit, in the spinney, sir. And he's not after telling us why he was there.' Kelly swallowed. 'An' the Police have been all round the village, the bastards – '

'I know that.' Audley gestured dismissively. 'I stopped off at the *Bells* – '

'They didn't get anything, sir,' cut in Kelly quickly. 'The till was open, an' the curtains closed – an' the door locked, an' Davey knew the names an' addresses of everyone that was drinkin' there, as was his guests after hours – we've taken no trouble from that, I swear.'

'No trouble? Christ, man – the Police weren't born yesterday! There should have been *nobody* there, with the ford covered – and Rachel should have been in her transparent nightgown to make them ashamed for knocking at her door.' Audley shook his head angrily. 'I leave the Chase for a few hours . . . and every damn thing falls apart, as though I'd never been here. You're not fit to take a punt from one side of the Cam to the other!'

Kelly drew a breath. 'But sir – '

'*Silence,* Gunner Kelly!' Audley sniffed. 'Small bloody wonder you couldn't hold the stripe of a lance-bombardier from one pay day to the next – you wouldn't have held any rank in my regiment either, that did the real work at the sharp end, where there were real Germans, by Christ!'

'Sir!' Doubt and outrage warred in Kelly's objection.

'Don't you dare *sir* me, with that *souvenir,* taken by a better man than you, in your hand! Christ, almighty! As if I didn't know all I wanted to know about gunners – I should have my head examined . . . *Becky* now – my god-daughter, who's no fool, so I've fondly believed until now, says you're no idiot – *you* tell *me* . . . what's supposed to be happening – if you can?'

Benedikt was much reassured by this outburst of anger, in spite of appearances to the contrary. Because . . . if the Kommissar in Wiesbaden had nothing to say about

152

Gunner Kelly and Miss Rebecca Maxwell-Smith, it had had quite a lot to reveal about David Audley, if not who his god-daughter was; and nothing had been about losing his cool, except for some very good reason, so there had to be a very good reason for this.

'David – it's exactly as Michael says: when the Police crossed the water we went on the Yellow Alert . . . But until we get the walkie-talkie radios we can't reach everyone – Blackie's collecting them tomorrow – '

'Today,' corrected Kelly. 'Today – promised, they are, and he'll be there at eight-thirty to collect them . . . And then we'll be ready for anything, begod, sir!'

'But . . ,' Miss Becky blinked at Benedikt '. . . but then the warning went off, and that was the Red Alert, and Michael went out to check it – we weren't expecting it so soon, of course, but he wouldn't let me go – '

'Aaargh! And isn't that the truth!' Kelly came to her rescue. 'Would I be lettin' her go – orders or no orders? Ye weren't here, an' it was dark as the pit – '

'Kelly . . .' Audley's voice turned dangerous. 'Don't you dare play the bloody stage Irishman with me!'

'So to hell with that!' Kelly cut back at him in a new voice, different from all its predecessors. 'He was in the trap and I wanted to have a look at him – so what? I know what I'm looking for better than you do, Dr Audley.'

Audley looked down over his big broken nose at the Irishman. 'So you do, Mr Kelly – so you do. And what did you find, then? Someone you knew?'

The face-in-the-crowd was inscrutable, as anonymous as ever, but the eyes glittered with dislike. 'No, Dr Audley – only someone you so kindly let me see from afar this afternoon, I grant you that. But it was a justifiable risk, nevertheless.'

'It was *not* a justifiable risk – it was unnecessary.'

Kelly shrugged. 'Not in my judgement.'

'And since when has your judgement been worth a

153

brass farthing?' Audley looked at Benedikt suddenly. 'Do you know him?'

'No, sir.' Kelly squirmed uncomfortably. 'But you were right about him, sir.'

'I was?' Audley continued to study Benedikt. 'What has he told you?'

'He hasn't told us anything. But now I've seen him close up . . . He's good . . . But I know the type.'

'What type?' Audley returned to Kelly.

'Never a civil servant. Soldier or policeman – soldier for choice . . . I've seen enough of them in my time. Regular soldiering marks a man – I don't care whose army. And I've seen his type before – it's an obstinate look, they have, even when you've got the bastards at gunpoint – I know that look, sir!'

Miss Becky stirred. 'Michael – David – '

Audley's expression changed. 'Yes, Becky?'

'He *does* wear contact lenses – he admitted that . . . I mean . . . he's wearing them *now,* you see.'

Audley shook his head. 'Doesn't mean a thing, my dear. Or rather . . . it does mean quite a lot, to put it another way: it means exceptional attention to detail, as you would expect of him. It means he's good, as Kelly says.' He turned the look on Benedikt, but with a suggestion of sympathy. 'You had bad luck there, I'm afraid. My wife wears contact lenses, and I've watched her with them a thousand times. I made her wear them – as a matter of fact, I've tried wearing them myself, but I could never really get to terms with them . . . But I know all about them, anyway . . . And there's a particular way some people touch the area under the eye, instead of wiping the eye – my wife does it, and so do you, and it's as good as a nod to me . . . It's a game I play – identifying people who wear them. You can even change eye-colour with them. But you'd know that, of course.' He shook his head. 'Still . . . belt and brace is one thing, but contact lenses and spectacles is another, Hauptmann Schneider. Bad luck, you had there.'

Bad luck – Hauptmann Schneider –

For a moment no one spoke, then Miss Becky said 'Haupt – ?' cutting the rank off into a hiccup of surprise.

'Captain,' translated Audley. 'Captain Benedikt Schneider, formerly of the Army of the Federal Republic . . . more recently of Grenzschutzgruppe 9, and now of the NATO Anti-Terrorist Liaison Group of the Bundesnachrichtendienst, attached to the West German Embassy in London as of next week.'

'Holy Mother of God!' said Kelly. 'Grenzschutzgruppe 9!'

Miss Becky frowned at him. 'Grenzschutz – who are they, Michael?'

'GSG9, for short – I read about them in the *Mirror* a while back, Madam – what the Germans call their SAS – the real hard boys.' Kelly shook his head. 'I think we caught the wrong tiger, Madam.'

6

In daylight, finishing his breakfast coffee on the terrace, Benedikt could understand even better how Gunner Kelly had felt the night before. The broad sweep of the manor lawn, wide between thick plantations of woodland on either side of it, rose gently to the ridge itself, without any intervening obstacle: the splendid view, which had surely delighted generations of the Maxwell family, would be no less satisfactory downwards from the crest, almost a thousand metres distant, to delight any well-trained and properly-equipped marksman, day or night; while from the edges of those woods, for those who first looked where they put their feet, even a tiro could hardly miss his mark.

The *clunk* of the postern door latch, which he had heard for the second time when the nervous servant-girl had ushered him on to the terrace, sounded behind him.

He held his gaze on the ridge deliberately. Nerves were for servant-girls and Thomas Wiesehöfer, not for Benedikt Schneider: that at least he must pretend, now that he could be something like himself.

'Captain Schneider – good morning.'

It was Audley behind him – and that was good, for with Audley he knew more nearly where he was.

He turned slowly. 'Good morning, Dr Audley.'

'Was the English breakfast to your taste?' Audley inclined his head politely, and then smiled. 'But then perhaps your mother has accustomed you to it?'

I know all about you, Captain Schneider: that was the first signal. 'It was excellent.' Coolly, then. 'But my

156

mother never locked my bedroom door, even when I was a child. Is that an English custom with guests?'

'No. But it's a custom to protect them from accidents, and last night there were some very trigger-happy characters around.' Audley gestured towards the ridge. 'You were admiring the view?'

'I was, yes . . . But I was also remembering that last night Mr Kelly did not do the same. He regarded it as unsafe, as I recall. And so, I think, did you?'

'So I did – quite right!' Audley raised his hand again, indicating the stone steps in front of them, down which Benedikt had stumbled not many hours before with a gun in his back. 'Shall we take a stroll? The view from up above, across the valley, is much more interesting . . . So I did, indeed. But not this morning – and not for *us* at any time, I'm sure.'

Benedikt mounted the steps. Far above, on the very skyline, the sheep which grazed the ridge scattered suddenly, catching his eye with their panic. A moment later a horseman appeared, and then another. They reined in together and conferred for a few seconds, then split left and right.

'The Dawn Patrol,' murmured Audley at his side. 'By autumn the Duntisbury Hunt should be in excellent shape, the exercise the horses are getting.'

They walked in silence for a time, until they came to a curious open grassy ditch which divided off the well-cut manor lawn from the rougher sheep-cropped pasture of the ridge. The upper side of it sloped gently, but the manor side was revetted vertically with stone to form a sunken wall protecting the garden without breaking the clear view from below.

Another sniper's post, thought Benedikt, running his eye along the trench until he reached its junction with the highest point of the wood on their left. But then he caught a glimpse of movement under the trees –

'It's all right,' said Audley soothingly. 'It's "one of ours", as they say. And we are not the target, as *I* say.'

157

Benedikt turned towards him. 'But Mr Kelly is?'

'Ah . . .' Audley stared back the way they had come. 'This will do well enough. We'd see more if we went higher, but you can get some idea of it from here.'

The rise of the lawn was greater than Benedikt had expected it to be. Beyond the manor house below, he could see the roofs of Duntisbury Royal peeping from among the village trees, with the squat church tower to their left marking the position of the Roman villa field on the edge of the inadequate River Addle.

'Peaceful little place, isn't it?' Audley invited him to disagree.

'I did not find it so last night,' Benedikt obliged him.

'No. But then you did rather invite trouble – like Mr King in Colonel Dabney's covers . . . Do you read Kipling?' Audley raised a mild eyebrow inquiringly. 'No . . . I suppose not . . . But what *am* I to do with you, then?'

Now they had come to it. 'I do not see that there is anything that you can do with me, Dr Audley – if you know me so well – ?'

'Oh, I do, Captain Schneider, I do. And it's a good report I have of you, too: good soldier, good officer . . . good son, good Christian . . . *good German,* I suppose one might say, even.' He looked sidelong at Benedikt. 'But you know what we used to say about *good Germans* in the old days? Your distinguished father would know – he was a damn good German, if ever there was one!'

'My father?' Audley's private source, whatever or whoever it was, was also a damn good one. 'He would be delighted to hear himself described as "distinguished", I am sure, Dr Audley.'

'"David" – do call me "David". It's so much harder to sound offensive with Christian names, don't you think? So may I call you "Benedikt"?' Audley hardly waited for a reply. 'He certainly is – and was – distinguished . . . Distinguished scholar now, and distinguished soldier once upon a time . . . An anti-tank gunner, I believe? Eighty-eights in the desert, with the 90th Light? I must say I'm extremely glad I was never in *his* sights!'

Benedikt realized the condition of the 'good Germans' to whom Audley had been referring, which would be the same for 'good Englishmen' – and 'good Indians' – down history, and which was hardly reassuring now.

'The trouble is, Benedikt, that now I appear to be in *your* sights. And I'm afraid that I must insist on your telling me why, without more ado,' concluded Audley.

'Insist?'

Audley gave a little shrug.

'Or else . . . what?' Benedikt did not like being leaned on. 'If you keep me here I shall be missed – and there will be those who will come to look for me. You can depend on that . . . David.'

'My dear fellow! They may look – ' Audley swept a hand over the valley ' – it may not seem so very big, but it hid one German in it for fifteen centuries . . . Also the people here are good at digging deep holes, as you discovered last night. And if that sounds rather barbarous . . . there is one thing I'd perhaps better explain which you must bear in mind.'

'And that is?' He sensed that Audley was not so much threatening, whatever he sounded like, as softening him up to make a deal – which might well be what Colonel Butler had intended all along. Yet whatever he could get for free he might as well get. 'And that is?'

'The Old General – "the Squire", interchangeably, as they call him . . . They really did love him . . . He seems to have been a *good* man in the oldest and best sense of the word – a man of instinctive . . . "goodness" is the only word for it: there simply wasn't badness in him – rather the way some men are utterly brave because they simply don't know how to be cowardly, like the rest of us . . . I met men like that in the war – I'm sure there were lots of Germans just like them – they generally get a lot of other

159

people killed without intending to, in my experience – but the completely good people are much rarer, and nicer . . . though it seems, from what is happening here, that they can produce the same unfortunate result . . .' He shook his head sadly. 'But they really did *love* him. And now they're very angry indeed, because Gunner Kelly has undertaken to bring the Old General's killer – or killers – back here, so they've got something to focus their anger on.'

'How is he bringing them back?'

'He won't say. All he'll say is that he was the real target of that bomb, so he has the contacts – '

'*He* was?' Benedikt simulated astonishment.

'That's right. And he won't explain that either – it'll only make them targets as well, he says. And – ' Audley stopped as he registered the change in Benedikt's demeanour. 'What's the matter?'

'If Mr Kelly was the target . . .' Things were going very well indeed: they could hardly go better. '. . .that changes everything, Dr – David!'

'Changes everything – how?'

'Why I am here.' Apologetic sincerity was the proper note to strike. 'You have been frank with me. I must return the compliment.'

'That would be nice, I agree.' Cautious relief, slightly coloured by disbelief, was returned to him.

'It was because of the Old General. We were not satisfied with the progress of your investigations.'

'You – ?' Audley frowned. 'I don't see what business the Bundesnachrichtendienst has with the Old General?'

Benedikt betrayed slight embarrassment. 'The bomb was of an Irish make . . . but you appear convinced that it was not the work of the IRA. And he was certainly not a logical Irish target.'

'So?'

'So he was a former second-in-command of the British Army of the Rhine, with special responsibility for missile deployment in liaison with the Americans.'

160

'So he was. And Count von Gneisenau was second-in-command to Blücher at Waterloo – and Flavius Vespasianus commanded the Second Legion – so what?'

Benedikt frowned. 'So – ?'

'It was a hell of a long time ago. Fifteen years? More, maybe . . .'

'But he was once a prime target for assassination – '

'Oh – come on, man! Once upon a time – maybe . . . But the Russians . . . whatever their faults, they're not vindictive about elderly generals.'

'Not the Russians, Dr Audley. Our own Red Army Faction, rather.'

'You're pulling my leg! They were in nappies when he was in uniform. And you've got them more or less buttoned up, anyway – '

'That is the point, Dr Audley – '

'David, please.'

'David . . . The survivors are looking for soft targets, to make headlines to show they aren't finished. And . . . they have a reciprocal arrangement with the Irish National Liberation Army, to help each other at need.' Benedikt spread his hands. 'We thought it just might be worth checking out, in case . . . And – I am sorry, David – but when I saw *you* down here yesterday . . . I was wrong – I acknowledge that now . . . But when I saw you, I thought I might take another look, to see what the British were up to. I did not think you would . . . tumble upon me so quickly.' He gave Audley a bitter smile. 'And I did not expect a big hole in the ground, either.' He pointed at the sentry on the corner of the wood. 'Or him.'

Audley grinned suddenly. 'Yes . . . I can imagine that. Although, oddly enough, it seems to come quite naturally to them. I suppose it's because they've been hunting things hereabouts since the beginning of time – wolves and deer and foxes and rabbits . . . and each other after dark often enough, playing gamekeepers and the poachers.' He nodded at Benedikt. 'If they'd had any man-traps still in working order it probably wouldn't have been a hole you'd have stepped into last night, by God!' Just as suddenly as it had appeared, the grin vanished. 'Or if Kelly had had his way there might have been fire-hardened stakes in it. Believe me, you weren't altogether unlucky.'

Benedikt shivered in spite of himself. But now he had everything. 'Then I must be glad you were here after all, in spite of what I did because of you . . . But . . . I am sorry to have caused you such trouble unnecessarily.'

'No trouble, my dear fellow! You tested our defences, actually.' Audley studied him. 'So now you want to go home, I suppose?'

Exactly right! 'I . . . I rather think I am in your way now, perhaps?' He mustn't seem too eager though. 'But if there is anything I can do . . . to make amends?'

'Yes . . .' Audley continued to study him. 'Well . . . as a matter of fact, perhaps there *is* something, you know.'

Damn! 'Yes?' *Damn*!

'It's rather awkward, really . . . You see, Benedikt, I'm here . . . as it were . . . unofficially, you might say . . . In fact, you *would* say – unofficially.'

'*What*?'

'Yes.' Audley looked uncomfortable. 'I'm on leave, actually.'

Benedikt stared at him for a moment, then looked round the Chase – from ridge to ridge, then down the Addle valley – and finally back to Audley. 'God in heaven! Then this – ?'

'Is unofficial too. Nobody knows about it except us.' Audley paused. 'You see, Benedikt, I came here as a favour . . . to a young friend . . . to stop Becky making a fool of herself.'

He really was getting everything now, thought Benedikt. But he must look worried, not satisfied.

Audley waved a hand. 'Oh . . . I could have stopped this easily enough. Just one word to the Police would have done that. But that wouldn't have stopped Becky and Gunner Kelly trying again – and trying somewhere where the odds were more against them.' He shook his head. 'And it wouldn't have answered any questions about Gunner Kelly, either.'

'Gunner Kelly?' Now a frown of concentration.

'He'd have vanished. And he knows well how to vanish, I very much suspect. England or Ireland . . . and he can pass as English.' Audley looked at his watch. 'And then we'd never know.'

Curiosity? But it was more than that.

'Let's start slowly back . . . I have an appointment soon – an outing planned, in fact. And I'd like you to come along with me.'

What? 'You would like me . . . ?'

'You'll see some fine Dorset countryside – Hardy country too . . . you know, they never did really approve of him – it was the divorce, of course, that stuck in their respectable throats . . . and Badbury Rings, under their big Dorset sky if the clouds are right . . . and other things – you'll enjoy it, I promise you.'

There was more to this than a jaunt in the country. And whether he would enjoy it was another matter also.

'Or, to put it another way . . . they don't trust you, and they don't altogether trust me either, out of their sight – maybe Becky does, but Kelly and the rest don't . . . And if I let you go they'll trust me even less, and I wouldn't like that, with all the effort I've put in.'

Audley had never intended to let him go. He was merely sugaring the pill now.

'And, to be strictly honest, *I* don't trust you either, Benedikt, my dear fellow . . . "A good German", I'm sure you are . . . a loyal ally and all that, but goodness isn't the prime quality of the Bundesnachrichtendienst, in my experience – it's smart fellows they like . . . Or, let's say, that I *do* trust you nine parts out of ten – '

'Nine parts?' He had to react somehow to this.

'Nine parts – I do believe my contact, you see . . . And, to put it another way again, when I came here it was *killing* they were up to, and then burying deep. Only I've put a stop to that – it's *capturing* now, they've agreed on.' He looked hard at Benedikt. 'Now that we're close to the house again let's turn around and admire the view, eh?'

Benedikt turned obediently, and Audley pointed towards the ridge. 'See there – if those trees were a few feet lower we could see the banks of the Duntisbury Rings . . . No, I don't trust you one hundred per cent. But I trust them even less – and I don't trust Gunner Kelly at all out of my sight, because I've this lingering suspicion that he's still after blood. I want to know a lot more about him therefore.'

David Audley and Colonel Butler both.

'In fact . . . I want the Old General's killers *and* Gunner Kelly, you might say – ' Audley pointed to the right ' – that's the way Caesar's Camp lies, as you will know, for it was a full guided tour those two terrible children gave you, wasn't it? Yes . . . I'm greedy. I want to save Becky, because that's what I promised to do. But I want all my questions answered as well. Because that's the only way I'm going to be able to extricate myself from this business: bearing gifts to those above me . . . Indeed, if I wasn't afraid that my colleagues would come down here heavy-footed, to be spotted straight away as you were spotted, I'd have thrown in my hand already . . . But as it is – what Miss Becky and Kelly think I'm doing now is enlisting you as another ally in the Chase – I've promised them I can do that . . . I've told them that, as the Germans can have no axe to grind in this – and you're a decent chap – you may be willing to hang around and help . . . whereas if we knock you on the head, or more likely incarcerate you for a few days in the manor cellar – which would actually be a rather agreeable place in which to be detained, with what the Old General put in it – then there'd be hell to pay, with hordes of Teutonic Fighting Men descending on the

Chase again, and trampling the place flat.' He gave Benedikt another sidelong glance. 'Which, to be fair to me, is pretty much what you've already threatened me with – isn't it?'

Except, thought Benedikt, it would be Colonel Butler's British Fighting Men. But he could never admit that now.

He opened his mouth to reply, but the familiar snap of the postern latch cut the words off.

'Don't turn round.' Audley spoke conversationally, pointing again at nothing in front of them. 'Whereas in fact I'm doing no such thing. Although I am certainly trying to enlist you – true enough – '

Another enlistment? Colonel Butler had enlisted him once. And then the people of Duntisbury Chase, where no one seemed to trust anyone, had wanted him. And now –

'But I want you just for myself. Because I need an ally here more than anyone – *now* you can turn round – ' Audley followed his own instructions ' – ah! Gunner Kelly! Are the boys ready?'

'Ready and waiting, sir.' Kelly looked inquiringly from Audley to Benedikt. 'And the Captain?'

'He's coming with me.' Audley smiled at Benedikt. 'Okay, Benedikt?'

That was taking acceptance for granted – *alliance* for granted – without leaving the ally any real choice.

He smiled back at both of them. 'Okay, David,' he said.

There was at last another German *foederatus* in Duntisbury Chase. But this one, at least, would be on his guard, he decided.

7

All military establishments were somehow alike, decided Benedikt critically, but one had to allow for national peculiarities.

The alikeness here – the true alikeness, apart from the unnaturally tidy ugliness – was its aura of impermanence. It wasn't that the buildings weren't substantial . . . the brick-built barracks and married quarters which he had glimpsed were if anything more solid than some of the ancient Dorset villages through which they had passed . . . But those little thatched cottages and small corner shops were part of the landscape, where God and man both intended them to be, while this place had merely been drawn on a map by some far-off bureaucrat to serve a finite need, and when that need evaporated it would decay quickly.

Yet at this moment, as Audley slowed the car to turn across the traffic, the British peculiarities were more obvious: not only was this camp bisected by a public road, without any visible sign of security, but there were children climbing on that tank – and wasn't that an ice-cream van –

The last of the oncoming vehicles passed by, and his view was no longer partially obstructed.

It *was* an ice-cream van. And there were several tanks, and they were all festooned with children, the nearest of whom machine-gunned them noisily with his pointing fingers as they came within his range.

And there were *more* tanks – and a pale grey howitzer of ancient aspect – it was all antediluvian equipment in a graveyard of armoured elephants: he craned his neck to the left as the car halted, towards a harassed mother shepherding her ice-cream-licking offspring from the van to the nearest monster; and then to the right, where on the roadside forecourt in front of a hangar-sized shed, he caught sight of the distinctive rhomboid of the sire of all these beasts, squatting on an angled concrete plinth facing the road, which until now he had seen only in old photographs, but which had once crawled out of the smoke and mud against Grandpapa.

'These are the ones they don't care about,' said Benje disdainfully from behind him. 'The proper ones are inside.'

'These are just for kids to climb on,' supplemented Darren. 'You can't climb on the ones inside.'

Benedikt looked questioningly from one to the other. 'Inside?'

'Inside the museum.' Benje raised an eyebrow. 'Didn't you know where we were going?'

'The museum?' The progression of questions were beginning to make him feel a trifle foolish, but Audley was too busy finding a space in an already well-filled car park to rescue him.

'The tank museum,' said Darren.

'*Museum machinationum,*' said Benje, seizing this un-likely opportunity to demonstrate his Latin vocabulary further. 'Or it could be plain *machinarum lacuum* doesn't sound right . . . But David says why not *testudinum,* from the way the Romans used to lock their shields together into a *testudo* – what do you think?'

'Yes.' What he thought was that Benje's obsession with all things Roman, unleashed on the mistaken assumption that Herr Wiesehöfer was a fellow enthusiast, was as exhausting as it was surprising. But Papa would never forgive him for discouraging a young classicist, so he must consider the problem seriously. '*Testudo* – a tortoise . . . I suspect, if there had been armoured vehicles in the Roman Army they would have had a proper name, as we have in my country – whatever the Latin for *Panzerkamp-*

fwagen may be . . . or perhaps *Schuetzenpanzerwagen* might be closer to what they might have had. But for a nickname I think *testudo* does very well – unless the Roman who invented that objected to such an infringement of his copyright.' He frowned at Benje. 'Was there a Roman copyright law?'

Benje returned the frown. 'I don't know. I hadn't thought of that. They had a lot of laws . . . What do you think, David?'

Audley had finally found a space and was nosing into it. 'I think *testudo* – there is actually an appalling monster in there called "The Tortoise" . . . 78 tons and quite useless – we started building it in '42 and finally got it to move in '46, to no possible purpose that I can imagine, unless they wanted to play snooker inside it under fire.' He applied the handbrake fiercely. 'But I think also that I do owe you an apology for failing to tell you where we were going, Herr Wiesehöfer. Actually, I thought I had – but it's young Benjamin's fault for monopolizing you with his theories on Boadicea – '

'*Boudicca*,' the boy corrected Audley sharply. 'Everyone gets it wrong, Mr Burton says. "Boadicea" is a spelling error – "Boudicca" means "Victoria", and she was Queen Victoria I, not to be confused with Victoria II, 1837 to 1901.'

Darren shook his head at Benedikt. 'He just talks *all* the time, that's his trouble.'

'It's not me. It's what Mr Burton says,' snapped Benje.

'What Mr Burton says is that you've got verbal diarrhoea – ' As he spoke, Darren squared up to resist physical assault.

'Out of the car!' Audley shot an arm between them. 'I've got a surprise for you both.' He winked at Benedikt.

Benedikt climbed out of the car, and then stared at Audley across its roof. 'And for me – a surprise also?'

'For you the museum is the surprise. It's strictly old hat for these two time-expired legionaries.' Audley led the way towards the entrance to the hangar. 'They have to have something new every time – *semper aliquid novi ex Bovingtonio,* as Mr Burton would say.'

'What's new?' Darren skipping backwards in order to face them, overtook them.

'They do collect new things all the time – ' Benje started out in a blasé tone for Benedikt's benefit, but suddenly an idea lit up his face and he switched to Audley ' – have they got one of those Argentinian personnel carriers from the Falklands? Is that it, David? Is that it?'

'No . . . but you're warm, young Benjamin.' Audley cocked an eye at Benedikt. 'They may very well have bits of General Galtieri's war surplus before long, they do collect such unconsidered trifles . . . They acquired their Russian SU-100 self-propelled gun from Suez in '56 – they're probably negotiating with the Israelis for a Syrian T62, I shouldn't wonder. Though where they'll put it, God only knows.'

Benedikt measured the enormous hangar with his eye. 'That is filled with tanks?'

'Bursting at the seams.' Audley nodded proprietorially. 'They've got pretty well the whole British range, from 1915 onwards, including experimental vehicles and the "funnies" from the last war – Crabs and suchlike . . . and armoured cars . . . And a very fair foreign cross-section, too – French and American, and all your Panzer marks.' He closed his eyes for a moment. 'They're particularly good on Tigers. Got a 1942 one, and a Royal Tiger with the Porsche turret . . . *and* a bloody great Hunting Tiger the size of a London bus.' He squeezed his eyes shut again, and then looked directly at Benedikt. 'I met a Tiger once, on the edge of a wood in Normandy . . . I don't know which one it was, I didn't wait to find out. All I remember is this *enormous* gun traversing, and I knew we couldn't get out of the way quick enough – it was like looking Death himself in the eye and knowing that it was me he'd been expecting all morning . . . We were in a

Cromwell, half his size, and we'd lost half our troop already since breakfast.' He shrugged. 'Very nasty moment.'

'What happened?' inquired Benje politely. 'Did you shoot him – the Tiger?'

'With my pea-shooter? Not likely! We just looked at each other for about a quarter of a second – maybe he was out of ammunition, having used it all on my late comrades . . . or maybe he'd had his ration of Cromwells for that morning, and he was feeling generous – I don't know – but in the next quarter-second he didn't shoot, and after that I'd remembered a pressing engagement for lunch elsewhere.'

'You retreated?' Benje sounded disappointed.

'Well . . . let's say I advanced in the opposite direction.'

Audley looked at Benedikt. 'You know, for years I couldn't bring myself to visit this place. I hated the very thought of tanks, Cromwells as well as Tigers – and Panthers, they were just as bad, if not worse . . . And then one day it didn't matter at all: it was as though there was a Statute of Limitations on bad memories, and after a certain time the badness no longer had any power. Or perhaps men change, and I have changed . . . I don't know. It's interesting, though.'

The boys were fidgeting now, a little disappointed with Audley's lack of heroism and quite lost with his theories on the healing quality of time, but above all desperate to discover the nature of their surprise.

Audley observed their impatience. 'Shall we go in?'

It was a museum without an entrance fee, but the entrance hall was like a shop dedicated to selling tanks in every form: in books and booklets, pictures and picture postcards, models and elaborate construction kits; and through a wide opening to his right Benedikt caught a glimpse of a vast hall packed with Panzers.

But right in front of him were two soldiers in uniform who showed no sign of moving out of the way, and both of them were looking at Audley.

170

One of the soldiers came to attention. 'Mr Audley, sir?'

'Yes.' Audley's lack of surprise indicated that this, in some form, *was* the surprise. 'Major Kennedy sent you?'

'That's right, sir.' The soldier wore sergeant's chevrons on his arm and the mailed fist of the Armoured Corps on his beret. And now he was looking at Benje and Darren. 'And these are the lads, eh?'

'They are.' Audley turned to the boys. 'The sergeant here is going to take you both for a ride. In a Scorpion.'

'That's right.' The sergeant gave the boys a brisk nod. 'The Scorpion tracked reconnaissance vehicle, as used recently in the Falklands to put the fear of God up the Argies. Aluminium alloy armour, and a Jaguar 4.2 litre engine – road speed 55 miles per hour. A very nice little runabout if you don't have to pay for the petrol. What would you say to a ride in that, then?'

Surprisingly, Benje looked slightly doubtful.

The other soldier, a button-nosed corporal who reminded Benedikt slightly of Gunner Kelly, grinned at the boys. 'And you can drive it, too – what about that?'

Benje thought for a moment. 'We haven't got driving licences,' he demurred.

'Don't need 'em for where we're going, my lad,' said the sergeant. 'No coppers or traffic wardens to worry about, you take my word for it.' He looked at Audley. 'About an hour, sir – would that be right?'

'Come on, Ben!' Darren encouraged his friend. 'What's the matter with you?'

'Nothing to it, lad,' the sergeant supported Darren. 'Remember those pictures on the telly of the Scorpions coming ashore at San Carlos Bay?'

'Off you go, then!' Audley gestured to push the boys towards the door. 'I can look after Herr Wiesehöfer for an hour, don't worry.'

'*Ben –* ' Darren caught his friend's arm ' *– come on!*'

'All right!' Benje shrugged off the hand, but looked at

171

Audley. 'And you'll be here with . . . with Mr – Mr Veezehoffer?'

'I won't step out of this place. I'll just show him the tanks,' promised Audley. 'Don't worry about us, we'll be okay, young Benjamin.'

Benedikt watched them depart – Darren eagerly, Benje with the backward look of a prisoner going to the firing squad.

'Hmm . . .' murmured Audley. 'A clever little boy.'

Benedikt turned to him. 'But frightened? No . . . ?'

'No.' Audley met his gaze. 'Our young Benjamin has led a sheltered childhood – he hasn't learnt to be frightened yet. He's just too clever for comfort, that's all. God help Oxbridge when it gets him . . . Perhaps we should put his name on the list, though – to get him inside our tent.' He shook his head slowly.

Benedikt stared at the Englishman.

Audley sighed. 'He knew I was getting rid of him – the chance to drive a Scorpion . . . and he still knew it!' He shook his head again.

'Get . . . get rid of him?'

'Oh, yes. Kelly's got Benjamin sewed up tight – and I haven't had time to unsew him.' Audley nodded. 'Young Benjamin is Mr Gunner Kelly's spy-in-the-sky on this trip – make no mistake about that. I got away last night because I'd given them you and your contact lenses on a plate, and they had to trust me . . . And then I gave them Captain Benedikt Schneider for good measure, to justify that trust . . . But Kelly still doesn't like anything that happens where he can't see it – or overhear it . . . I told you – in Duntisbury Chase I'm still one of the *foederati* from outside, not one of the native Britons: when it comes to the crunch, they're not sure whose side I'm on.'

Benedikt struggled with this interpretation of reality, even though it coincided with his own. 'And that child . . . ?'

'That child is old enough to believe in a cause, if he

172

trusts whoever is feeding him the bull-shit.' Audley's jaw set hard. 'In a year or two he'll think for himself, and no one will make his mind up for him. But at the moment he can still remember the Old General, and he's got adolescent yearnings for the way Becky's shirt bulges, which he doesn't understand . . . And he believes Mr Gunner Kelly is an extension of those bulges, on the side of Good and Right. And if I tried to tamper with that I'd get my fingers burnt.'

Gunner Kelly. *Mr* Gunner Kelly . . . It always came down to *him*! But they were *here* now – and they had got rid of 'young Benjamin', however unsatisfactorily –

'What are we doing here, David?' The organization of 'Major Kennedy' and those Armoured Corps NCOs to get rid of the little spy could only have been encompassed during Audley's brief period of freedom, which meant that it had been planned in advance for a reason. And there could only be one reason worth such a risk. 'Kelly?'

'Kelly.' Audley pointed to the hall of the tanks. 'I had one opportunity, three days ago, to get a question out . . . Now we'll see whether I've got an answer to it. Shall we go and find out?'

Benedikt strolled into the hall alongside him. On one side there was a line of Panzers which could obviously hold their own on any modern battlefield, so far as any armoured vehicle could in the present state-of-play on the North German killing ground . . . while on the other – the museum was ranged anti-clockwise, he could see that at a glance – while on the other there were these crude rhomboid-shapes – God! But they must have been brave to have faced such things, crawling out of the smoke, crushing barbed-wire and men in their remorseless advance – the ultimate horror of machine against flesh-and-blood on the ground, before rockets and computers had abstracted the collision of the two to petty imagination –

'No time for a proper tour . . . Another day, maybe . . .' Audley's voice was casual. 'It's a good cautionary

173

tale, really – the story of the tank, right from the beginning . . . Ploughshares into swords, to start with, you might say.'

Benedikt looked at him. 'Ploughshares?'

'Oh, yes . . .' The big man gestured vaguely to his left, towards the anti-clockwise beginnings of the fully-fledged leviathans lined up on his right. 'The caterpillar track began its life as a bit of agricultural machinery, anyway – "to boldly plough where no horse had ploughed before" that sort of thing.' His voice was still casual, but there was something in his face which hinted to Benedikt that the Statute of Limitations on bad memories hadn't altogether run out, whatever had been said to the contrary. 'But it put paid to the cavalry charger much more comprehensively than to the farm-horse and the plough-ox – there are plenty of quadrupeds still at work in the fields in third-world countries well-equipped with tanks. Like I said, a cautionary tale – a matter of human priorities . . . Or, "How many armoured divisions has the Pope got?", as Stalin said – was it Stalin?' He twisted a lop-sided smile, unsmiling, at Benedikt. 'But our priority is over there – ' he pointed ' – past the DD-Sherman with its skirts right up, over by the Tunisian Tiger. Okay?'

Benedikt nodded, and followed the Englishman dumbly into the labyrinth. One thing was certain, he thought: if there ever was another day for him here, it would not be David Audley who presided over it. For some reason – perhaps to get rid of those juvenile spies without argument – it suited the man to set up a rendezvous here. But the place was still too painful for any casual visit.

But now Audley was moving purposefully ahead of him down the aisle, ignoring his surroundings. Only when he was half-way down the hangar, level with a cross-aisle, did he pause for Benedikt to catch up.

'We are meeting someone?' The question sounded foolish, but he qualified it by looking about him at the

174

other visitors thronging the museum. So far as he could observe they consisted mostly of family groups, with the fathers showing off their knowledge to their sons and the bored mothers more concerned with the whereabouts of stragglers.

'Trust me.' Audley answered without answering, moving down the side-aisle. 'That's my old tank, the Cromwell. Would have been good in the desert in '42 . . . bloody death-trap in the Normandy bocage in '44 – not too safe against your old Mark IVs, and suicide against those big sods over there . . . unless you could find one all by itself and get in a shot from the rear . . . which I certainly never did.'

Audley was nodding down another aisle, directly ahead of him, at a sinister desert-yellow Tiger facing them.

'Head-on – that's not the way to say "hullo" to a Tiger.' Audley shivered. 'One of your chaps – a bright lad named Wittmann – bagged a whole squadron of London Yeomanry outside Villers Bocage with just this one Tiger of his, so we were told. And apparently he'd already got over a hundred Russian tanks on his score-card – he must have been the Richthofen of his team.' He eyed the Tiger silently for a moment. 'They used to start up with a sort of cough . . . quite distinctive. Once heard, never forgotten, but not wanted to be heard again – '

'Hullo there, David.' The voice which cut off Audley's reverie came from behind them. 'Telling how David slew Goliath?'

Benedikt turned towards the voice.

'Why – hullo, friendly cousin!' Audley greeted the newcomer with cheerful innocence. 'Good to see you.'

'A pleasure shared, as always.' Smooth black hair, thin moustache . . . swarthy, almost Mexican complexion . . . and the dark eyes were fixed on Benedikt, appraising him frankly. 'You have a friend, I see.' The voice, by contrast, was mid-Atlantic rather than trans-Atlantic, educated American.

'A friend *and* colleague,' Audley corrected him smoothly. '*Allied* colleague.'

'Is that so?' The American continued to scrutinize Benedikt. 'But additional to our deal, maybe?'

Audley gave a tiny shrug. 'Additionally necessary, say. But I have thrown in a little more to balance him. I don't think you'll be disappointed.'

'Hell – I'm sure I won't, at that!' The American flashed white teeth at the Englishman. 'It's just that my . . . acquaintance back there may not find your allied friend and colleague so easy to take on board, that's all – no offence, allied friend and colleague.' He gave Benedikt a share of the teeth. 'Just . . . I get this feeling he already wishes he didn't owe me so many favours.'

'He's nervous, you mean?' Audley contrived to mix innocence and satisfaction in the question. 'But not on account of me, surely?'

The American considered Audley coolly. 'On account of you . . . maybe a little. He doesn't know you as well as I do, I guess.' He paused. 'On account of what he's gotten for you . . . about which, because of our agreement, I have not as yet inquired, you understand . . . on account of that, I think he now knows something he'd rather not know.'

'Ah!' Audley's satisfaction increased. 'That's good.'

'Good isn't his word for it. In fact, it took all my powers of persuasion to get him down here today. It seems he's conceived a sudden urge to visit his second cousin in Boston – an overwhelming urge to be somewhere else for the time being – to get away from it all . . . You know the feeling?'

'I know the feeling.' Audley smiled. 'So you'll just have to use your charm – or whatever – again, won't you?'

Another cool look. 'Seems that way.'

'Which would bring benefits all round, remember.'

'All round?'

'To you and me all round. It's all waiting for you at the

176

usual place, what you want – plus the bonus on behalf of my colleague here. All pure and unadulterated.'

The American came to his decision. 'Okay, David. You can have him. Half an hour, no more – and don't frighten him if you can help it, he's not a bad guy. Just give me a minute to convince him.'

'Agreed. I'll be sweetness and light itself.'

'And I get this too . . . whatever it is . . . in due course?'

'If it concerns you – yes.'

'Fair enough.' The American acknowledged Benedikt. 'Watch yourself with this English gentleman, friendly ally. *Auf Wiedersehen.*' He nodded finally at Audley. 'See you, David.'

Benedikt watched the man disappear among the tanks, then he looked at Audley.

'CIA?' It felt like the first thing he had said in hours.

'At its best.'

Benedikt digested that. Praise from Audley was worth remembering. 'He knew me.'

'Of course – he would. It's his business to know you. He just met you face to face a week or two before he expected to, that's all.' Audley grinned. 'Sorry about all that horse-trading. You inhibited us both, rather.'

Horse-trading was how Audley operated, Benedikt remembered. 'You have a special relationship?'

'Of a sort . . . when it's in our respective national interests. Otherwise we have this old-fashioned gentleman's agreement about declarations of war preceding hostilities. Short of that we play dead straight with each other, which makes for much greater efficiency as well as simplicity. And we trade on that basis.'

'You gave him something – ?

'That's right.' Audley caught the expression on his face. 'Nothing out of our files – nothing like that . . . Something of *mine* . . . I have these private Israeli contacts, and they want the Americans to know something. But they don't

177

want it to come from them directly, for the record. Only . . . not everything they've given him is strictly kosher, so I've given him good value on my own account.'

Benedikt glanced round, but couldn't see anyone answering to his imagination. 'Value for what?' The front runner in the race was obvious. 'Gunner Kelly?'

'Gunner Kelly.' Audley double-checked on his own account. 'I've given you some of it, and you must have put more of it together by now . . .'

'The bomb was for Kelly.' He studied a middle-aged man who was loitering near the panel bearing the Tiger's biography. But then the man's family joined him. 'He knows who was responsible, and he had some way of communicating with him, to get him to try again. Only this time he'll be ready for him.' Now there was another possibility: a good-looking young man in a beautifully-cut lightweight suit had joined the family group, but was not part of it.

'Correct.' Audley pointed suddenly towards the Tiger's turret. 'See that gouge on the trunnion there? That was made by an anti-tank shot . . . six-pounder AP, most likely . . .' He waited until the young man had sauntered past them, to disappear beyond a neighbouring Mark V Panther in the direction of the armoured car hall. 'Go on.'

Benedikt stared at him. 'Is it really vengeance that he wants? What does he really want?'

'Yes . . .' Audley met his gaze for a moment, then let his glance wander again. 'That is the heart of the matter: what is he really up to?'

There was still no likely prospect in sight, only one harassed mother being dragged by one small boy while trying vainly to keep two others in view simultaneously.

'What did he tell the people in the Chase?' Benedikt fended off one of the small boys who was about to collide with him. 'Miss Becky? And Blackie Nabb . . . and Old Cecil?'

'And others. Wally Grant and Ron Turnbull, the two

178

main tenant farmers. And Ken Tailor, who runs the shop. And Mike Kramer at the garage up on the road and Dave and Rachel in the *Bells*.' Audley nodded. 'He started with them . . . the ones with the influence.'

'What did he say?'

Audley thought for a time without replying. 'Yes . . . I've told you how they all felt about the Old General – the Squire . . . *their* Squire.' He looked at Benedikt candidly. 'I've never come across anything quite like it before. I've heard about it – I've *read* about it . . . but I didn't think it still existed.' He half-smiled. 'It's like stumbling on a secret valley and finding an extinct animal grazing peacefully there . . . Or a mythical beast, even – a unicorn, maybe?'

'But this unicorn has a sharp horn.'

'Oh yes! And sharp hoofs to kick with, and teeth to bite with. Unicorns were only gentle with virgins.' The half-smile faded. 'He told them at least some of the truth, it seems – perhaps he told them all of it that could be told. That's what he says, anyway.'

Benedikt waited. There were two youths in jeans passing by, with two little painted girls, oblivious to everything but each other.

'He said it was all his fault – that the bomb was for him. He admitted that straight off. His fault. But not *deliberately* his fault – not expected . . . and not deserved, either – '

'Not *deserved*?' Benedikt frowned.

Audley held up a finger. 'I'll come back to that. What he said was that there'd been someone hunting him for a long time, trying to get the crossed wires on him – that he'd been running for a long time before he'd come to Duntisbury Chase. And even then he hadn't come for the job the Squire had advertised – *"Man Friday wanted, ex-gunner preferred"* – he'd simply remembered his officer from long ago, when killing was in fashion, and he'd only come for advice. *"In a tight corner, the Squire always knew what to do"*, was what he remembered.'

So what followed had been inevitable, thought Benedikt. At least, inevitable, the Old General being the man he had been. 'So he got the job instead?'

'Not instead – because, more likely. The Chase was off the beaten track . . . no one comes to Duntisbury Royal, it isn't on the way to anywhere. And what the job entailed didn't involve going anywhere, either . . . So four years, he's been here . . . and the first three of them he didn't step further than Kramer's garage, to take the Old General's car for its occasional service. It was only the last few months he'd driven the old boy to Salisbury and Bournemouth, to his tailor and his wine merchant, and such like . . . Between them, they reckoned the trail must have gone cold . . . Or, it wouldn't likely be very hot in Salisbury or Bournemouth.'

Benedikt thought of the cathedral and its quiet close, with its old houses and cool green grass; and Bournemouth was the seaside town to which the elderly English gentlefolk retired on their pensions and their dividends. Bombs and snipers belonged in neither of them.

'"Sanctuary" – that was Kelly's word for it: "He gave me sanctuary", he told them – Becky and the rest. "And now I've killed him for it, as sure as if I'd set that bomb meself.'

They should have known better, the Old General and Gunner Kelly between them, thought Benedikt – that there was no place safe from sudden death if defenders were not vigilant – not the bishop's Salisbury, not the pensioners' Bournemouth . . . and not peaceful Duntisbury Royal either – there was the Fighting Man to remind him of that.

No safe place . . . He looked round again, and saw that for the first time they were quite alone beside the Tiger. It must be getting near to the museum's lunchtime closure.

'So now the Squire was dead, and he was still a target. Which meant it was time for him to start running again.'

'Why was he a target?'

'All in good time, my dear chap. I'm telling it to you

how he told it to them. He could run again – nothing easier. He had his pension from the army, he could have that sent anywhere. And he had his savings, and four years' wages that he'd hardly touched – he could run a long way on that, and maybe even far enough this time.'

Still no one. The American must be having difficulty persuading his contact that Audley could be trusted.

'But this time was different. He wasn't going to run this time. There was a score to settle this time.' Audley paused.

'He'd been lying low in the Chase, working that out. Those that were after him would reckon he'd run already, but when he was ready he had a way of letting them know where he was. And then when they came he was going to repay them in their own coin. He owed that for the Squire. What happened afterwards was no matter. But, also because of the Squire, he owed them in the Chase the telling of what he was going to do. That was all.'

All? thought Benedikt, lining up what he had observed of the people of the Chase as well as what he had been told about them, and then adding Gunner Kelly to it. Because then, *all* was what it wasn't: it wasn't an end, it could only be – and had been – merely a beginning.

So he could jump the next question, having the answer to it, and go on to the more interesting one that followed it.

'He knew they'd insist on helping him?' As he spoke he saw that Audley had been watching him. 'He calculated it?'

The big Englishman relaxed slightly. 'Right. No proof . . . but . . . *right*!'

'Do they know?' He thought of Blackie Nabb handling the police at the ford. 'They are not stupid, all of them.'

'You're dead right they're not stupid, all of them!' Audley spoke feelingly. 'But Kelly is a remarkable man, you know.'

'A man of many voices?' He remembered the previous night's events.

Audley smiled. 'You've encountered that, have you?'

'The question is . . . how many of his tongues are forked

. . . ?' He did not find it easy to smile back. The rôles Gunner Kelly was playing ranged too widely for that: he could be the ultimately loyal soldier, devoted to the avenging of his liegelord's murder at the risk of his own life, and therefore not too scrupulous about manipulating others who owed the same service. But he could also be a clever man planning to end a long pursuit by using others to destroy his pursuers.

'I agree.' Audley nodded. 'The trouble is . . . he is a great performer – but is he really that good? Because they aren't stupid – you're right . . . but at the same time they're not professionals.' He turned the nod into a slow shake. 'In his place . . . he's taking one hell of a risk . . . *in his place I'd run, you know.*'

But run from what? thought Benedikt: that was still the final question. 'Who wants him dead?'

'Yes. That's where we have a problem, I'm afraid.' Audley rubbed his chin as though in doubt. 'A real problem . . .'

'He is an Irishman.' That ought to simplify matters, and was surely not to be ignored when it came to killing. With an Englishman, or a German, the possibilities were too numerous to make mere nationality significant; with an Italian, even though the Red Brigades were as good as beaten, there was now the Bulgarian connection as well as the Mafia and the terrorists of the far right. But with Irishmen, as with Basques and Corsicans and Palestinians, there was a single starting point nine times out of ten, no matter how it splintered afterwards.

'But only of a sort.' Audley studied him. 'If I may say so without offence, you continental Europeans don't understand the Irish at all, you know.'

'And you British do?' Even at the risk of offence, he couldn't let that pass. 'Forgive me for not being able to see the evidence for that.'

Audley smiled. 'Oh . . . culturally, perhaps you have some inkling of them. I'm not decrying what the cultivated

182

German tourist observes, even though he probably relishes romantic notions of the pre-urban society . . . just as you are inclined to see Britain in somewhat idyllic Dickensian terms – '

'Now you are patronizing me, Dr Audley – '

'Then I'm sorry! But I don't mean to, I assure you. Would it help if I admitted that the British have no worthwhile insights at all about foreigners? You at least see *something* – we see nothing at all . . . It's the curse of insularity . . . No matter how many millions of us go abroad, we're still the most cretinously ignorant nation in Europe – I admit it.' He smiled again, disarmingly. 'And I admit quoting your Nobel prize-winner Böll – Heinrich Böll – at you. But at least I didn't suggest he lived in Ireland for tax reasons – you must admit that, Benedikt.'

How Father would love to cross swords with this man! thought Benedikt. At least it would be a fairer and more rewarding match than Audley's Cromwell against Father's deadly 8.8s.

'No . . . what I meant was that it's *Gunner* Kelly we're up against – not *Michael* Kelly.' Audley shook his head. 'He was a Royal Artilleryman longer than he was an Irishman in Ireland, you know. And on a time-span, he's twice as English as he is Irish.' Another shake. 'Apart from which, what he did tell Becky was . . . that his problem was nothing directly to do with "the ould country" . . . whatever that means, and if we can believe it – '

The words stopped suddenly, and the open expression on Audley's face closed in the same instant as he stared past Benedikt.

'My dear How – ' Audley bit off the rest of the name as though it had burnt his tongue. 'Hello, there, *cher cousin*!'

'David.' The mid-Atlantic voice came from behind Benedikt, almost lazily, encouraging him to turn towards it without any indication of surprise.

It was the good-looking young man in the well-cut suit who stood at the CIA man's shoulder. Only, close-up the suit was even better-cut, as only the finest English tailor could mould a suit, and the man inside it wasn't quite so young, with crow's feet corrugating the corners of the eyes which were as dark brown and as wary as had ever focussed on him.

'Dr Audley.' The eyes flicked to the Englishman, and then came back to Benedikt. 'Captain Schneider.'

God in heaven, thought Benedikt. *Another Irishman!*

8

Audley studied the Irishman for a long moment. 'You have the advantage of us . . . Mr – ?'

'Smith.' The Irishness of the voice was there, but it was unobtrusive, only just across the median line between the two countries. 'But I doubt that, Dr Audley. For I have heard tell of you.'

'Indeed?' Audley's eyes moved to the American.

'I have asked my friend to stay,' said the Irishman. 'For the record.'

Audley came back to him. 'But there is no record.'

'There's always a record.' Under its softness the voice was hard. 'But . . . shall we say . . . you have a friend with you, who wasn't in the small print. So now I have a friend, too.' The man's expression concealed the same contradiction as his voice, decided Benedikt: beneath its superficial amiability there lay distrust as well as apprehension.

The American's shoulder lifted slightly in apology: those, plainly, were the Irishman's terms, and they could take it or leave it.

'I see.' Just as plainly, the terms were not to Audley's liking, even though he could hardly refuse them.

'Do you, Dr Audley?' One corner of the Irishman's mouth lifted. 'You know . . . they say you have no liking for my country – and its inhabitants. And is that the truth, would you say?'

Benedikt was torn by the need to watch the Irishman while checking on Audley's reaction to such baiting.

'"They say"?' Suddenly Audley's voice was as soft as the Irishman's. 'I would say . . . that if you paid a ha'penny for that information you were shamefully overcharged, Mr Smith.'

'Is that so?' The man seemed perversely pleased by the denial. 'And yet, is it not a fact that you'll take no job across the water?' He cocked his head knowingly at the Englishman. 'That when they put you down for Dublin once, it was a letter of resignation that they got back? What would you say to that, now?'

Audley looked at his watch. 'I would say that I am at last beginning to get an inkling of why they beatified Pope Innocent XI in 1956, Mr Smith. And I'm grateful to you for that, because it's rather been preying on my mind.'

'What?' Mr Smith frowned.

'It simply has to be because he rang the bells of Rome to celebrate Protestant King Billy's victory over Catholic King James – 1688 and all that.' Audley turned towards Benedikt. 'Do you spend a lot of time discussing the relative merits and demerits of North Germans and South Germans, Captain Schneider? Let's see now . . . the North Germans are like the Southern English, aren't they? Rather more anonymous than the . . . it would be the Bavarians, wouldn't it be? And the Bavarians are the Yorkshiremen of Germany? Or the Lancashiremen? And then there are the Prussians – I presume they rather frighten you, the way the Scots frighten the English . . . But the Ulstermen, who are really only transplanted Scots, frighten us even more – damn good assault troops, I'm told, but dirty in the trenches . . . And then there are the Welsh – far too clever . . . not intelligent, mind you – it's the Scots who are intelligent – but *clever*. Good rugger players, though. And I always think a man can't be all bad, who plays rugby, so there must be some good in the Argentinians . . . And the Rumanians – and the Fijians . . . It's not the colour of a man's skin – it's whether he plays rugger, that's what counts, in my view. Black, white or khaki. Jehovah's Witnesses, Freemasons, Frenchmen – you can always tell – tell at a glance.' He turned back suddenly. 'Now, I don't care whether you like the English

186

or you remember Drogheda and Wexford every time you see one, and spit. You can have any prejudice you like – and if you want to believe that I think the moon is made of green cheese, you're welcome. All I want to know is who wants Michael Kelly dead, and why. Nothing more, and nothing less.'

The Irishman had a curious expression on his face now, which seemed to Benedikt to be compounded of conflicting emotions, and was altogether incomprehensible to him. But his mouth stayed closed and the silence between them lengthened.

The American stirred. 'You could try giving him your word, David. That you'll play straight.'

'Word of an Englishman?'

'Just *your* word. No generalizations – you've made your point there, I guess.' The American drew a slow breath. 'Hell, man – he may have something which you can play your "Great Game" with. But it's *his* skin that could end up nailed to the wall.'

Audley looked down his nose at the American. 'I said there was no record. He said there was, not I.'

'So he doesn't know you. Him and two billion others.'

Audley thought for a moment. 'Very well . . . For what it's worth, Mr Smith . . . I haven't met you today. I have no memory of you. Your name – your *face* – will never be identified by me. You do not exist . . . You have my word on that.' He looked to Benedikt. 'Captain Schneider?'

Benedikt stiffened. 'My word is as Dr Audley's.'

The American looked at Mr Smith. 'If the Captain's word is good enough for David, it's good enough for me, Jim.' Then he smiled. 'So who the hell is Michael Kelly, then?'

The Irishman looked at all of them in turn. 'Who is Michael Kelly? And you with your great machines that can count the nine billion names of God Himself? He's nobody, that's who he is . . . He's John Doe, and William Rowe . . . and William Smith and Wilhelm Schmidt, who never did any harm to anyone – that was all his own harm, and not the harm others gave him to do.' The Irishman spread his glance between them. 'He was a British soldier, for his sins – his father's sins – ' the glance fixed momentarily on Benedikt ' – and probably killed a few Germans in his time, that he never set eyes on at all.'

'We know that.'

'You do? And he was a Bradford taxi-driver after that – you'll know that, too? And no one looked twice at him, because no one ever looks twice at a taxi-driver, providing he's there on time and doesn't over-charge – eh?'

'We know that, too.'

'So you do . . . Michael Kelly – John Doe, William Rowe, William Smith, Wilhelm Smith, Wilhelm Kelly, William Kelly, Aloysius Kelly – '

'*Aloysius Kelly*?'

'A common name. *Two* common names – *Aloysius* and *Kelly* . . . Though maybe *Aloysius* is not so common hereabouts. But – '

'Aloysius Kelly.' Audley repeated the name quickly, as though he'd only just heard it the second before. 'But he's dead – ' He looked at the American.

'Dead – so he is!' agreed the Irishman. 'Dead and gone these six years – seven years?'

'Four years,' the American corrected him.

'Four years, is it?' The Irishman accepted the correction. 'But you're right – it was seven years they were after him, but it's only four years since they caught up with him – you have the right of it as always, Howard. But dead and gone – four years, or seven years, or seventy years, it's all the same: dead and gone with all that was locked up in his head. And there are those that sleep a lot sounder for that, by God!'

Benedikt looked at Audley. 'Aloysius . . . Kelly?'

'Yes.' Audley didn't return the look. 'What is Michael Kelly's connection with him?'

'Ah . . . now that machine of yours is good, but not

good enough – eh?' The black-brown eyes dismissed the Kommissar as well as the British computer's memory-bank. 'The best connection of all, he had – the one that's thicker than water, through the sister-son, which is one that counted strong from the old days.'

'Hell!' The swarthy American shared his surprise with Audley. 'He had no next-of-kin, damn it – '

'There now!' Pure satisfaction peeled off the veneer of the Englishness in the man's voice. 'You have to go back . . . and you have to have the connections to get the sense of it, which your man prying wouldn't take from it in a month of Sundays! For there was an age-gap you wouldn't credit, between the one of them marrying young, and the other marrying late – and the scandal of the first one, that had to marry, that they always like to forget so they had the chance to . . . And it was a Kelly marrying a Kelly, that was no relation at all – and a difference of opinion between the families as well . . .'

Benedikt gave up trying to disentangle that convoluted relationship. Michael Kelly's father had served with the British Army, and that might have made for enmity. But he wasn't sure which generation the man was talking about.

'What has Michael Kelly got to do with Aloysius Kelly?' The edge of anger in Audley's voice indicated that he had the same problem, and was cutting through it.

'They grew up together – I'm trying to tell you, Dr Audley. The same church and the same school, and houses in adjoining streets. And they kissed the same girls down by the river, and put their hands where they shouldn't under the same skirts . . . Or, perhaps Michael didn't, because he was the good one, that did as he was told – and enlisted in the British Army, like his father before him . . . Not like Aloysius – he was the clever one – and the *bad* one, to your way of thinking, Dr Audley.'

'The bad one?' Benedikt was tired of the nuances of their fools' quarrels, which evidently encompassed Ireland's own enmities as well as those he more or less understood.

'*His* father was a Republican. They say he was one of those that lay in wait for Michael Collins.' The Irishman's mouth twitched. 'Michael's was a Free Stater. And he wasn't ashamed of wearing his medal ribbons – the DCM among them – the old man wasn't. Out of their frame beside the fireplace, for all to see.'

Mit Eliot zu Ruhm und Sieg, thought Benedikt: like the Elector of Hanover, the King of England had scattered his battle honours far and wide in the days of the empire.

'But . . . the two families – it was like there was an armed truce between them, the generation of the Troubles, and the Partition, and the Civil War, because there was blood between them as well as common to them . . . But the boys would have none of that – they were like brothers in the mischief they got up to between them . . . There's this auntie, blind as a bat and sharp as the razor the barber shaves himself with – she remembers them both . . . until Aloysius went off to the seminary and Michael went to fight for the English – which was maybe just a little better than being a butcher's boy, which was all the work he could get when they wouldn't have him at the garage . . . It was always cars he was into, the auntie said: it was a driver he wanted to be for the English, but his father said it was a gunner he must be, because it was only the presence of the guns on the battlefield that turned mere fisticuffs into proper warfare – ' The Irishman looked around him quizzically ' – which is all these things are, I suppose, if you think about it – just bloody great guns on wheels, with an engine bolted to them . . . *Anyway,* that's when the two boys split up – ' He slapped his hand on the Tiger ' – and went their own ways – and very different ways, by God!'

It was time, decided Benedikt, to cut his own losses ruthlessly: both the Englishman and the American clearly knew what the Irishman was talking about, but he did not.

'Who is Aloysius Kelly?' He could have asked the question of any of them, but Audley was the most likely to give a straight answer. 'David?'

'Hah!' It was the Irishman who reacted first. 'Now that's a question that's been asked a time or two!'

Benedikt waited. The big Englishman wasn't looking at him, he was staring past him, past the Tiger, at nothing, as though he hadn't heard. 'David?'

Finally Audley drew a breath. 'Who *was* Aloysius Kelly . . .'

'Of course.' They had all said as much: the Englishman and the American had argued over the length of time since that event, and the Irishman had agreed that *it was four years since they caught up with him.* 'Who was he?'

Audley looked at him. Then he looked at the American. 'It was in Spain he was first spotted, wasn't it?' He frowned. 'With General O'Duffy's Blue Shirts on Franco's side?'

'That's probably just a story. He would have been absurdly young to have been with them on the Jarama.' The American frowned back at him. 'Too young.'

'They say he lied about his age.' The Irishman turned to Benedikt. 'They say he first went into action alongside your General von Thoma's tanks – they say the General wanted O'Duffy's men with him because he reckoned they wouldn't run away.'

'But I don't go for it.' The American shook his head. 'I don't reckon he was there so early.'

'But he did go straight from the seminary,' countered the Irishman. 'And he lied about his age, they say.'

'Maybe. But if he was there he changed sides damn quick, that's for sure.'

'Ah . . . well, isn't that the Irish for you!' Mr Smith smiled. 'Going over from the winners to the losers.'

'*If* he went over – '

'And nothing out of character.' The Irishman stuck to his guns. 'He went there as a True Believer, straight from

191

the seminary. And he went across like St Paul on the road to Damascus, when he found another faith he liked better, having seen both sides – '

'No!' The American shook his head again. ''38 – late '38 – is the first year I'll buy. With Frank Ryan in the International Brigade – and the Abraham Lincoln Battalion, not the British one, because it was long after the Cordoba trouble.'

'Ah . . . Frank Ryan! Now he was a lovely man in his way, you know.' The Irishman half-closed his eyes. 'A great gentleman, they say . . .'

'And IRA since 1918.' The American looked at Audley.

'And in contact with the Nazis, along with Sean Russell, in '41 – they had a radio link going,' said Audley.

'Which was a great waste of time for them both, to be sure,' murmured the Irishman.

'But not for lack of trying,' said Audley.

'That's not what I mean, Dr Audley,' replied the Irishman mildly. 'What I mean is that Aloysius Kelly was there beside him – and wasn't he feeding it all back to Moscow, on his account, eh?'

Audley sniffed abruptly, and turned to Benedikt. 'Yes. So there you have it in a nutshell, Captain Schneider. Aloysius Kelly went to Spain and teamed up with Ryan, who was a long-time IRA man – '

'Who'd fought alongside his father, in the Troubles and the Civil War,' supplemented Mr Smith.

'But before that he'd been talent-scouted by one of their Political Commissars,' said the American laconically. 'He was ordered to attach himself to Frank Ryan, who was an Irishman first and last – whoever was England's enemy was his friend, it didn't matter who – '

'Which made him politically unreliable – Frank, I mean – '

'Jim! For God's sake!'

'I was only explaining – '

192

Audley cut them both off with a gesture. 'What they both mean, Benedikt, is that the IRA originated as the military wing of a nationalist movement – a nationalist sectarian movement. The fashionable idea now is that all twentieth-century guerrilla organizations tick because Marx and Lenin wound them up – that it's all Marxist-Leninist magic that makes them work. But the truth is that most of them owe damn all to Marx, and even less to Lenin – the halfways successful ones, anyway . . . from Pancho Villa to Fidel Castro, by way of the Jews and the Algerians and the Cypriots . . . and even the Chinese and Vietnamese too. You could say they owe a lot more to any classical guerrilla leader in history – to Francis Marion, say – ' he pointed at the American ' – his "Swamp Fox" in the Carolinas, fighting Cornwallis and Tarleton in the American War of Independence – Marx and Lenin didn't teach *him* anything . . . And the IRA has always derived a hundred times more from the United States than from Soviet Russia and Colonel Gaddafi . . . But to do that, it was the end of British colonialism – not the beginning of the socialist revolution – that they campaigned for. The shift to the left in the IRA didn't start until the '60s.'

'Aha!' Mr Smith gave Audley a shrewd look. 'And you not an expert on Ireland, eh?' Then he nodded. 'Ah – but it was you who said what I had was not worth a ha'penny, wasn't it! So I can't say you didn't tell me.'

'I'm not an expert on Ireland, damn it!' snapped Audley irritably. 'We're not talking about Ireland – we're talking about Aloysius Kelly.'

'And the Debreczen meetings.' Almost imperceptibly the American had shifted his position from alongside the Irishman, until now he was nearly facing him. And there was a note in his voice which matched his change of position: the mention of 'Aloysius Kelly' had ranged him alongside Audley as an ally, he was no longer a neutral 'friend'.

'Oh no! *Debreczen* is something else – ' Mr Smith held

up his hand, fingers widely spread, as though to ward both men off ' – there's nothing at all I know about that! It's none of my business . . . what it was, or when it was. And I'm not having any part of it, either.' He looked around him, and Benedikt couldn't help following his action. But now there was no one at all in sight: the great hall of tanks was inhabited only by fighting machines.

'Fair enough.' Audley's flash of irritability was gone. 'No one could blame you for that. So . . . we'll just forget Debreczen – it's something else that never existed. Right? And Aloysius Kelly too!'

Debreczen?

The Debreczen *meetings*? Benedikt frowned as the *meetings* fixed Debreczen for him. But what would an Irish veteran of the Spanish Civil War be doing in a nowhere-town in eastern Hungary, which – so far as he could recall – lay somewhere just on the better side of the Carpathians, almost equidistant from the borders of Slovakia and Rumania and the Ukraine?

The Irishman looked at Audley wordlessly, and Benedikt could see that Audley friendly frightened him more than Audley hostile. But then, perhaps that was what Audley intended.

'It's Michael Kelly – our very own Gunner Kelly – who interests us, Mr Smith, you see?' Audley smiled, first at the Irishman, and then transferred the smile to Benedikt for confirmation. 'Correct, Captain?'

Benedikt nodded. 'That is correct.' If anything, he thought, a smiling Audley was *more* disturbing.

'And we left him taking the King's shilling . . . forty years ago? No – forty-five, it must be . . .' Audley carried the nod back to Mr Smith. 'Which is a long time ago, when you think about it.'

A long time, indeed! Benedikt tried, and failed, to conjure up pictures of the Ireland of their time – the two Irish youths, one a butcher's boy, the other a young seminarian . . . one to become a British soldier, the other to travel a very different road, serving under a newer flag and exchanging the true God for a false one. But both of them had grown old since then, over those long years . . . and yet now one was mysteriously dead, and the other plotted murderous vengeance, when they both ought to have been drowsing in front of the television sets by their firesides among grandchildren.

'So when did they meet again, Michael and Aloysius?' Audley prodded the Irishman gently. 'Because they did meet again, didn't they?'

As a guess, it was nothing extraordinary, really: it was the only computation of the possibilities which made any sense of what was happening now.

'They met.' The hand resting on the tank clenched.

'Four years ago?'

'Ten years ago.'

'So long as that?' Audley frowned, and fell silent for a moment. 'Well now . . . ten years . . . and not by chance?'

The Irishman didn't reply.

'Not by chance, let's assume. And it was Aloysius who sought out Michael – right?' Audley nodded, but more to himself than to Mr Smith, and then turned to the American. 'It was about ten years ago that they put the word out on him, wasn't it?'

The American stared into space for a couple of seconds. 'No. Not so long – more like seven . . . '75 – not earlier than that, David.'

'Humm . . . But then he could have seen the writing on the wall before they did. So he could have been setting up his bolt-holes in advance . . . That's what I'd have done in his place.'

'They' . . . ? Both because Audley was who he was and because Aloysius Kelly had been who he had been, *they* were not the IRA, estimated Benedikt coldly. The long hunt for him – which now seemed to have extended to a pursuit of Gunner Kelly – sounded much more like the KGB's Special Bureau No 1 on both accounts.

'So how did Aloysius trace Michael?' Audley came round to Mr Smith again, and beamed suddenly at him. 'Ah! He'd go about it just like you did, wouldn't he!' He nodded at Benedikt. 'There now – that's a lesson for both of us: the computer gives back only what it's already been given, and if it lacks that one special bit of knowledge . . .' He switched back quickly to the Irishman. 'And *that's* what's bothering *you* at the moment, isn't it?'

The man's source – of course! Because once Audley had that, the man himself was superfluous.

'The old auntie.' This time Audley didn't bother to smile, because he no longer needed to do so.

'No – '

'Yes. You slipped, and now you're kicking yourself for it – although it's easily done, and we all do it when we're scared . . . And I could be charitable, and assume that you don't want the old lady bothered by great gallumphing Britishers with Irish accents . . . Or I could be *un*charitable, and suspect that you're more worried about someone remembering that you'd been to see her just recently, and putting one and one together to make two – eh?'

The Irishman had composed his features, but the knuckles on his fist betrayed him to Benedikt. 'No. I was just thinking . . . word of an Irishman – that's all.'

'And quite properly.' Audley looked down his nose. 'She's your contact. But you don't exist, so she doesn't exist either.' He shrugged. 'Simple.'

'Your word on it?' Apart from the knuckles Mr Smith was steady now.

'No. You already have my word, I can't give it to you twice. Over here . . . a gentleman only has one word – would you have insulted Michael Collins or Frank Ryan like that?'

The Irishman rolled a glance at the American. 'Insufferable! And you wonder why we're as we are, by God!' Then he relaxed slowly, with a light in his eye not present before. 'And yet . . . you have no Irish blood in you by any far remote mischance, Dr Audley?'

'Not a drop. No Irish raiders ever reached Sussex – fortunately for them. Good Anglo-Saxon, Mr Smith, I'm afraid. King Alfred's men . . . the ones who beat the Danes in the end – remember?'

'But not the Romans. Or the Normans?'

'The Romans were before our time. The Normans were no more than a useful tincture, to tone us up. We assimilated them – as you have assimilated your English aristocracy, Mr Smith . . . We've done the same with anyone prepared to stay the course – French Huguenots and German Jews – and the Poles and GIs left quite a few souvenirs behind them more recently.'

'And now the Pakistanis and the West Indians?'

'Nothing wrong with them. They may not play rugger, but they play damn good cricket. In a hundred years' time they'll have improved us – ' Audley grinned at the CIA man ' – they'll be as English as Howard is American . . . It's you Irish who make a tragedy of your history – you have this boring obsession with re-living it, as though it mattered what Cromwell did in Drogheda and Wexford any more than what Vespasian did to Maiden Castle with his legion just down the road from here, outside Dorchester . . . It doesn't worry *me* that we were once a Roman colony – it lends a touch of class to what would otherwise be rather dim tribal history . . . and it makes the archaeology much more interesting.' He waved a hand. 'It's all a joke, so long as we don't have to live through it, and we can laugh at our ancestors slipping on the historical banana skins, don't you see?'

He was challenging the Irishman to disagree with him in a way that no Irishman could disagree, thought Benedikt.

'So what did Auntie tell Aloysius Kelly ten years ago?' Audley came on frontally, like any good tank commander who reckoned he could break through the centre now, with no more messing around on the flanks to draw the Irishman's reserves away.

'Aargh . . . it wasn't Aloysius she'd kept in touch with – it was Michael who was her boy . . . it was always him that she'd been close to – her man had been with Michael Collins, not one of the Republicans – a Free Stater, when it came to the Treaty – and he'd been alongside the English in the trenches too, before that, so it was Michael that was always closer to her. And it was Michael that kept in touch with her over the years.'

'But then Aloysius turned up – ?'

'Out of the blue. Asking after Michael.' The Irishman had lost his wary look. 'He said there was this debt he had, that had been on his conscience for more years than he cared to remember. But now he'd come into a bit of money – and he showed her a wad of notes to prove it . . . It was before the darkness had come on her, while she could still see what was close-up . . .'

'What did she make of him?'

'She didn't like the sound of it – of him . . . There were too many notes – and it was English money – and she'd not a lot of time for the English, but she'd no time at all for Aloysius – it was Michael who'd written to her over the years, with never a word from Aloysius until he came through her door as bold as brass, with his handful of money . . . No, she didn't like it at all. But just at that time Michael had been having some bad luck: a bit of bother with his insurance, he said, after he'd had this knock in his taxi . . . but she reckoned it was more likely it was a knock in the betting shop he'd taken, the way he fancied the horses as every good man should . . . So in the end, balancing that against the other, she let him have Michael's address. And that was the last she saw of him –' he stopped suddenly.

'Yes?' Audley was right: there was more.

'It was some time later . . . It was the next year her sight went, and she's a bit vague about time after that. A year or two, maybe . . . there were these two fellas came looking for Aloysius – had he been to see her? Did she know where he might be? "Old friends", they were, and for old times' sake, having lost touch with him, they wanted to meet up again.' Mr Smith paused. 'It was just her in the house, with her great-grand-niece for company – and these two fellas.'

An old blind woman, and a child, thought Benedikt. And . . . would that be two "old friends" from Special Bureau No 1, come to ask questions only the very brave or the very foolish refused to answer?

'They didn't have a chance, of course – not a chance!' The Irishman settled his glance finally on Benedikt himself, as though it was he who needed education most. '"Oh, yes", says she – and thinking it'd serve Aloysius right, whatever he was into, but now there was Michael to remember, which was the name and address they were after – "Oh yes", says she, "that fine boy Aloysius – him that put those two Black-an'-Tans in the gas works furnace at Tralee – a fine boy!" And that flummoxed them, because they were foreigners, and if they'd heard of "Black-an'-Tan" it was in the history books – or a drink across an English bar, more likely. "Oh no", says one of them. "This is Aloysius Kelly, our old friend – him that was Frank Ryan's friend in Spain, auntie." And she looks into the air between them and nods. "Frankie Ryan?" she says. "No – but he was a fine boy too! Yet he had no part in what was done at Tralee – it was Kilmichael he was at, when they took that Auxie patrol – an' it was Tralee, where the Tans burnt down the Town Hall afterwards, that Aloysius was – with young Seamus, that was killed by the Free Staters afterwards, and little Patrick Barry, who'd made his fortune in America an' wanted me to join him. Only it was Mr Kelly that I'd given my word to – that you see there on the mantelpiece, above the fireplace, in his silver frame." . . . And every time they asked her a question, she gave them an answer that was more than fifty years out-of-date, would you believe it!' Mr Smith shook his head admiringly. 'And when I was there, not a week ago, it was Cruise missiles she wanted to know about – it's her great-grand-niece, that's still not married, who has to read the paper to her every day – *The Irish Times,* is what she takes – and her an admirer of Margaret Thatcher, by God! Not a chance, they had: they went away thinking her senile – and she'd run twenty rings round them!'

Audley swayed forwards. 'So how did you get her to talk to you?'

'Aargh! She knew my mother – and my grandmother before her. And she knows where I stand.' The Irishman gave Audley an uncompromising look. 'And I told her that Aloysius was dead, and that Michael was on the run because of it . . . And not a postcard she's had from him, these four years. But I said I'd maybe pass on the word, if I could.' The look softened suddenly. 'Is that something I can do – with a clear conscience?'

Audley compressed his lips into a thin line. 'To be honest . . . I don't know.' He considered the Irishman. 'But I'll put it to him, and he can choose for himself. That's a promise I'll include with my word, if you like.'

The Irishman gave him back the same consideration. 'She would take that as a kindness, for she set great store by him. And . . . and I would take it kindly, too.'

Audley shook his head. 'Better not say that, Mr Smith. Better say a debt repaid, and the slate clean – since we have never met.'

The Irishman looked at Audley for another moment, and then turned to his American. 'I think it is time for my other appointment. And I'm thinking I would not like to miss it, now, more than ever.'

'Okay.' The CIA man looked at his watch, and then at Audley. 'David . . . ?' But there was something in the question that was looking for more than mere permission to withdraw.

'Hail and farewell, trusted ally.' Audley lifted a hand. 'I'll be seeing you . . . very soon . . . Is that soon enough?'

'Okay.' The American gave Benedikt a nod. 'And I guess I'll be seeing you too, Captain . . . Let's go, Jim.'

The Irishman started to move, and then paused suddenly, twisting back towards them in mid-step. 'Michael . . . Michael was the *easy* one, and that's the truth. But that was a long time ago, Dr Audley, and there's things that a long time teaches.' He closed his eyes for a second. 'And if he's been running . . . running changes a man. And . . . most of all . . . whatever Aloysius touched – *don't you be trusting it not to turn in your hand, Dr Audley.* That's all I'm saying.'

Benedikt watched the two men weave between the tanks, until Audley's voice recalled him.

'Well . . . coming from "Jim Smith", that was a gipsy's warning, and no mistake!' Audley spoke wonderingly.

'You knew him?'

'I think maybe I do . . . by reputation.' Audley half-shrugged. 'Not my field, though. But our loyal ally certainly did us proud, no doubt about that, by golly!'

Benedikt frowned. 'But he only gave you a connection between . . . Aloysius Kelly and Michael Kelly that was years ago – ten years?'

Audley gave him a sidelong look. 'He didn't bother telling me what we both knew. Waste of time, don't you know!'

That was far enough, decided Benedikt. 'No, I do not know. So you need to tell me, I think. And preferably without patronizing me.'

The Englishman's ugly face broke up quite surprisingly. 'My God! I'm sorry, Benedikt! I was, wasn't I! And quite without justification too. In fact . . . *in fact,* I wouldn't like you to put it down to damned insufferable British delusions of superiority – quite the opposite, rather . . . More like butterflies in the stomach making me nervous.' He grimaced.

'About Aloysius Kelly?'

'About Aloysius Kelly – right.'

'And . . . Debreczen?' It was hard to stay angry with him, even allowing for the certainty that he was also a clever man. 'Is it that important?'

'Aloysius Kelly and Debreczen!' Audley drew a breath. 'You feed either of them into your computer, and the little red lights will start flashing.' He looked at Benedikt. 'I don't know why . . . but I had this pricking of the thumbs that I was on to something here.' He looked around. 'Only . . . I'm not really intuitive – I like little sharp facts, like diamonds – or juicy soft ones, like currants and raisins in a suet pudding.' He came back to Benedikt again. 'And now I've got something I can't wear and I can't swallow, by Christ!'

Benedikt made a disturbing discovery: the disadvantage of playing second fiddle to David Audley was that the man's confidence and omniscience was irritating. But David Audley suddenly nervous was rather frightening.

Audley seemed to sense his disquiet. 'Not to worry, though. We've maybe got a bit of time . . . The point is that he knew I'd know where Aloysius was killed.' He gave Benedikt an evil grin. 'Car bomb in his garage. Spread him like strawberry jam.'

'Where?'

'Airedale. Little cottage on the far side of the valley from Keighley . . . lovely country. Just down the road from Bingley. Which is just down the road from Bradford, you see.'

'Where Michael Kelly drove his taxi?'

'Just so. And altogether too coincidental.' Audley sighed. 'At least, it is *now* – in retrospect . . . At the time, the bomb brought in the Special Branch, and they brought in our people . . . who in turn picked up enough evidence in the cottage to identify the strawberry jam as Aloysius Kelly. And what made him so very interesting was not simply that he'd been on our wanted list for years, but that more recently we'd had word that he was on *their* wanted list as well. In fact, it was a toss-up who wanted him more – them or us.'

'Them being the KGB?'

'Them being Spetsburo One – the strawberry jam makers.' Audley showed his teeth. 'So now you're going to ask me why he ran? And the short and humiliating answer to that is – we don't know.'

Benedikt frowned. 'You mean . . . he was not defecting?'

'From them he was. But not to us, and not to the Americans either. He went to ground, and he never surfaced – and he had time to pick and choose, too. The way it seems to have been . . . when the troubles began again the Russians sent him back to Ireland – to Dublin – to stir the pot maybe, certainly to watch out for their interests. But then something went sour.' The big man shrugged. 'What went sour – we don't know . . . He'd been away a long time . . . it was the same old enemy, but not the same old country as it was in Frank Ryan's day . . . and he was older, so maybe he was wiser – or maybe he was just older and very tired. Only God knows now, anyway.' He looked at Benedikt. 'All *we* know is that he ran. Because one day we wanted him – to get what he knew – and the next day they were after him to make sure we didn't get it.'

'But the KGB found him first.'

'Yes.' Audley grimaced. 'And on our home ground too . . . Though they had advantages we lacked, to be fair.'

'Such as?'

'He was one of theirs from way back, all nicely filed. So they knew what they were looking for. We never did.' Audley shook his head. 'We never even had a decent photo of him – just one smudgy face in an International Brigade group picture that might have been him in his teens. But no real face, let alone prints or distinguishing marks. He was always a man for the shadows, not the sunlight . . . *Shit*!'

The uncharacteristic obscenity surprised Benedikt, and he looked questioningly at Audley.

'I was just thinking . . . They were damn good: they let us pick up their sighs of relief after he was dead – that *Kelly, Aloysius* could be filed as *deceased,* and the matter was closed. But they must already have had a *Kelly, Michael* file. And we didn't even know of his existence, let alone the connection between them. So they've been hunting Michael while we've been sitting on our arses and twiddling our thumbs – hunting him in *our* territory.'

Benedikt forgave the lapse, sensing more than wounded pride behind it. 'So Aloysius must have passed on information to Michael.'

Audley gestured helplessly. 'What other interpretation is there? He ran – and they're after him, damn it! *Damn it*!'

Now there was only one thing he needed. And although the Kommissar at Wiesbaden could give it to him in no more than the time it took to key the question he wanted it now. 'About the Debreczen meeting?'

Audley was studying the Tiger critically as though he was seeing it for the first time, his eye running along the barrel of the deadly 8.8cm gun to the massive armoured shield which fronted its turret.

'What happened at Debreczen?' asked Benedikt.

'What happened at Debreczen?' Audley turned a critical eye towards him. 'It was before your time – just about *literally* before your time, Captain Schneider . . . Damn it! It was before even *my* time, professionally speaking.'

Early to mid-1950s, that would make it, estimated Benedikt. At least, if one discounted the unconfirmed report that a very young Lieutenant Audley had not been a simple tank commander in the last months of the war . . .

'Debreczen is out of the deeps of time – it's still part rumour and part legend . . . we didn't even get a whiff of it until years afterwards, from the Gorbatov de-briefing, and Gorbatov's been dead . . . for a long time – ' Audley smiled suddenly, reminiscently ' – of cirrhosis, I should add. In a piece of Canada which most resembled his native land . . . At least the rat-catchers never caught up with *him!* Just the booze.'

Debreczen? Benedikt wanted to say. But he said nothing.

'It wasn't actually in Debreczen . . . There was this old Hapsburg castle in the woods. Or . . . it was more like a Ruritanian hunting lodge, though God only knows what they hunted there . . . But the Germans had added some huts, and there was perimeter wire – all mod. cons., Nazi-style . . . And, for some reason – perhaps it was accessibility, with no questions asked – for some reason the Russians liked it for what they had in mind.'

Hapsburg castles Benedikt knew, and hunting lodges and huts and perimeter wire too. But he had never visited Debreczen . . . and where was Ruritania?

'First, it was like a seminar centre for experts – not only the KGB specials, but also the foreigners that they really trusted, who could lecture on political conditions in their own countries . . . Like, what they couldn't do and what they could do – what they'd done wrong in the past, but where the opportunities lay in the future . . . The sort of thing Philby and Co did a few years later – okay?'

Philby and Co had cut the British deep – so deep that for some of them the very names were taboo. But in this, as in so many other things, Audley was different, even though as a Cambridge man himself his wound must be particularly painful.

'And then, over the next year or so, they slipped in people from the West one by one – the promising ones they wanted properly educated for the long-term future . . . Not types connected with the intelligence services – not people who were already actively working for them, nothing like that . . . These were the young ones who had good prospects in civilian life – in business and industry, and banking and the law, and the arts and academic life . . . The sort who might go over to politics eventually, or turn up in think-tanks. The policy-makers, if you like.' The Englishman regarded Benedikt bleakly. 'They came for just a week, or a fortnight at the most . . . The sort of time they could lose quite easily in a European holiday – almost untraceable . . . As I well know, because I was eventually one of those who drew the shitty job of trying to short-list our Debreczen possibles. *And* without alerting them, that we were vetting the vacation they'd taken five or six years before . . . whether they'd really been tasting the wine in Burgundy, or skiing in Austria, or counting the Madonnas and Children in the Uffizi. And it was damn near impossible: I got two "certainties" – one of which turned out to be wrong . . . and two probables, both of which were probably wrong . . . and four possibles, who could be pure as driven snow but have my black question mark against their names for evermore, because I couldn't absolutely clear them.' He scowled, and shook his head at the memory. 'The best part of four months' work, and really only one name to show for it. I wished to God I'd never heard of Colonel Gorbatov and Debreczen by the end of it – it was a damned *shitty* job!'

The adjective was not inappropriate this time, thought Benedikt: an assignment which left other men soiled by unconfirmed suspicion *was* a dirty one, however prudent and necessary in a dirty world. 'But Aloysius Kelly was the name you obtained?'

'Good God – no!' Audley blinked at him. 'Aloysius wasn't one of the pupils – he was one of the *teachers,* man – one of the experts running the course. One of the trusted foreigners, don't you see.'

One of the trusted ones –

'He'd been on the game for years by then,' Audley elaborated. 'He'd nothing to learn, but a hell of a lot to teach.'

Benedikt kicked himself. Both Aloysius Kelly's years of service, from the Spanish Civil War onwards, and the implacability of the KGB's pursuit pointed to that truth. And, more than that, of all men a defecting instructor could not be allowed to live: where any Debreczen 'student' might, or might not, have glimpsed a fellow-student, their instructors would know them *all* –

'It was the CIA who identified him, when they squeezed *their* Debreczen graduate.' Audley's eyes clouded. 'Ours shot himself before we could get to him – he got wind that we were on his tail . . . But the Yanks got theirs – the one they managed to identify. He was an Irish-American, that's probably why he remembered Aloysius particularly: there were no names in Debreczen, only numbers and letters . . . The pupils never saw each other, only their teachers – it was a sort of Oxbridge tutorial system, very élitist and security-conscious . . . Anyway, this Irish American made Aloysius sure enough – ex-Abraham Lincoln battalion in the International Brigade, ex-sidekick of Frank Ryan . . . But he had a low opinion of the IRA at that time, did Aloysius – it was the early fifties, and he said they weren't worth a row of beans in Ireland then, but there was good anti-British work the American end could do, playing up British colonialism to weaken the Atlantic alliance, that sort of thing . . .' Audley paused. 'Unfortunately, the third day the Yanks had this chap – in a supposedly safe house outside Washington – somebody sniped him at about seven hundred yards while he was taking a breath of air.' Audley's shoulders lifted. 'A real good shot . . . and I always wondered whether our chap really pulled his own trigger . . . But it goes to show how much they valued Debreczen, eh?'

Benedikt nodded, and thought of the wide-open view of Duntisbury Manor from the ridge, down across the lawn to the terrace . . . And was the fate of the Irish American – and possibly that unknown English traitor too – one of the things that Aloysius Kelly had passed on to Michael Kelly?

'So the Yanks never finished squeezing their man, anyway – who was the only one they got a line on. And they put Aloysius Kelly's name on the red side of the tablets – ' Audley looked at his watch suddenly ' – and didn't forget about him either.' He looked up at Benedikt equally suddenly. 'You saw how our loyal ally perked up at the mention of him?'

'Yes.' Benedikt's mind was beginning to accelerate, moving from his own thought – *one of the things that Aloysius had passed on to Michael* – even before Audley had reminded him that the CIA was in the game now. 'How much do you trust your American friend, David?'

'To leave the field to us?' Audley pursed his lips. 'In theory . . . quite a lot.' Then he frowned. 'But Aloysius Kelly's memoirs – or whatever he may have passed on to Michael to make a target of him . . . that'll be a sore temptation to him, I fear. A sore temptation.'

'And he didn't give his word to Mr Smith.'

'Nor he did! And he's *got* Mr Smith, too.' Audley's features contorted into ugliness. 'And any lead to those Debreczen graduates . . . They were just the likely lads in the mid-fifties – they'll be the top dogs and the bosses now, the ones who've stayed the course.' He shook his head. 'A sore temptation!'

Quite suddenly the only course of action open to him became clear to Benedikt: there would have been Germans among those Debreczen traitors – *graduates* was a weak euphemism for such swine – so his service had an equal interest now in what had started as a purely British affair.

'We cannot sit on this any longer, David.' He shook his head at the big Englishman. 'Neither of us can. It is too big for us both.' Yet he had to leave the man an honourable escape route. 'The Americans know. But this is your territory.'

'Yes.' Audley faced reality with traditional British phlegm. Or perhaps, thought Benedikt, he had recognized it at the first mention of Aloysius Kelly. 'You're quite right.'

'Who is your chief?' He hoped his expression was impassive. 'Colonel Butler?'

Audley smiled painfully. 'Yes. Jack Butler.'

'He will be angry?' He pretended to think about Colonel Jack Butler. 'But he is a good man, is he not?'

The smile twisted. 'Yes – and yes.'

Benedikt searched for the right words. 'We have no choice. But not much time, I think.'

Audley studied him. 'Not much time is right. But I still have a choice.'

Benedikt frowned. 'What choice?'

Audley continued to study him. 'Duntisbury Chase should hold for a few more hours. But how far can I trust you, Captain Benedikt Schneider?'

'Me?' Had he betrayed something?

'Yes. I need to talk to Jack Butler face to face. But I need someone I can trust in the Chase – someone who won't make Michael Kelly run. But can I trust you?'

He had betrayed something, but Audley didn't know what it was. And the only way the man's dilemma could be resolved would complicate his loyalties even more, by adding Audley's to them. Yet there was no alternative. 'Would my word-of-honour help you?' He managed to avoid sounding quite humourless. 'My father's used to be good enough for your people in the war.'

For a moment Audley's face recalled Mr Smith's. Then, like Mr Smith, he relaxed. 'Yes, of course.' The big man looked around. 'We need another car for you, so that you can get back with those boys . . . No need to hurry back – take them to lunch somewhere, and then round about, to be in the Chase by tea-time – four or five . . . And tell Becky I phoned my wife and she called me home – say my daughter's sick, and they can get me at home – ' Audley was leading him through the tanks towards the entrance ' – I'll be allegedly in the bath when she phones – if she checks up – and my wife will know where I really am, so that I can phone back . . . Okay?'

They were passing through a line of modern giants, a British Chieftain and an early German Leopard among them. The entrance ahead of them was empty, except for one of the armoured corps NCOs standing guard in it.

'I want a car, Corporal.' Audley didn't mince matters. 'For the captain here – quick as you can. Hire it or borrow it, I don't mind. Major Kennedy will help you.'

'Yes, sir.' The Corporal rolled his eyes at Benedikt, but reacted like any intelligent NCO to a clear and concise order delivered by someone whom he recognized as being in a position to give such orders. 'Right away, sir . . . Quarter of an hour, sir?'

'That would do well. I shan't be here when you come back. The Captain will be in charge of the boys.'

'Right, sir.' The Corporal very nearly saluted, but restrained himself with an effort before striding off.

Audley looked at Benedikt. 'They could give you a hard time – or young Benjamin could, anyway . . . Darren should be full of tanks, but young Benjamin is a Kelly-admirer and will stick to his orders . . . Tell him more or less who you really are, and that you've agreed to help Miss Becky and Gunner Kelly and me – that should give him something to chew on . . . And when you get back latch on to Kelly and try not to let him out of your sight – interrogate him as much as you like, he'll expect you to . . . . And if you're sticking your neck out, you've got a right to, after all.'

'But you're not expecting anything to happen . . . for the next few hours?'

Audley nodded. 'That's right. They only acquired their walkie-talkie radios this morning, and they're reckoning on a practice run tonight. Mrs Bradley's boy, Peter, at the village shop, has been "Larnin' 'em", as Old Cecil puts it – he's a CB radio enthusiast . . . There's a lot of quite unlooked-for expertise in Duntisbury Royal, and not just the ancient village skills . . . from Peter in the shop to Blackie Nabb, who was a Royal Marine Commando in Korea.' The Englishman's voice was quietly proud. 'Blackie was one of Drysdale's men who fought their way up Hellfire Valley to link with the American marines south of the Chosin Reservoir – the Falklands was a Sunday stroll compared with that . . . Besides which, anyway, it's Gunner Kelly who knows how to summon up the demons on his tail – he won't do that until the Chase is ready for them.' He half smiled at Benedikt. 'You were an altogether unexpected test of our defences, you know . . .'

'And I did not get far?' Benedict completed the sentence. 'True. But I was a man alone. And I am not the Special Bureau No 1 of the KGB.'

'True.' Audley's face creased suddenly, as though with doubt, and then cleared slowly as the doubts resolved themselves. 'But there is . . . something else which I think you should know.'

'Something else?' It was disturbing that the Englishman had not been frank with him. 'Something you haven't told me?'

'No – not really . . . Something which has only occurred to me since Aloysius Kelly came into the reckoning, you see.'

'Yes?' An instinct told Benedikt that the man was not lying. He had seen that creased look not long before, while Mr Smith had still been with them.

'I don't know quite how to put it . . . Aloysius Kelly's not been my concern for years – never was, really, I've only read the reports . . . The American one originally, and then the others, four or five years back, when he was killed.'

'Yes?' But this was the man's true skill; to distil truth from the merest broken shards of knowledge buried in ground thickly sown with lies and rumour.

'I swear there's something Gunner Kelly knows that we

211

don't . . . a certainty – almost a serendipity . . . But more than that.' The creases were back. 'It *could* be just that he's stopped running and started fighting . . .'

'Or?'

Audley faced him. 'Or we can turn the whole thing round.' He paused. 'Like, bring it back to Mr Smith's old auntie. Because if there was one thing Comrade Aloysius Kelly was, he was a damned downy bird, and he wouldn't be easy to kill.' Another pause. '*So let's suppose he wasn't killed.*'

'Wasn't – ?' Those creases were justified. 'Then who – ?'

'Any tramp by the wayside would do. Any homeless vagrant – any drifter . . . Aloysius Kelly could have spotted the bomb – he knew the form: he'd more likely set one than be caught by one. But if the KGB set it – if he gave them a body . . . then no more pursuit: *out of this nettle, danger, we pluck this flower, safety* – the old, old story, Benedikt, man!'

Benedikt stared at him. *More likely to set a bomb than be caught by one* –

'And Michael Kelly?'

'And Michael Kelly . . . It would have been Michael who set him up in that cottage – if he gave Michael money years before, some of it would have been for the betting shop debts, and some for the bolt-hole . . . But after the bomb, if Michael knew he was still alive, then Michael was a little nettle still growing among the flowers. And little nettles have a way of growing bigger.'

But that didn't fit. 'Are you suggesting that Michael got away from Aloysius? That he realized he'd be next?' He shook his head. 'No.'

Audley frowned. 'Michael's no fool. Damn it – you can see that for yourself.' But then he shook his head. 'No . . . I take your point – it isn't likely. But there was something that bound them together: blood had been thick enough for Michael. It could have been thick enough for Aloysius . . . at least to start with, until the idea of being *absolutely* safe began to corrode his mind.' Pause. 'Remember Mr Smith's parting shot? *Running changes a man*?'

That was more like it. To kill a blood-relative who had also been a friend . . . that might daunt any man; and the Irish were a strange race, in which poetry and romantic chivalry mingled with dark notions of blood sacrifice. Yet also that image of *corrosion* was right: to leave one's life in another man's hands . . . for Aloysius Kelly could never be sure that the KGB would not reach Audley's conclusion, and look to confirm their suspicion from Michael. And Aloysius of all men would know how unremitting they were in pursuit, too . . . to leave one's life to such a chance –

'Perhaps he just gave Michael a sporting chance, for old times' sake. "I'll count from one to a hundred – and then watch yourself, me boyo."' Audley's eyes widened in amazement at his own imagination. 'That's the trouble – why I'd never take an Irish job: I like them too much as people, and I find them totally incomprehensible – I studied their history at Cambridge from Strongbow to Parnell and Gladstone, and I could never answer a single question right, even when I knew the facts. And I wish to hell I'd never promised Jane and Becky – that I'd never promised to make sense of this, damn it!'

Jane?

But Jane didn't matter. Audley had lifted the stakes far above little girls with the possibility of this final duel between the two Kellys, Aloysius and Michael.

The outer door of the museum banged behind him, and the Corporal's boots cracked like rifle-shots on the concrete floor.

'I have a car for you, sir.' The Corporal addressed Benedikt as though Audley was as invisible as he'd promised to be. 'Major Kennedy's wife's car actually, that the lady brought back with her from our last posting . . . I hope you have no objection to a foreign car, sir?'

Benedikt goggled at him. 'A f-foreign car, Corporal?'

213

'Yes, sir. A Volkswagen *Sci*-rocco GL – a Jerry car, but very nippy, and I think your young *lads* will like it . . . If you've no objection?'

Benedikt looked at Audley, then back at the Corporal. 'No objection, Corporal. A Jerry car will do very well for me, thank you. No objection at all.'

Zu Ruhm und Sieg! A Volkswagen would be just right for that.

PART THREE

You pays your money, and you takes your choice

The Old House,
Steeple Horley,
Sussex

My dear Jack,

You will, of course, be getting my official report of occurrences in Duntisbury Chase both before and after my somewhat traumatic meeting with you. But that will be couched in the proper jargon, abbreviated and bowdlerized so as not to offend less understanding official eyes and ears than yours, furnished and ornamented with such excuses and explanations as may mitigate my crimes if not altogether exculpate me from censure, and – apart from the usual *suppressio veri suggestio falsi* – with one or two outright falsehoods which I consider necessary and which I confide they will swallow.

This private letter I am writing partly to set the record straight, but partly also because you may find out more from another source; and – not least because I must admit a gross original error of judgement – I would not wish you to be wrong-footed in such an event. I must also admit that if I was sure we could get away with it I would not be putting pen to paper now. But better from me now than from some enemy – or innocent source – later.

By 'we', you see, I mean your daughter Jane and me.

The fault, however, is all mine, not Jane's. Becky Maxwell-Smith, a friend of hers at Bristol University, confided in her. Being your cleverest one Jane smelt bad trouble. But – still being your cleverest – she also knew that you were up to your ears in work (Cheltenham) and that I was on leave, so she turned to me. Unwisely, as it turned out, but she can hardly be blamed for assuming that I represented Age and Wisdom, for not knowing that I was going through one of my *accidie* periods (why the hell didn't you give me Cheltenham? I've a friend teaching modern languages there at school) – bored out of my mind and ready for any mischief.

The moment I arrived at Duntisbury Chase I was lost: that marvellous place – a little world of its own under its unbelievable sky – and *that Irishman*.

You know my hang-ups about the Irish – which probably date from the time I fluffed a question at Cambridge on Elizabeth Tudor's Irish policy: I just don't understand them. But I'd read the Maxwell memo (saying that it was definitely not an IRA hit) before I went on leave. So he seemed a safe enough object for close study – at least, that's what I told myself.

Self-indulgence and stupidity – I know! But it was good fun – and I was able to watch over Becky, as I'd promised – until our loyal Bundesnachrichtendienst ally turned up out of the blue. I should have reported to you then, but I thought I'd stand a better chance with you if I came bearing gifts – namely, how and why the Germans had reached Duntisbury Chase ahead of us (or, in this case, you, Jack – to be brutally frank), as well as Gunner Kelly's secret, whatever it might be.

As it turned out, Captain Schneider's explanation for his presence was – and is – decidedly thin, which made me all the more curious about his appearance. I wanted more, but I had an appointment with one of my American contacts, who was digging dirt on Gunner Kelly for me in recompense for past favours.

And that, of course, produced the dynamite too unstable for me to handle, which I brought to you with my tail between my legs – not least because I was terrified that the next thing we'd get in Duntisbury Chase was a herd of CIA tourists sampling the rural charms of the place, and making Michael bolt – and scaring off Aloysius (if he was alive).

218

The problem was, as I explained briefly when I saw you, that I couldn't be in two places at once, for only saints have the gift of bi-location. But I had to see you – so I had to trust Captain Schneider.

Had to? That's unfair to him: I sent him back to the Chase because I trusted him – not because I had no choice.

Or trusted him on one level, anyway. Because I'm damn sure he lied about his reason for being there. More likely – more humiliatingly likely, if their Wiesbaden computer is as good as rumour has it – he was there because he already knew about Aloysius Kelly's connection with Michael Kelly and they surely wanted Aloysius just as much as we did, if not more. He put on a damn good show of innocence, right to the end. And he's a very sharp and resourceful young man, as well as being a brave one (like we said in the war: when they're bad, they're very, very bad . . . but when they're good, they're sometimes a damn sight better than us; and he's very much his father's son, and his father by all accounts was very good indeed).

The point is, I had my source on him (but mostly on his father), and I liked the cut of his jib. You might say he's everything I'm not – or, seeing that I'm the wrong generation (the war-wounded one), he's everything that our pupil Paul Mitchell isn't: Paul is English, with a cynical-pragmatic French strain – Benedikt Schneider is half-English, but actually all German . . . serious (Christian), efficient, perhaps rather sentimental-romantic, but above all honourable. In fact, allowing that he wasn't old and bruised and rubbed all over with alcohol, and more than half-crazy and Prussian with it, he was like old Blücher after Ligny and before Waterloo. When I left him in the tank museum, he'd given me his word and he meant to keep it.

So I trusted him, anyway – I even told him about Aloysius Kelly, if he didn't know already, so that he wouldn't go back to the Chase not knowing who he might end up against.

And you know how things went wrong after that, at our end – your end – with you at Cheltenham, and the time we lost because of that: my fault – my sin – mihi paenitet – or is it me paenitet, I can't remember, my Latin's getting rustier every day – but I lost the hours of life and death that mattered there, Jack. So I was on the road back, south from Cheltenham, when it all blew up. And every time I get it wrong, someone dies – like that young policeman died, and like lovely Frances died –

'Captain Schneider!' Miss Becky exhibited equal measures of surprise and envy. 'Where's David? And where *did* you get that car? What a beautiful colour!'

Smile. 'It's called "Champagne".' It was a woman's colour, certainly: left to himself, he would have chosen silver in Germany, and British Racing Green in Britain if Volkswagen offered that shade. 'I borrowed it from one of his armoured corps friends.' Smile again. 'He is a Panzer man, from long ago, Fraülein – I have learnt that this day, at the tank museum which is in the middle of nowhere.'

The smile came back to him. 'At Bovington?' Her face lit up. 'He's a dragoon, actually. It's rather nice – how they still have "dragoons" and "hussars" – and "the Household Cavalry", who ride horses only for the Queen, but really drive tanks and such things.' The smile embraced him. 'Not that *he* did – he's a terrible driver – he crashes the gears on his Cavalier something awful, I'd never let him ride one of my horses – ' the smile edited itself ' – but where is he?'

'He's gone home.' He fabricated slight embarrassment. 'He spoke with his wife upon the telephone, from – from the museum of Panzers, Fraülein.'

'Faith?'

'Faith?'

'His wife – Faith.'

'Ach so – Faith – his wife.' He was conscious of serving

up another inadequate explanation which needed more substance. 'There was some pressing family matter, I believe. But he said for you to telephone him at his home – the number I have for you.' He felt in his pocket. 'And he said that he would return very soon, perhaps by nightfall.'

'Oh.' Audley's absence had worried her, but now she was at least partially reassured. 'He said to phone him?'

'Yes. At his home.' As he handed over the slip of paper he remembered his duty. 'And Mr Kelly? I am to speak with him, if you please.'

'Yes – of course . . .' More and more she was over-matched by the deadly games she had allowed herself to play, he could see that very clearly. But she was a long way from giving in to her fear even now. 'He's in the West Tower. Peter Bradley and Blackie are up there with him at the moment, running over our plans for this evening.'

'Our plans?'

'Didn't David tell you?' She thought for a moment. 'It was Michael's idea . . . now that we've got the radios – to have two practice runs this evening, just after dark.' She smiled again. 'When you . . . arrived last night there was a certain amount of . . . confusion. We don't want that next time, so Michael's arranged two intrusions for this evening – one will be coming over the top, by Caesar's Camp, and the other will come down the stream, from the ford.'

That was interesting – interesting that Gunner Kelly had marked the stream as an approach route into the heart of the village . . . and interesting also that he had chosen to test the defences at two points which single intruders might favour. Whereas the KGB . . . the Special Bureau would send in a three man squad for this sort of operation: one man to make the hit, one backing him up, and a driver to get them in close and out quickly. For though they might expect the target to be on his guard after the Old General's death, they would not – *could not* – imagine a community-in-arms waiting for them.

But then, equally, what did Michael Kelly expect? Or . . . if Audley had warned him of KGB practices . . . why was he practising for a single intruder? Why – unless Audley was right, and he already knew that it would be just that – just Aloysius Kelly –

'Captain?'

Benedikt blinked quickly, aware too late that he had been staring the poor girl out of countenance. 'Forgive me, Fräulein! I was thinking . . . you are being very careful. And that is good: you are right to be very careful.' He smiled.

'Yes.' She did not find his smile reassuring, but she bore up bravely. 'David said not to relax for a moment. And not to trust anyone we don't know.'

'Including me?' Mother would not approve of her – of what she was doing. But Papa's attitude would be more relaxed.

'Oh no! David said . . . ' She trailed off. 'Is what we are doing so very wrong, Captain Schneider?'

'Wrong?' He played for time.

'We're not going to kill anyone. If we can help it.'

'You were going to kill someone – at first – weren't you?' He watched her. 'Or Mr Kelly was, anyway.'

She bit her lip. 'Yes. That would have been wrong – David made us see that. But . . . these people . . . who do things like this – killing Grandfather . . .'

'It was Mr Kelly they were after, though – yes?'

'That makes it worse. Killing Grandfather – or it might have been anyone passing by – just as though he didn't matter one way or the other . . . as though he was *nothing* – and ordinary people are *nothing*.' Suddenly she was defiant. 'Well, we're going to show them that people aren't *nothing*. That's what we're going to do.'

'Them?' The phenomenon of the worm turning – and turning into a cobra as it turned – was an old and interesting one. But he had no time for it today. 'And who is "them", Fräulein?'

'Whoever comes. It doesn't matter.'

'But only Mr Kelly knows. Because only Mr Kelly can summon them. Does that not worry you?'

'Why should it worry us?'

'For two reasons, Fräulein. Do you not want to know why they want him dead? Suppose Mr Kelly is a *bad* man . . . ?'

Her chin came up. 'Michael served with Grandfather. If he was good enough for Grandfather, he's good enough for us.' She looked at him proudly. 'You never met Grandfather, so you can't understand. But that's the way it is.'

Amazing! But also wonderful in its ancient meaning: full of wonder – the faith out of which great good and great evil came, according to its inspiration, from Jesus Christ to Karl Marx and Adolf Hitler.

'So – '

'Michael would have died for Grandfather.' She cut him off. 'You should have seen him after . . . after the bomb. He could never have pretended that – the way he was . . . And he could have run away afterwards. But he didn't, Captain Schneider.'

'No. He didn't.' She was beautiful, thought Benedikt. *God grant me another time, another place*!

'And he may still die for him, Captain Schneider. Because he's the target here – no one else is in danger.'

He nodded. 'Yes. But he is also an old soldier. So are you sure he will not prefer to kill for your Grandfather still?'

She smiled suddenly. 'Because he has Grandfather's old gun? Captain . . . he doesn't know it, but that gun has no firing pin. It wouldn't hurt a baby.' The smile became almost tender. 'We know Michael . . . That was the only part of him we didn't trust – that's why I gave him the gun, you see. Just in case.'

God in heaven! thought Benedikt. And that was a complication if things went wrong, too.

223

'But don't you dare tell him that, though,' she admonished him. 'The moment he sends off for them, to let them know he's here, we shan't let him out of our sight for a moment – David's got it all worked out – that was why David was so angry when he went out to see you last night . . . But . . . you go and talk to him – ask him about Grandfather . . . I must go and see about supper – '

The rooms passed him by, dreamlike . . . Gunner Kelly – *Michael* Kelly – up against Aloysius, if not the KGB . . . with a useless weapon in his hand – *God in heaven!*

At the foot of the spiral staircase in the West Tower he met Blackie Nabb coming down, with a bearded young man at his back.

'Evenin', sir,' Blackie acknowledged him with an air of armed neutrality, his shot-gun safely broken open under his arm, while the bearded young man studied him in silence, frankly curious, as he squeezed past up the narrow stair.

Duntisbury Chase was going on the alert between the two of them, guessed Benedikt: old and new skills, they had . . . but would that alliance be enough against Aloysius Kelly, whose own experience went back to General Franco's war?

'*Ahhh* – Mr David's German gentleman – Captain!' Kelly chose his Irish voice with which to greet him. But then he peered past him, towards the empty landing. 'An' the Great Man himself – ?'

'Dr Audley is at home. His wife summoned him.' The thin excuse again.

'Did she now?' Polite – but absolute – disbelief. 'An' him a good family man? Well!'

'Miss Rebecca is telephoning him at his home now.' With Kelly that somehow only stretched the lie even more thinly.

'Is she so?' Kelly cocked an eyebrow at him. 'An' not checkin' up on me, then?'

'Checking up on you?'

'Uh-huh,' agreed Kelly equably. 'After exchangin' notes with you, Captain.' Then he grinned. 'I should have shot you last night, I'm thinkin', an' said "sorry" afterwards.'

Benedikt decided to be very German. 'Please?'

'Ah now – don't be givin' me that!' Kelly brushed his incomprehension aside. 'You know what I mean very well. For I've fought you fellas – six long years . . . An' if it was one thing you never were, it was foolish. 'Twas only when that little man – him with the Charlie Chaplin moustache – 'twas only when *he* interfered that you made mistakes . . . You never let us down otherwise, the Squire always said. So don't be disappointin' me, eh? Checkin' on me, he'll be.'

Better to say nothing at all, Benedikt corrected himself.

'Or maybe he doesn't need to check now?' Kelly stared at him for a moment, and then stood up suddenly and turned towards the window behind him for another moment, and then swung back just as quickly. 'The hell with that! There was a fella I knew once, that's dead and gone, but you lot can never rest easy because of him – that's why you're here. Because there's no other reason worth a damn – deny that if you can!'

There was no point in arguing. 'And if I do not choose to deny it, Mr Kelly?'

'Faith – then you've wasted your time! For he told me nothing – *nothing* – would you believe that?' He paused for only half a second. 'But of course you would not! It's the one thing that none of you will believe – because you can't afford to believe it! Because the thing that he had – whatever it was . . . it was too big for you – is that a fact, now?'

Nothing?

'But I tell a lie! It was not nothing he told me – ' Kelly

leaned towards him ' – he did tell me *one* thing. And you know what that was?'

Nothing? Or *one* thing?

'He said to me: *"I think I'm safe home at last, Michael – me that hates 'em all, for the black bastards they are, both sides of 'em, that'll never let a man rest . . . But if anything happens to me, then you start runnin', Michael, an' don't look over your shoulder, an' don't ever stop, because it'll be you they'll be after then, in case I've given it to you!"'* Gunner Kelly wiped his hand across his mouth. 'An' it did happen to him – so I ran. That's all.'

'He gave you nothing?'

'Captain – don't you think that if he'd given me anything I'd not have given it up by now? Mary, Mother of God! But how can you prove that you don't know what you don't know? You can only *run* – that's all you can do!'

Suddenly his face changed. 'But then there was the Old General – the Squire . . . that was the best man that God ever made out of clay . . . I asked him for a bed for the night, an' I told him why I was running. And he gave me four years and his own life in exchange, is what he did.'

The man wasn't lying. Aloysius Kelly was dead and it was the KGB who were coming to Duntisbury Chase – Benedikt had never been more certain of anything in his life.

'So this time – just for this time – I'm not running.' Kelly shook his head quickly. 'Oh – I know we'll not get them as have given the orders . . . I know we'll never get them – they'll die in their beds most likely, one way – another way . . . But we'll get the bastards who did their dirty work – it'll be the same fellas, I'll be bound . . . An' we'll make a great scandal, an' get the headlines in all the papers – an' that'll be big trouble for them, back home, that they'll not be forgiven for. An' that'll be something that's better than nothing. They'll not forget us, by God!'

In his own way he was saying what Miss Becky had said, thought Benedikt. And even if it wasn't true Gunner Kelly believed it to be true.

And more, also: this would be a killing, not a capturing, if Gunner Kelly could make it so. Of that he was also certain.

So Audley had been right not to trust Gunner Kelly, whether it was Aloysius or the KGB out there: and prudence, in the most remote possibility that they were both wrong about Aloysius, decreed that he should be slowed down.

'But what about Miss Becky? Do you not have an obligation to her?'

'Ah – she'll be all right. It'll all be over, and her no part of it.' Gunner Kelly looked at him. 'I mind a time . . . Dr Audley said your dad was an anti-tank gunner – is that a fact, now?'

'Yes.' Benedikt frowned. What had Papa to do with this – with Gunner Kelly and Miss Becky?

'So he was, then! Well, I mind a time – it was in Tunisia it was, when I was with the Squire . . . And we bedded down in this little valley, minding our own business, an' thinking there wasn't a Jerry within fifteen miles of us – an' nothing in front of us, do you see . . . not that it was our affair what was in front of us – it was 25-pounders we had, and gunners we were . . . An' then there was all this terrible row one night – and it was bloody Jerries – ' Kelly registered Benedikt suddenly ' – that's to say, it was *Germans* out in front of us somewhere, where they'd no right to be at all . . . It was a wearying night, we had, not knowing what was going on over the ridge in front. But the Squire and all, they reckoned there was nothing we could do, an' it was best to leave it to whoever was busy there, because the Germans weren't coming forward, so far as we could make out, an' they weren't shooting at us – they didn't seem to be shooting at anything much, they were just shooting over our little valley . . . I think the Squire did get out for a bit, because that was the sort of thing he did. But he came back pretty smartish . . . Anyway, in the morning, a whole lot of Gordons came through – Scotsmen, anyway – infantry, clearing up the way they do . . . walking along an' shooting a few people, and taking prisoners, an' that . . . An' the Squire says to me "Come on, Kelly, an' let's go an' have a look over the top there." And the first thing we saw was these Bofors guns – anti-aircraft guns . . . But they hadn't been attacked, the crews had spent the whole night cowering in their emplacement, just like us . . . So we went on a bit – for they said there was guns in front of them down the ridge, which we took to be more Bofors . . . But then we came upon this extraordinary gun – begod, we more like tripped over it, for it was almost invisible, with no shield that I recall, an' no more than knee-high to a little fella . . . but with this great long barrel along the ground, pointing across the next valley. And there were its owners in their slit-trench just nearby, brewing up. So the Squire says: "Who the devil are you, then?" And looks at the long gun, "An' what the devil is *that?*" says he, pointing at it . . . An' they says "Why, that's the new 17-pounder, that is – an' if you want to know what it does, just you look across yonder". An' they points across the valley, an' there's four – maybe half a dozen – Jerry tanks, that's come round the side across their front, poor devils – twelve hundred yards away . . . *twelve hundred yards, if it was an inch!*' He shook his head in wonderment which had evidently not decreased in forty years. 'That was the first time the 17-pounder ever went into action – in front of our gun position, saving our bacon. We couldn't believe our eyes, I tell you!'

Benedikt looked at the Irishman questioningly. 'Yes?'

'Aargh! Do ye not see?' Kelly cocked his head at such obtuseness. ''Tis us that are the 17-pounders here – you and me, and Dr Audley . . . An' maybe Blackie Nabb and one or two others at a pinch. So if it's Miss Becky you're worried about – why, she shall sleep sound in her bed while we're doing the business that has to be done, an' her none the wiser.' Then he smiled at Benedikt, and for the first time there was a hint of something more than mere calculation in his eye. 'I understand you, Captain: a fine young lady, she is – and with a heart as big as her grandsire's. But she has her life before her . . . And the rest of us can look after ourselves well enough.'

Somewhere far away, but still within the house, a bell rang out a tuneless electrical alarm.

Kelly looked at his watch. 'There now! That'll be young Mr Bradley calling me to my duty with him, havin' all our people placed where they should be. The marvels of science!' He smiled at Benedikt again. 'Your concern does you credit, Captain. Once upon a time it would have been a pleasure to have fought you – an' now it's glad I am you're on the same side. But you must excuse me while I go to see how young Peter's getting on. Then I'll be with you for supper in the kitchen before we put our defences through their paces – eh?'

Schneider knew there was something wrong then, but only by instinct, not by reason, so he says. Kelly was too calm and confident – 'laid back', is it? 'Serene' almost, Schneider says: not so much like the old phoenix before it goes into the fire, but more like the new one which comes out of the flames, born again.

So he knew something was wrong, just as I always knew something was wrong, but he couldn't put his finger on it any more than I could, because neither of us is a computer with total instantaneous recall. But he thought he still had some time in his pocket, and he knew Kelly was with Peter Bradley in what passed for their control room, so he went to look for Becky to find out whether she'd confirmed my alleged whereabouts.

Becky was making the supper. She'd phoned my wife, who had said that I was in the bath and would phone back, as I'd instructed her to do. And he talked with her for a few minutes, for the sake of politeness. Only, by that time the

229

thing in the back of his mind, which had been nagging him, but which he still couldn't reach, was on the way to driving him half frantic. He went out from the kitchen, down the passage and into the main hall.

The main hall at Duntisbury Manor is where a lot of the family portraits are: a selection of military Maxwells down the years, with the Sargent picture of Colonel Julian, the poet, in pride of place. No picture of the Old General, of course – he was never self-considering enough to have one painted. And yet he was there all the same, said Schneider: it was the Old General – the Squire – who filled his mind, not Kelly. Not either of the Kellys. Just the Old General.

And then he had it. 'Like it was the Old General gave it to me,' he says. And you can make what you like of that –

'Miss Rebecca – do not argue, I beg of you! He must not leave the Chase! I have told Peter Bradley to give that order, but he does not know me – he will not obey me. But he will obey *you*, Fräulein!' He had to reach her somehow.

'But, Captain – he is with Peter, surely – '

'No! He has gone, I tell you!' He felt time accelerating away from him. 'When Peter rang the bell it was to tell him that a car had passed the ford – a car with three men in it.'

'Yes, but – '

'He told Peter not to worry – that they were accounted for and expected. *Expected*?' If it frightened her – he had no choice. '*What men*?'

'I don't know. But – '

'*He* knows.' He was committed now. 'He was expecting them – and he has gone to meet them.' He cast around desperately in his memory for something with which to convince her. But the truth would be meaningless to her, even if he had had time for it. 'This is what he planned – from the start . . . Where are most of your people now?

They are out of the way on the ridge and along the stream where he sent them. *You must believe me, Miss Rebecca!'*

Suddenly her hand came to her mouth. 'That gun he has – ! Oh God!'

Huh! thought Benedikt. But if that would move her, then that must be his way. 'I will go, Miss Rebecca – I have the car outside. But you must give that order: he is to be stopped at all costs.'

'Yes – yes –'

'Has he a car?' Without a car the man couldn't get far.

'No – yes . . . My Metro is at Blackie's – he'll know that – ' She didn't stop to wonder why he was asking her.

'Well, you've got your road-blocks – set them up, then. And stop him at gun-point – ' God in heaven! What would that lead to? But he had no more time to worry about that. ' – but give that order, Miss Rebecca – now!'

'Yes.' Her decision reached, she started to move. And then stopped. 'You won't get past the lodge gates. But the key's hanging up by the backdoor – on a hook – '

Odd how last-minute thoughts make the difference. But then odd about that 17-pounder story . . . of all the stories he could have told. Though perhaps not so odd, on second thoughts, Jack: he told a story for Captain Schneider, and no one else, I suppose

But if she hadn't remembered about the locked gates . . . Kelly just nipped over the wall, and headed for Blackie Nabb's garage. But Schneider went round the back to get the key – and there was this KGB heavy lying stone-cold dead (or still warm, rather) by the open backdoor. Three shots for him – he was the back-up man, so maybe he'd smelt something wrong and was moving when Kelly hit him; whereas the squad leader inside the lodge – the one who'd expected to wait for Kelly, and had found Kelly waiting for him – just one head-shot for him, nice and clean. Gunner Kelly indeed, by God! But not with an old

231

*25-pounder – and not with an old war souvenir with no firing
pin either, which told Schneider all he needed to know,
which he'd only suspected until then, but was sure now – the
neat head-shot – and also warned him of what lay ahead: two
hundred yards away up the road, nicely parked on the verge,
under the trees by the estate wall where Kelly had crossed out
of the wood – a brown 2-litre Cortina, six years old and as
anonymous as you could wish for, except for the driver lying
dead across the front seat – another head-shot at close
quarters for him, he never knew what hit him.*

So Schneider put his foot down then –

It was the same tableau he had seen once before, but with
differences out of a nightmare.

The farm tractor and its hay-bale-loaded trailer were
slewed across the road, out of the same gateway. But now a
pale blue Metro was nosed against it, driver's door wide.
That was one difference.

Inconsequential things: the Metro's engine was still
running . . . one of the gate-posts leaned out of true, beside
a buckled fence, from yesterday's charade –

Blackie Nabb stood up from where he had been squatting beside the body on the verge. And, in the same
movement, his shot-gun came up to cover Benedikt. And
death brushed across him, light as a cobweb, as he faced the
man in the long moment which it took to lift his empty
hands.

Inconsequential things: the dead man's legs – how did he
know the man was dead? – stretched out of the tall summer
grass into the road – old scuffed leather boots, hob-nailed
with iron studs.

Benedikt found his voice. 'Miss Rebecca sent me.' The
words sounded foreign.

Blackie Nabb made a sound in his throat. 'Too late.' His
eyes left Benedikt's face for an instant. 'Over there.' The
shot-gun lowered slowly.

Benedikt moved cautiously. There was a silenced Heckler and Koch pistol in the road, lying beside the Metro's toy-like nearside wheel. Then he saw Kelly.

'He is dead?' More foreign words.

'I dunno. An' I don't much care, neither.' Blackie's voice was matter-of-fact.

Benedikt looked at him.

'Down by the stream, we were.' Blackie drew breath. 'An' the message come – to stop 'un. An' Old Cecil drove the tractor, an' I sets on the back. We got 'ere just before 'im.'

There were sounds in the distance.

''E says to Old Cecil "Open up the road" . . . An', for an answer, Old Cecil just gets off the tractor.' Another breath, almost a sigh. 'An' 'e says again, "Open up the road". An' Old Cecil says "No". An' then there's this . . . like a *thump*, as I was a-comin' round the side.' He looked straight at Benedikt. ''E didn't give 'im no chance. An' I didn't give him none, neither.'

Benedikt went to where the shot-gun blast had blown Kelly, on the opposite verge. Blackie must have been very quick to have got that shot in like that, against an expert; and, more than that, because with killing it needed will as well as reflexes. But the old soldier's training must have reinforced the poacher's instinct in that instant, so Kelly had been unlucky at the last when he was almost clear.

He knelt down beside the man. The blast had taken him midway, and not spread much, but there was a lot of blood. The unmarked face was grey-white, and old. He thought . . . *old men shouldn't die like this –*

And then the eyes opened suddenly, and the chest moved, blowing a bubble of blood.

'Captain.' Kelly looked up at him, expressionless as Blackie. 'Ahh . . .'

With a wound like that . . . it was hard to tell if there was nothing to lose – or anything to gain?

Nothing to gain of value now, he estimated coldly. Only curiosity was left now.

He bent a little closer. 'Why did you kill them?'

Kelly gazed at him. 'Told you. Personal matter.'

That wouldn't do. 'No . . . *Aloysius.*'

Just as suddenly as they had opened, the eyes were no longer without expression. 'Ahh . . . You knew?' Now they were sharing curiosity. 'How long?' Almost a frown now.

Truth? 'Minutes.' Truth. 'The long gun – the 17-pounder . . . The Old General wasn't there, he was away sick at the time. So you lied. But you had no reason to lie . . . Or you weren't there yourself, either . . . And that made me think of other things . . .' Yet – what other things? wondered Benedikt. Because it still didn't add up.

'Ahh . . .' The frown was smoothed away. 'True story, though – Michael's story . . . Had to be Michael, for you . . . little mistake – big mistake. Clever – too clever.' Almost imperceptible nod. 'Michael always said . . . *Jerries* clever.' Against the odds the voice was stronger. 'Forgot that.'

And, even more strangely, the voice was no longer Irish, but had no country. 'It was Michael who was killed?'

Another tiny movement of the head. 'Bad luck. Both going . . . running . . . Spotted one of *them* – can always tell . . . *bastards* . . . Michael had talked of going to the Squire – safe with him . . . I went instead.'

And that was where it didn't make sense. 'And he accepted you? As Michael?'

'Michael?' Aloysius Kelly closed his eyes, and for a moment Benedikt thought he had lost him. 'Ahh . . . I *was* Michael – Michael Kelly . . . 834 Gunner Kelly, *sir!*' Another frothy bubble expanded, bigger than the rest. 'Best troop in the battery, best battery in the regiment, best regiment in the brigade, best brigade in the division, best fucking division in the whole fucking army! 834 Gunner Kelly, *sir!*'

He still couldn't believe it. 'The Old General accepted you as Michael?'

The eyes opened. 'What?'

'He-accepted-you-as-Michael?'

'Accept me? The Squire? Never!' There was blood at the corner of Kelly's mouth. 'Told you true . . . told *him* true . . . not all of it, of course – couldn't do that . . . But told him I was done with it – their lies, my lies – over and done with it for ever, and no going back in this world . . . Told him a lie – told him Michael had gone back to Ireland, where he'd be safe – not him they were after, only me – couldn't tell him about Michael . . . Asked him if I could lay up for a few days, till I got my breath back.'

More blood now. What had the newspapers said about Michael Kelly's death? An accidental explosion of petrol in a garage? And nothing about a victim, of course . . . all hushed up . . .

'He was a man, he was – the Squire. "If Gunner Kelly's safe in Ireland," he said, "then you be Gunner Kelly safe in England – how about that, then?"' Impossibly, Aloysius Kelly was moving one hand, as though to touch Benedikt. 'How about that, then – 834 Gunner Kelly – the Squire and Gunner Kelly – the bastards'll not forget them so quickly, not now – '

Then the blood came with a great rush, choking him.

How we put all that together is according to taste, I suppose, Jack!

So far as Captain Benedikt Schneider is concerned, the fact that he knew every detail of the Old General's military career only demonstrates once again how thoroughly the BND does its homework – thanks, presumably, to the Wiesbaden computer. But even so, his catching the one mistake Kelly made – that 17-pounder lie which the real Gunner Kelly wouldn't have told – marks him as someone special: young Schneider has that rare gift which is better than a good memory, the wild faculty of plucking truth from untruth.

For his part, he maintains that the lie sparked all his subconscious suspicions into consciousness. I had fed him my doubts about Aloysius Kelly's supposed death (though perhaps he already knew that); and all along he'd picked up contradictory vibrations from 'Gunner Kelly'. The man was a cunning hunter, like Esau in the Bible, but that could have been the old soldier's skills surfacing. Yet he was also a smooth man, like Joseph in the Bible – sometimes falsely wearing Esau's hairy skin, but also Joseph's coat-of-many-colours.

Of course, I'd picked up Kelly vibes too. But I was blinded by the Old General's acceptance of him as 'Gunner Kelly': my experience of pure Christ-like goodness, which gives sanctuary to sinners without listening to the Devil's Advocate, is sadly defective, I fear . . . Besides which I was too busy looking for danger from outside the Chase – perhaps that's how that original Fighting Man came unstuck.

Excuses, excuses! Maybe if I'd known the Old General's military history I would have sussed out the real Kelly from the false one – and maybe if Schneider hadn't been his father's son, come fresh from the tank museum, he wouldn't have done. But the fact is that I didn't and he did.

When it comes to Aloysius Kelly and his motivation, there is a difference of opinion between Schneider and myself. Of course, I watched the man over several days, but Schneider saw him die.

My somewhat unromantic Anglo-Saxon view, anyway, is that the leopard does not change his spots – that however much Kelly may have admired the Old General he always intended to survive. So his vengeance was intended to leave us believing that he was indeed Gunner Kelly, while the blood-bath in Duntisbury Chase – the elimination of an entire hit-squad – was intended to dampen the KGB's ardour for continued pursuit (plus, of course, the scandal of such a massacre on our territory). I believe he had another bolt-hole set up.

While he thinks differently, Schneider does agree that by the end Aloysius was running very scared – he had been using Becky Maxwell-Smith and her people in the Chase to give him early warning; because he never underrated the KGB, even though he was obviously pretty sure he could get them where he wanted, when he wanted (with a pretended IRA call? They wanted him dead too). Anyway, my arrival was bad enough, but Schneider's positively stampeded him: it was that evening or never, he must have reckoned.

It's on the 'why' that we diverge. For Schneider is romantically obsessed with the sanctity of the Old General, which he thinks somehow transmuted ex-Comrade Kelly into ex-Gunner Kelly, like base metal into gold – or even made a single man out of them, with the ex-comrade's brains and the ex-gunner's loyalty: a sort of super Irishman, but without the luck of the Irish.

Maybe we're both right – and it was Comrade Aloysius who shot Old Cecil like a dog, and died for it; but it was Gunner Kelly who left that letter on the mantelpiece of the Lodge, claiming his ancient right of vengeance and exculpating the Chase from blame. You pays your money, and you takes your choice, Jack.

As for me – the same applies. Captain Schneider is a loyal ally, and as blameless as your Jane. But Old Cecil's blood is on my hands and I've lost you whatever was in Kelly's head, so my resignation is attached. Use that or give me Cheltenham and I'll win for you there, I promise. Losing is not to my taste.

Yours,

David

The world's greatest thriller writers now available in Panther Books

Jack Higgins

A Game for Heroes	£1.95	☐
The Wrath of God	£1.95	☐
The Khufra Run	£1.95	☐
Bloody Passage	£1.95	☐

Gerald A Browne

11 Harrowhouse	£1.25	☐

Trevanian

The Loo Sanction	£1.95	☐
The Eiger Sanction	£1.95	☐
Shibumi	£2.50	☐
The Summer of Katya	£1.95	☐

Anthony Price

Soldier No More	£1.95	☐
The Old Vengeful	£1.95	☐
Gunner Kelly	£1.95	☐

Jonathan Ryder

Trevayne	£1.95	☐
The Cry of the Halidon	£1.95	☐

To order direct from the publisher just tick the titles you want and fill in the order form.

All these books are available at your local bookshop or newsagent, or can be ordered direct from the publisher..

To order direct from the publisher just tick the titles you want and fill in the form below.

Name

Address

Send to:
Panther Cash Sales
PO Box 11, Falmouth, Cornwall TR10 9EN.

Please enclose remittance to the value of the cover price plus:

UK 45p for the first book, 20p for the second book plus 14p per copy for each additional book ordered to a maximum charge of £1.63.

BFPO and Eire 45p for the first book, 20p for the second book plus 14p per copy for the next 7 books, thereafter 8p per book.

Overseas 75p for the first book and 21p for each additional book.

Panther Books reserve the right to show new retail prices on covers, which may differ from those previously advertised in the text or elsewhere.